WICKEDLY
Charming

KRISTINE GRAYSON

sourcebooks
casablanca

For Dean:
You will always be my Prince Charming

The Idea

Chapter 1

BOOK FAIR

The very words of the sign filled Mellie with loathing. Book Fair indeed. More like Book Unfair.

Every time people wrote something down, they got it wrong. She'd learned that in her exceptionally long life.

Not that she was old—not by any stretch. In fact, by the standards of her people, she was in early middle age. She'd been in early middle age, it seemed, for most of her adult life. Of course that wasn't true. She'd only been in early middle age for her life in the public eye— two very different things.

And now she was paying for it.

She stood in a huge but nearly empty parking lot in the bright morning sun. It was going to be hot— California, too-dry-to-tolerate hot, fifty-bottles-of-Gatorade hot—but it wasn't hot yet. Still, she hoped she had on enough sunscreen (even if it did make her smell like a weird, chemical coconut). She had her hands on her hips (which hadn't expanded [much] since she was a beautiful young girl, who caught the eye of every man) as she surveyed the stunningly large building in front of her, with the banner strung across its multitude of doors.

The Largest Book Fair in the World!, the banner proclaimed in bright red letters. The largest book fair with the largest number of publishers, writers, readers and moguls—movie and gaming and every other type of mogul the entertainment industry had come up with.

It probably should be called *Mogul Fair* (Mogul Unfair?). But people were pitching books, not pitching moguls (although someone probably should pitch moguls; it was her experience that anyone with a shred of power should be pitched across a room [or down a staircase] every now and then).

This season's books, next season's books, books for every race, creed, and constituency, large books, small books, and the all-important evergreen books which were not, as she once believed, books about evergreens, but books that never went out of style, like *Little Women* or anything by Jane Austen or, dammit, by that villain Hans Christian Andersen.

Not that Andersen started it all. He didn't. It was those Grimm brothers, two better named individuals she had never met.

It didn't matter that Mellie had set them straight. By then, their "tales" were already on the market, poisoning the well, so to speak. (Or the apple. Those boys did love their poisons. It would have been so much better for all concerned if they had turned their attention to crime fiction. They could have invented the entire category. But *noooo*. They had to focus on what they called "fairies," as misnamed as their little "tales.")

She made herself breathe. Even alone with her own thoughts, she couldn't help going on a bit of a rant about those creepy little men.

She made herself turn away from the gigantic building and walk to the back of her minivan. With the push of a button, the hatchback unlocked (now *that* was magic) and she pulled the thing open.

Fifty signs and placards leaned haphazardly against each other. Last time, she'd only needed twenty. She hoped she would use all fifty this time.

She glanced at her watch. One hour until the Book Unfair opened.

Half an hour until her group showed up.

Mellie glared at the building again. Sometimes she thought of these things like a maze she needed to thread her way through. But this was a fortress, one she needed to conquer. All those entrances intimidated her. It was impossible to tell where she'd get the most media exposure. Certainly not at the front doors, with the handicapped ramp blocking access along one side.

Once someone else arrived to help her hand out the placards, she could leave for a few minutes and reconnoiter.

She wanted the maximum amount of air time for the minimum amount of exposure. She'd learned long ago that if she gave the media too much time in the beginning, they'd distort everything she said.

Better to parcel out information bit by bit.

The Book Unfair was only her first salvo.

But she knew it would be the most important.

He parked his silver Mercedes at the far end of the massive parking lot. He did it not so that he wouldn't be recognized—he wouldn't be, anyway—but because he'd learned long ago that if he parked his Mercedes anywhere near the front, the car would either end up with door dings and key scratches, or would go missing.

He reached into the glove box and removed his prized purple bookseller's badge. He had worked for two years to acquire that thing. Not that he minded. It still amazed him that no one at the palace had thought of opening a bookstore on the grounds.

He could still hear his father's initial objection: *We are not shopkeepers!* He'd said it in that tone that meant shopkeepers were lower than scullery maids. In fact, shopkeepers had become his father's favorite epithet in the past few decades, scullery maid being both politically and familially incorrect.

It took some convincing—the resident scholars had to prove to his father's satisfaction that true shopkeepers made a living at what they did, and in no way would a bookstore on the palace grounds provide anyone's living—but the bookstore finally happened.

With it came myriad book catalogues and discounts and advance reading copies and a little bit of bookish swag.

He'd been in heaven. Particularly when he realized he could attend every single book fair in the Greater World and get free books.

Not that he couldn't pay for his own books—he could, as well as books for each person in the entire Third Kingdom (which he did last year, to much complaint: it seemed everyone thought they would be tested on the contents of said gift books. Not everyone loved reading as much as he did, more's the pity).

Books had been his retreat since boyhood. He loved hiding in imaginary worlds. Back then, books were harder to come by, often hidden in monasteries (and going to those had caused some consternation for his parents until they realized he was reading, not practicing for his future profession). Once the printing press caught on, he bought his own books—he now devoted the entire winter palace to his collection—but it still wasn't enough.

If he could, he would read every single book ever written—or at least scan them, trying to get a sense of them. Even with the unusually long life granted to people of the Third Kingdom, especially when compared with people in the Greater World (the world that had provided his Mercedes and this quite exciting book fair), he would never achieve it. There were simply too many existing books in too many languages, with too many more being written all the time.

He felt overwhelmed when he thought of all the books he hadn't read, all the books he wanted to read, and all the books he would want to read. Not to mention all the books that he hadn't heard of.

Those dismayed him the most.

Hence, the book fair.

He was told to come early. There was a breakfast for booksellers—coffee and doughnuts, the website said, free of charge. He loved this idea of free as an enticement. He wondered if he could use it for anything back home.

The morning was clear, with the promise of great heat. A smog bank had started to form over Los Angeles, and he couldn't see the ocean, although the brochures assured him it was somewhere nearby. The parking lot looked like a city all by itself. It went on for blocks, delineated only by signs that labeled the rows with double letters.

The only other car in this part of the lot wasn't a car at all but one of those minivans built so that families could take their possessions and their entertainment systems with them.

The attractive black-haired woman unloading a passel of signs from the van looked familiar to him, but he couldn't remember where he had seen her before.

He wasn't about to go ask her either. His divorce had left him feeling very insecure, especially around women. Whenever he saw a pretty woman, the words of his ex-wife rose in his head.

She had screamed them at him in that very last fight, the horrible, unforgettable fight when she took the glass slipper—the thing that defined all that was good and pure in their relationship—and heaved it against the wall above his head.

Not so charming now, are you, asshole? Nope, not charming at all.

He had to concede she had a point—although he never would have conceded it to her. Still, those formerly dulcet tones echoed in his brain whenever he looked in the mirror and saw not the square-jawed hero who saved her from a life of poverty, but a balding, paunchy middle-aged man who would never achieve his full potential—not without killing his father, and that was a different story entirely.

Charming squared his shoulders and pinned his precious name badge to his shirt. The name badge did not use his real name. It used his *nom de plume*—which sounded a lot more romantic than The Name He Used Because His Real Name Was Stupid.

He called himself Dave. Dave Encanto, for those who required last names. His family didn't even have a last name—that's how long they'd been around—and even though he knew Prince was now considered a last name, he couldn't bring himself to use it.

He couldn't bring himself to use any name, really. He still thought of himself as Charming even though he knew his ex was right—he wasn't "charming" anymore. Not that he didn't try. It was just that charming used to come easily to him, when he had a head full of black, black hair, and an unwrinkled face, and the squarest of square jaws.

Prince Charming was a young man's name, in truth, and then only the name of an arrogant young man. To use that name now would seem like wish fulfillment or a really bad joke. He couldn't go with P.C. because the initials had been usurped, and people would catch the double irony of a prince trying to be p.c. with his own name change.

And as for Prince—that name was overused. In addition to the musician, Princes abounded. People named their horses Prince, for heaven's sake, and their dogs, and their surrogate children. In other words, only the nutty named a human being Prince these days, and much as Charming resented his father, he couldn't put either of his parents in the nutty category.

So he told people to call him Dave, which was emphatically not a family name. Too many family names had been co-opted as well—Edward, George, Louis, Philippe, even Harry, not just by another prince, but by some very famous, very fictional, magical potter's kid.

Dave, not David, a man who could go anywhere incognito any time he liked. Gone were the days when people would do a double-take, and some would say, *Aren't you…?* or *You know you look just like that prince—whatsisname?—Charming.*

Now they nodded and looked past him, hoping to see

someone more important. Which was why he preferred the Greater World to the Third Kingdom. In the Greater World, they knew he wasn't *the* Prince Charming. To them, *the* Prince Charming was a man in a fairy tale, a creature of unattainable perfection, or—more accurately (he believed) a cartoon character, an animated hero.

He was none of those things. True, he had a longer-than-usual life, but that caused longer than usual problems—like waiting for his father, who also had a longer-than-usual life, to kick the proverbial bucket (which in the Third Kingdom, wasn't as proverbial as you might think).

But as for magical powers, Charming had none, be-sides that all-encompassing charm, that Ella had told him, in no uncertain terms, was gone now. Ella, who got his estates, half of his money, and custody of their two daughters because—true to form—his father wouldn't let Charming contest the divorce over *girls*.

Charming sighed and started across the monstrous parking lot. Several other cars were pouring into the first entrance, way up front, near the doors. The park-ing there, he knew from the emails he had gotten, was reserved for booksellers and the disabled—or the dif-ferently abled, as he had been bidden to say. The emails claimed he would need the close-in parking for the hun-dreds of pounds of books he would lug back to his car at regular intervals. But he had lugged chain mail and two injured companions over a hundred miles. He figured he could handle a few books.

The attractive woman had pulled out the last sign. He saw the initials—PETA—and felt a surge of disap-pointment. He'd seen what those animal rights lovers had done to his mother's favorite fur coat the one and only time he had taken her to the Metropolitan Opera in Manhattan. His mother had been horribly traumatized, although not so traumatized that she forgot to command him to bring the entire cast of the Met to the Third Kingdom at the end of every opera season.

Charming walked around the attractive woman, resisting the urge to stare at her. Instead, he glanced at her out of the corner of his eye.

She had hit that age when women moved from cute and perky to beautiful and sometimes even handsome. This woman had a narrow face and raven black hair, the kind that always attracted him. She wore a short-sleeved black jacket over matching black pants, along with a red blouse that accented her unlined skin.

She looked like the kind of woman who knew exactly what she wanted and exactly how to get it. The kind of woman who ran boardrooms and households with equal ease.

The kind of woman his ex most certainly was not.

He shuddered at the thought of Ella. No matter how much he tried to forget her, he couldn't. He'd had hopes for that relationship. He had hoped it wouldn't be an empty relationship, like his parents' relationship. He had hoped it would be based on trust and mutual interests, and most of all, on love.

He had loved Ella. He had loved her a lot.

But he had paid for his myopia time and time again, for the fact he hadn't recognized her when he had seen her covered with ash from her stepmother's fireplace, a fact that Ella—in all the years of their marriage—never let him forget.

In those days, he hadn't known he needed glasses. No one used glasses back then, well, no one important anyway. A few people wore a magnifying glass over their eyes, but a king's son certainly couldn't, not if he wished to maintain his dignity.

His mother had paid for a few spells to improve his eyesight, but the damn things always wore off at the most inconvenient times. He'd been married a year when he got his first pair of glasses—and he'd gotten them in defiance of his entire family, including his wife. But none of them had nearly died on the field of battle, because the damn spell wore off as he was in the middle of hand-to-hand combat with one of the champions from the other side. The entire world went from crystal clear to blurry in a half a second, and he flailed miserably.

Fortunately, in the flailing, he'd managed to disarm (and accidentally dismember) his opponent. It ended well for Charming—in those days, things usually did—making him even more of a hero to his people.

But they didn't know it was an accident because he couldn't see anything.

Not that he ever wore his glasses on the field of battle. His family wouldn't hear of that (and truthfully, the thought frightened him—glasses *broke* at the most inopportune times and in the most inopportune ways. Eye-gouging was a favorite practice in those days—one of the few things the early fairy tales [misnamed stories of his—and other people's—exploits] got right).

He had passed the woman now. For a brief moment, he fantasized that she would look up from her struggle with the PETA signs (why did the gorgeous ones always have a tinge of nutcase to them?) and would see him. She would watch him walk with great interest, as if he were still the Charming of old, thinking how much she'd like to meet him (and maybe how much she'd like to do other things with him).

The very thought made him blush. Then it made him grimace. He didn't do himself any favors by letting his imagination run wild. That had been the problem the first time. He'd seen a pretty, petite girl at a ball—honestly, the prettiest girl he'd seen up until that time—and he'd convinced himself he was in love. He had been in lust, but fairy tales didn't deal with lust. And neither did virtuous king's sons—at least, not in their conscious mind. But the subconscious… well, that was a different story.

Back then, he hadn't known what a subconscious was. Or what failure was.

Or how it felt to be balding and no longer distinguished. Just another middle-aged man with a purple badge, heading into a book fair.

Charming sighed. He tried to put the attractive woman out of his mind. He still had something to look forward to—something he enjoyed greatly. Something he couldn't get back home.

Coffee. Doughnuts. And insight into this season's bestsellers.

Mellie watched the handsome man walk the length of the parking lot. She had only caught a glimpse of his profile, but it was classic: high cheekbones, square jaw, aquiline nose. The frame of his glasses was so thin that it looked like an arrow pointing to his stunning salt-and-pepper hair.

He wore what was known as business casual—a long-sleeved shirt and dark pants (no suit coat, no tie) but he still looked elegant. Some of that was the clothing itself; there was nothing casual about it. It was tailored to fit—and fit it did, over a well-muscled back, broad shoulders, and a nice tight—

She shook her head and looked away. If she really thought about it, she had to acknowledge that men were the source of her troubles. From her beloved first husband who had left her a young widow with two extremely young daughters to her know-it-all second husband who stupidly introduced her as a fait accompli to his own daughter starting a resentment that continued to this day, men had been the root cause of her dilemmas from the moment Mellie had hit the public eye.

Of course, she had handled things badly. She always thought that any publicity was good publicity. Little did she realize that once someone had defined you to the media, then it didn't matter how many charities you gave to or how many advanced degrees you had, you would always be the evil stepmother, the wicked witch, or worse, the aging malignant crone.

At least she had avoided that last category—for now, anyway. She felt it hovering around her, like the flying monkeys from the stupid Hollywood version of *The Wizard of Oz*.

She heard a sound and turned. The man behind her was exceptionally attractive. He had pale blue eyes and glossy black hair that fell like a mane around his face. He also left a trail of wet footprints heading west. He was a selkie whose real name she did not (of course) know. He carried his pelt over his right arm and this time he wore human clothing.

He had actually stopped their first protest earlier this year by pulling off his pelt and having nothing suitable on underneath it. (Although she could see why the human storytellers had felt threatened by these creatures from the sea: not only were they preternaturally good-looking, they were also very well endowed.)

"As people show up, will you hand out signs?" she asked. "I need to figure out where we'll stage our protest."

She shoved the last pile of signs at him, not giving him a chance to say anything, and then she hurried along the parking lot.

Midway there, she realized she was trying to catch that ever-so-elegant man and she slowed her steps.

She had sworn off men decades ago.

She wasn't about to let one distract her now.

Chapter 2

THE COFFEE WAS BITTER AND ONLY THE INEDIBLE COCONUT-covered doughnuts were left. Charming should have arrived earlier. Still he poured himself a cup, grabbed one of the few remaining paper plates, and found a maple bar crammed against the back of the doughnut box. Then he settled into a chair at the back of the room.

The panel was already talking about social media and whether or not it meant the death of the book, a topic that always broke his heart. He understood the importance of stories—he'd been raised on stories. Bards had come to his father's court before Charming could even read. But the best stories were the ones he accessed privately—and a screen never really felt private to him.

Still, he listened politely, getting more and more discouraged, until he finished his maple bar and fled.

The doors to the main exhibition hall were locked, with guards standing out front. The guards didn't look that formidable—two fat security guards in uniform, and several bookish types with their arms crossed, trying to look tough.

Too late for doughnuts; too early to see the books. Story of his life.

Still, he had some time before the exhibition hall opened, so he decided to explore. He knew from his convention packet that there were side rooms, meeting rooms, conference rooms, and the all-important media room where the famous people, from the writers to the politicians/actors/musicians who loaned their names to books, gave interviews about whatever seemed important at the time.

The hallways were unbelievably wide so that they could accommodate crowds and wheelchairs, and yet he was the only person in them, except for the occasional publishing house salesman scrambling to put the finishing touches on a booth. From a distance, he caught the scent of cafeteria food, and remembered that they would all be able to buy lunch here if they were so inclined.

He was inclined, especially after that maple bar. There were no restaurants nearby, and he didn't want to lose his parking space.

He meandered, glancing at computer-generated signs telling him that the small press area was in a building to his left, the affiliated organizations were in the basement, and the media room was down the hall.

The media room was closest. Besides, he had a hunch he'd spend time in the media room and wouldn't in the affiliated organizations area. He didn't want to leave the building—not yet, maybe not ever. This wasn't his first book fair, and he'd learned that he couldn't see everything in the main exhibit hall, let alone everything in the other wings and buildings.

The amount of things published in English alone scared him. In English in the United States. Not counting England, Canada, or Australia. Not counting all the other countries and their own presses in their own languages.

Sometimes he thought of starting his own publishing company back home, but these things tended to spawn more publishing companies, and then there'd be book fairs, and then he'd have to read everything published in the Kingdoms—not just everything *written* about the Kingdoms, which had been going on for centuries.

He felt overwhelmed just thinking about it.

The media room signs pointed to both a flight of stairs and to a bank of elevators. He stopped and looked at the map for this network of buildings. The media room wasn't a room; it was an entire wing.

Which made sense, since most of the programming he wanted to see was held in the media room. He'd had to get tickets ahead of time, sometimes at extra cost, just so that he could see his favorite authors expound on something he probably didn't care about.

Still, he was enough of a geek to want to see the people whose work he enjoyed, even if they were talking about something else. He'd gotten as many tickets to as many events as he could. He'd sit in the back of the room, though, because there would be cameras.

Not that he was famous here in the Greater World— he wasn't (unless you counted that whole Prince Charming thing [every girl was looking for one, or so he was told]). He had simply learned over the years that the camera loved him. He had a bit more charisma than the average author, so camera operators would focus on his reactions to various speeches.

He became the "average reader" nodding and smiling as his favorite author spoke. No one recognized him as Prince Charming. No one even thought he was a celebrity. But for a year or so, he became "Reaction Man"—the go-to guy on *Book TV*. If Charming had been near an author who gave a speech, and that speech was filmed, then inevitably, Charming would find his own face flittering across *Book TV*—laughing, looking very serious, or applauding as the writer said something worthwhile.

Charming hated that. At first, he'd thought it a simple error. Then he saw it repeated over and over again. Then, at one of the smaller book fairs, he overheard segment producers asking if someone could find Reaction Man so that they could actually interview him.

From that point on, Charming hid in the back of the room, in the dark, away from the lights, never raised his hand and—sadly—never asked his favorite writers for autographs at the end of their talk.

But to get that coveted back-of-the-room spot, he had to scope out the room and find the darkest corner. Moments like this were the best time to do so, when no one important was around—especially not the camera operators or the producers.

The wing had several function rooms. He stopped in the hall and double-checked his program. He might have to investigate more than one room.

He would just have to find out which one.

———————

Mellie pulled her badge out of her purse. The badge was a disgusting orange, the designated color for "affiliated organizations." She had registered PETA with the book fair right at the start, although she'd had to use the organization's full name—People for the Ethical Treatment of Archetypes—because (apparently) the other, more famous, PETA was both hated and feared.

Rather like she had been once, for a brief span of her life, back when she was searching for Snow White.

Mellie sighed. She didn't miss those days. In fact,

she wished she could wipe them out entirely. But they defined her life, whether she wanted them to or not.

She rounded the building—which was bigger than half the castles in the Kingdoms (uglier too)—and found the double doors leading into the north wing. The north wing, according to her book fair materials packet, held the media room, and the publicity area, and the interview room—all the places she cared most about.

She carried flyers in her book bag. The flyers would get her into the publicity area. Savvy book fair attendees knew to put their flyers in the publicity area *and* on their booth. Especially when their badge category was relegated to the basement like hers was.

She'd tried to get a press badge, which would have given her the run of this wing. She'd even started a newsletter, with book reviews and everything. But the book fair committee—while not exactly telling her she was an amateur, implied it:

Due to the preponderance of regular media, the refusal letter had said, *we are unable to give more than one hundred passes to smaller media organizations. We thank you for your interest in our fair*.

"We thank you for your interest in our fair," she mouthed, still annoyed at that. Apparently there were limitations on press, but none on affiliated organizations. If you were willing to pony up the exorbitant fee—damn near ten times the fee for the booksellers (those folks got in almost for free)—then you could have a booth in the affiliated organizations area.

She'd gotten Griselda, Hansel and Gretel's stepmother, to man the booth most of the time. Griselda—or Selda, as she preferred—could talk about their cause without getting furious. She was a true asset. But she had gone through counseling and done lots of work here in the Greater World. Selda wasn't even angry at her former husband for making up all the lies about her. She said such things happened all the time in abusive relationships.

Mellie slipped through the double doors into the loading dock. The media area always got the best loading dock, mostly because it needed a place to safely park the various trucks—including satellite trucks, which got brought in on the second day for the keynote speaker.

This year's keynote wasn't all that spectacular— some bestselling writer who wrote thrillers. In previous years, there'd been former presidents. Mellie had been hoping a former president this time. The former presidents did force the place to have added security, but that didn't matter as much as the added media coverage. Just because one of those former heads of state visited—and they were, in her mind, rather minor, considering they only ruled for a maximum of eight years (why would anyone agree to that?)—every major news organization showed up in droves. And the fair got coverage on all the major channels as well as the minor ones.

No such luck this year. She'd been disappointed when she figured that out. But, she decided, this book fair would be a practice run at a bigger media blitz. She'd convince places to report on her grievances, and then maybe—if she got lucky—she'd become a keynote speaker at one of these things. Her goal this weekend was minor. All she wanted was local press coverage.

Although "local" in Los Angeles was a misnomer. If nothing else, her footage would air on major affiliates from here to New York. If this worked, she'd head from here to the publishing capital of the United States to press her case.

Her breath caught. Beneath it all, she was very, very nervous. She had a lot resting on this.

She really wanted to make a difference in countless lives, and this was the only way she knew how.

She wound her way around cables strewn across the concrete floor, past trucks with station logos emblazoned on the side, past brawny men with droopy pants carrying light and sound equipment up a small flight of stairs.

A number of the men smiled at her as they went by. She still looked good. Her old self—the pre-disaster self—would've seen that as a positive sign. Now she knew it for what it was, a symptom of the world's—both worlds' (hers and this one's)—obsession with beauty over substance.

When she'd had real beauty, she'd had little substance. Now that she was older, she had a lot of substance, but she was nowhere near as beautiful as she had been before.

Although she did have a bit of glamour. A touch of the magical that made her seem larger than life here in the Greater World. She'd learn to use that to press for her cause.

She waited until another group of sweaty men carrying equipment went up the small flight of stairs into the main part of the building. Then she scurried up the steps behind them.

She had a few missions: First, she'd scout out the locations, find the green room, find the interview room, and find the celebrity hideout for the on-air talent consigned to this place. Then she'd see if she could line up an interview or two. If some security guard saw her badge and told her that she didn't belong, she'd pull out her flyers, and bat her eyes, and ask (oh-so-dejectedly) where the publicity room was.

She'd also find the best place to stage a protest. Maybe she'd do it during the keynote speech, which wasn't until mid-afternoon tomorrow. She knew from experience that she could probably store her signs in the loading dock or one of the small, unused closets alongside it.

She stepped into the hall. The lights were brighter here, the air cooler (air conditioning—one of the best inventions *ever* in the Greater World), and the floor softly carpeted. The color scheme left a lot to be desired— whoever thought rose red and sky blue made for a good combination?—but she wasn't the one who had to put all that garishness on film.

She just had to use it to her advantage.

She clutched her book bag to her side, flipped her badge over so that its white back was the only visible part, and made her way to the keynote speech area. First she'd figure out if she had room for a protest there. Then she'd find the interview room.

The hallway was surprisingly empty—no sweaty men carrying equipment, no overly made-up on-air talent trying to find the green room. No one except that elegant man she'd seen earlier.

He stood with his back to her as he peered at the program listing outside one of the function rooms.

His back *was* stunning. She really couldn't get over those broad shoulders, the hint of muscle through the beautifully tailored shirt, the way that it all tucked into the form-fitting pants—

She shook off the thought and made herself look

away, her cheeks warm as if she were a young maiden like she'd been before her first marriage.

Of course the elegant man would be down here. He was probably on-air talent. He wouldn't be national—she would've recognized him, even from (especially from?) the back. He was probably the main anchor at one of the local affiliates. They liked their main anchors to have some judiciously silver hair—sometimes they even made the men dye the silver in, so they had that classy salt-and-pepper look.

Male anchors had to look authoritative, but approachable. The knowledgeable, trustworthy guy on the block, not too handsome, but handsome enough.

Or in the parlance of fairy tales: Just Right.

He was Just Right, even from the back. *Especially* from the back.

Her cheeks grew even warmer. She pressed her hands against them, willing the reaction to go away. She didn't need to get all hot and bothered over some local anchor.

Although he might make a good contact. Maybe she could even sweet-talk him into an interview.

She let her hands drop away from her cheeks. She took off her badge and smoothed her clothes. She swept one hand over her hair—it felt like all the strands were in place—and she suddenly felt thankful for that blush. It would highlight her skin (still flawless after all these years) and make her seem more vibrant.

She straightened, then sashayed toward him, trying to figure out how, exactly, she would approach him. Maybe she'd pretend to be an expert on the building. Or better yet, someone who was as lost as he was. They'd have something in common, a bit of instant camaraderie.

As she approached, she saw him turn slightly. He reached for the door, then stopped as if he thought the better of it. He glanced over each shoulder quickly, as if he were doing something wrong.

He didn't see her.

Which was a good thing.

Because she stopped walking, her heart in her throat.

He wasn't an anchor at all.

He was a Charming.

Chapter 3

CHARMING SLIPPED INSIDE THE MAIN FUNCTION ROOM AND shivered. Someone had turned the air conditioning on "icicle," probably in anticipation of large crowds for the various speeches. This room was huge—as big, if not bigger, than most hotel ballrooms. At least five hundred seats had been placed too close together, and a bit too close to the makeshift stage.

The room had already been set up for a panel discussion. A long table sat on top of a dais, with microphones in front of four seats. No names yet—someone always set the name placards out just before the thing started—but an ice-filled pitcher of water along with four glasses sat on a little coaster in the middle of the table.

It was so cold in here that ice probably wouldn't melt.

He rubbed his hands together. Someone had taped x's to the floor on either side of the table, a suggestion for the camera operators—a suggestion that would probably irritate them. A sound board sat near the door, already hooked up, which was good for him. That meant that no one from the media would be anywhere near the back.

He walked to the back of the room, realized there was space for at least another two hundred chairs (some of which were stacked against the far wall), and glanced up at the lighting. It was regular conical lighting—more flattering than fluorescents—but also good for him. Conical lights created circles. Circles overlapped, but they also created shadows.

The door banged.

He froze, glanced over, not wanting to be caught in the room alone. Not that there was anything wrong with it. He just hated the hassle.

But no one had come in.

He let out a small sigh, then looked up again, double-checking what he already sensed. He walked over to the farthest chair deep in the shadows, and took out the extra program he'd filched off one of the doughnut tables. He set the program on his chair, and wrote "reserved" across it in Magic Marker.

Even if someone moved the program, they'd only move it a seat or two away. He had his spot for the first panel discussion.

Now all he had to do was find similar spots in the other function rooms. By the time he was done, the exhibition hall would be open.

And he'd be ready to enjoy the book fair.

Like he always did.

~~~

A Charming.

A Charming in the middle of a book fair.

What was a Charming doing here?

He was trying to get in the way of Mellie's message, that's what. Charmings benefited from the archetype. Charmings were the flip side of the Wicked Stepmother motif. Charmings were desired and desirable.

Charmings were the bane of her existence.

Now there was one in the middle of her book fair, about to destroy her carefully laid plans.

And she couldn't stand for that.

Mellie hurried to the door as it eased closed. She managed to catch it before it latched.

She peered through the opening.

He was surveying the room, probably going over his speech, dammit.

She finally saw him full-on. He was breathtakingly handsome—all of the Charmings were—albeit a little older than the last time she had seen him. She could at least pinpoint that date.

The end of what the Greater World called the nineteenth century. Those horrible Grimm brothers had already published their lies for the entire world to see. The lies had seeped into the Kingdoms, and they were making life difficult for everyone concerned.

Well, not everyone. The younger women came off rather well (if they didn't mind being considered beautiful victims) and the Charmings had become heroes. None of them were called Charming then; they were "the king's son" or "the prince"—always single and perfectly willing to marry beneath them, unlike most princes now.

If she was really being honest, the people who came off poorly were the older women (evil stepmothers, witches hiding in the woods), the ugly men (Bluebeard—who really was indefensible; and the cursed Beast, who wasn't), and Those Who Were Different.

Some of Those Who Were Different got a pass, even if they didn't get the girl—the so-called Dwarfs in the so-called Snow White tale; good old Tom Thumb (who was small, but not as tiny as everyone said); and that conniving little tailor. All of these men were abnormally short (she later figured it was probably due to a failure of nutrition in the Kingdoms), but somehow positive role models.

Unlike her old friend Rumpelstiltskin, who was also short. And loud. And a bit of a con man. He didn't deserve to be the bad guy any more than she deserved to be a witch and a murderer.

But so it went in storyland.

Those who didn't mind the lies told about them felt that no one should do anything about Jakob and Wilhelm Grimm. Or Hans Christian Andersen for that matter. Or Oscar Wilde (although, if she told the truth, she had to admit she liked the wry tone of some of his fairy tales).

She held a meeting way back then, and nothing had come of it, except the first (and only) meeting of all of the so-called fairy tale characters in one place.

All those Charmings. They looked so different—Sleeping Beauty's self-assured Charming; Cinderella's handsomer, slightly shy Charming; and of course, the Charming Mellie knew well, her former son-in-law, Snow White's Charming. Who was charming on first glance, and got more and more creepy as time went on.

Mellie sighed. She knew the man in the room wasn't Snow's Charming. But she wasn't sure if he was Beauty's Charming or Ella's Charming. He could've been one of the lesser Charmings—the Goose Girl's Charming or Rapunzel's Charming. They all had that bit of look-at-me glamour, whether they wanted it or not.

The hundred-plus years had changed this Charming just enough to make him hard to recognize. At the meeting, none of the Charmings had silver highlights, and none of them wore glasses. This Charming's glasses accented his square face and strong features, making him look intelligent and oh-so-handsome all at the same time.

In fact, his front was much better than his back, and his back had been spectacular. It had been a long time since she'd seen a man this desirable and—

She backed away from the door. It banged closed and she cursed.

The last thing she wanted to do was interact with a Charming. They were all so handsome and so sure of themselves, and so dismissive of older women—even though all of the Charmings were more of an age with the stepmothers than with the girls they married.

She wasn't sure what to do or how to confront him. Or even if she should confront him at all.

Maybe she should just follow him around and see what subversive activity he was up to.

Of course, if she did that, she'd never accomplish her mission.

Better to stop him in his tracks now, to let him know she was here and she wasn't going away.

No matter what lies he told.

Chapter 4

ONE FUNCTION ROOM DOWN, TWO MORE TO GO. CHARMING pulled open the door and stepped into the hallway, checking his watch as he did so. Twenty minutes before the main exhibit hall opened. Then he'd scurry through it, looking for the best galleys and free giveaways before he filled up his first four book bags. Then he'd head back to the car, and sprint back for more.

He'd worn sensible shoes at least. He'd learned that much from previous book fairs, which had left him with blisters.

Air moved around him. He looked up, expecting a security guard, but didn't see anyone. Still, the air smelled faintly of roses. Delicate, sun-warmed roses—the old-fashioned kind, the kind you could only find on ancient rose plants or in the Kingdoms. Not the kind you got at stores here in the Greater World. Those roses had almost no scent at all—which, as far as he was concerned, defeated the whole purpose of roses.

He turned, and collided with the woman from the parking lot. He put his hands on her arms to steady her, felt the smoothness of her skin, and was surprised when he realized he didn't have to look down to see her face.

She was even more beautiful up close than she had been from far away. Her eyes were filled with intelligence, accented by her very good bone structure. She would be lovely even into old age, so long as she didn't let that mouth of hers remain twisted like that.

"Charming, right?" she said, sounding disappointed. "The question is which one?"

He let go of her arms and stepped back, his heart pounding. Her beauty made it hard for him to focus on her words. He blinked, thought, remembered, and then felt startled.

She recognized him.

Worse, she recognized him as a Charming. Not just Prince Charming, but one of many Charmings.

Which meant she wasn't a native of the Greater World. She came from one of the Kingdoms. But again, the question was which one.

"My name is Dave," he said trying to sound calm when his heart was pounding, and his hands still felt the softness of her skin. He couldn't quite get past how beautiful she was.

He hadn't been attracted to a woman in a long time.

"Yeah, I see that your name is Dave." She grabbed his prized purple badge, looked at it, and then dropped it against his shirt. "Dave Encanto. You're not fooling anyone, 'Dave.' Why are you here? To shut me down?"

Her bitterness surprised him. Clearly—and not unexpectedly—she was not as attracted as he was. He was slowly getting used to women who weren't interested in him as a matter of course, but he didn't expect bitterness.

Obviously, he had met her before, but he couldn't remember when. He had probably been rude to her. He used to be rude a lot more often, before he realized how much words could hurt.

That still didn't help him understand her comment. He didn't have the power to shut down anyone. Not in the Greater World, anyway.

But he did remember her PETA sign. She had probably been at that protest at the Met. His mother had sounded deranged—at least to the people in the Greater World who had been on the sidewalk that day. *My son will punish you all*, she'd shouted after a haughty *How Dare You! No one angers Prince Charming*.

The woman in front of him must have remembered the entire incident—although he didn't know exactly how that translated into the question she'd asked about the Princes Charming. Maybe she was being sardonic.

"Listen," he said, "I know everyone has a right to their opinion, but I do think tossing paint on little old ladies going into the opera takes things a bit too far. When I said I would shut you all down, it was only because I was angry, and it was, after all, my mother's fur coat that you ruined—"

The woman made a sound of disgust. She crossed her well-toned arms. She looked almost amused. "You don't know who I am, do you?"

"No-oo," he said. "Just that you're with that animal rights group."

"Clearly we need a new acronym," she said more to herself than to him.

She seemed serious. And with that look, and the mutter, she seemed almost familiar. He had a sense of who she was, a half a memory, just out of his reach...

She sighed and straightened her shoulders, catching his attention. Her movements were graceful, almost dance-like. He hadn't seen a woman this elegant in a long time.

"I am," she said, "the founder of PETA which stands for People for the Ethical Treatment of *Archetypes*, not animals. We had the acronym long before those animal people stole it from us. They were just better at getting press coverage like everyone else on the planet, including you, 'Dave.'"

He tilted his head slightly. What was she talking about? Archetypes? Press coverage? He wasn't good at press coverage. It wasn't his fault the media filmed him at book signings.

"I'm not interested in the press," Charming said. "I don't vie for their attention."

"Of course you don't," she said. "That's why you're so very famous."

"I'm not." He hated having to explain the camera thing, but he was going to try. "I didn't ask—"

"You *are* famous. You're the most famous of all of us." A flush rose in her cheeks, accenting her startling emerald eyes. She leaned toward him. "Everyone wants to find their Prince Charming. *Everyone*, 'Dave.' Women. Gay guys. Even real men because they want what Prince Charming has. What *you* have. You don't need a publicist. You just need to bask in your princely charmingness."

He hadn't expected the attack. It had come at him sideways. He wasn't quite sure he understood it—the press and his "princely charmingness"? What was that all about?

"I don't bask in anything," he said.

"I'm sure you don't realize it," she said. "You're one of those people who glides through life. Everything goes well for you all the time because you're so handsome and charming."

He felt a half-second of surprise at the word "hand-some." She thought he was handsome. No one had used that in connection with him for a long time. But charming? He hadn't been charming to her. He hadn't even tried to be charming.

"You're making assumptions," he said.

"Am I?" She raised her pencil-thin eyebrows. He usually hated manicured eyebrows, but on her, they looked appropriate. They matched her thin, angular face.

"You're not one of the fairy godmothers," he said, deliberately changing the subject. He had to take the focus off himself. "The fairy godmothers are always unbelievably happy for no apparent reason. Disney got that right at least. *Bippidi Boppidi Boo* and all that."

Her breath caught, and she leaned back just a bit, as if she were seeing him for the first time.

He'd gotten her, and he felt a bit of disappointment at that. He was using his best weapon—his only weapon, really. Charm. He was so very good at charm, and one part of charm was to focus on the person you were talking to.

Not that it was hard, focusing on her. He wanted to focus on her. Despite the bitterness of her tone, despite the sarcasm she used against him, he wanted to be closer to her.

He wanted to kiss her.

And he knew that wouldn't go over well at all.

"You can't be one of the old crones either," he said, making himself concentrate on the charm and not on the woman. Although he couldn't help focusing on her a little. Real charm was based on truth, and truth came out of opinion, and opinion came out of personality. "Because the crones do look like the witches in *Macbeth*— Shakespeare had clearly been to one of the Kingdoms, maybe more than once."

The woman's delectable lips curved upwards slightly. That twisted, bitter look was gone, and with it, at least ten years, maybe more. She looked younger and even more striking than she had a moment ago.

So more truth:

"And you're beautiful, more beautiful now than you probably ever were as a girl." He didn't want to sound like he was coming on to her. He didn't dare, not with her being so bitter. So he made it sound like he was stating a fact.

Which he was.

"You're probably one of the stepmothers," he said. "I would guess Snow White's, because one of the step-mothers is my mother-in-law."

Whom he liked, truth be told. She was just a woman who had gotten a raw deal—her beloved husband had died, leaving her to fend for herself, and she hadn't known how.

"And the other stepmother…" He stopped himself before he said something he would regret. Sleeping Beauty's stepmother, Eris, was a witch in the classic sense of the word. And he really didn't want to think of her. So he kept talking, which he tended to do when he needed to work out a problem.

"Which means," he said, "you and I met at a party, gosh, a century or two ago, when someone decided we should clear up the Charming mess and the step-mother gossip and see if we could take care of those Brothers Grimm."

That look of almost-amusement the beautiful woman had vanished as if it had never been. Her eyebrows met in the middle as she mustered a truly formidable frown.

"*I* decided," she said. "It wasn't *someone* who decided we needed to clear up what you so politely call 'the Charming mess and the stepmother gossip.' It was me. *I* decided. I hosted that party."

He nodded, remembering now. It was one of the first large scale events ever held in the Greater World. There had been too many arguments about which kingdom would host the gathering, so someone—this woman maybe?—decided to rent a castle in Germany of all places, that white one with the towers along the Rhine that Disney later used in one of its films.

Nothing had gotten settled, and in fact, he could point to the entire event as the beginning of the end of his marriage. Ella met the wives of the other Charmings, and they started talking about their marriages, and Things Got Said. The other Charmings apparently treated their wives like princesses. Not that he hadn't. But he also expected Ella to think for herself, and do something other than spend the king's gold.

He'd said that more than once, and he'd made the mistake of saying it in front of his father, who then harped on it forever. Apparently—at least according to Charming's ex-wife, the other Charmings never said anything bad about their wives.

Charming thought that was just one-upsmanship. People—charming or not—said things they regretted. Maybe the other wives just hadn't been as sensitive to slights as Ella had been. Either way, Ella had been dissatisfied with the relationship ever since.

Charming looked at the beautiful woman before him. Now the memory was becoming clear. He had noticed how stunning she was in Germany all those years ago. He had noticed and thought she had gotten a bad rep, considering everything. All she and the other stepmothers wanted was a little respect.

"You never answered me," he said. "Are you Snow White's stepmother?"

"Are you Sleeping Beauty's Prince Charming?" she asked, apparently not willing to show him hers until he showed her his. But in asking the question, he got his answer. She was Snow White's stepmother.

"I married Ella," he said. "The fairy tales still call her CinderElla, which really isn't fair. She was only covered in a light dusting of ash, mostly because there was something wrong with the flue—"

"Thin and shapely and beautiful and oh, so young." That bitterness again.

What had made her so bitter? It was awful to see on a woman as beautiful as she was—as beautiful and as obviously intelligent.

"Why is it," she was saying, "that men like you always go for women like her?"

"Women like her?" He wasn't feeling defensive, exactly. More curious. "What do you mean, women like her?"

"I saw her," the woman said. "Petite and delicate and so pretty. She talked about clothes and jewelry, and I remembered thinking that she didn't have a thought in her head."

Oh, Ella had thoughts but she worked at suppressing them. And she did enjoy her wardrobe and her jewels, primarily because they'd been denied her as a teenage girl. She didn't want to put her mind to use. She'd used it too much—she said—to escape her wicked stepmother.

Charming wasn't going to lie (although he could have. What would it matter? He probably wasn't going to see this woman again [and that thought made his heart twist a little, but really, when had he pursued a relationship? He hadn't even pursued the relationship with Ella. That had been his father's idea]).

He didn't feel like defending Ella either. Or himself, really.

But this woman had asked, and despite her bitterness, he wanted to continue the conversation. She was the first person who had seen him—really seen him—in years.

And somehow that made her even more attractive.

"I was a boy when I met Ella," he said. "And she was a girl, not a woman. We weren't really old enough to commit to anything."

The woman let out a small *huh*. "So all three of the best known Charmings have divorced now."

That news made him grunt with surprise. He hadn't known that. He thought the other Charmings lived in perpetual wedded bliss. Happily ever after and all that.

Lost in her surprise, the woman didn't seem to notice his. She was saying, "Isn't that just the way of things? I suppose you blame the women's movement as well?"

"Excuse me?" It took Charming a moment to understand what she meant, and when he did, he almost let out another grunt of surprise.

The other Princes Charming had blamed the Greater

World's women's movement for the failure of their
marriages? Seriously?

He knew where the fault in his marriage was, and it
wasn't with some amorphous movement in another world.

"Ella and I weren't compatible from the beginning,"
he said. "She's very into the social whirl, the dresses, the
dancing, and me, well…"

He grabbed his badge. He was going to shake it ruefully. Instead, his fingers closed protectively around it.

"I'm bookish," he said. "Quiet. A bit of—what do
they call it here in the Greater World?—a nerd."

The beautiful woman took a step backwards. Of
course she did. Beautiful women, no matter what world
they were from, loathed nerds.

"A nerd," she repeated, as if she couldn't quite believe what she was hearing. "Prince Charming is a nerd."

"And," he said, mostly to cover the blush he could
feel warming his cheeks, "I'm certain my father didn't
help any. He wanted sons, and he blamed Ella when
we didn't have any. There was no explaining genetics
to him. X and Y chromosomes are beyond him. He'd
been urging me to throw her off after our first daughter
was born. But then, he also wanted me to use the old-
fashioned King Henry the Eighth method."

The woman frowned. Those pencil-thin eyebrows
didn't meet in the middle this time, though. They just
danced toward each other for a millisecond.

She had a wide range of frowns—and this one was
attractive.

"Divorce?" the woman asked, with an edge of worry
in her tone.

Another opportunity to lie. Of course, he didn't take

it—and normally he would have. He always lied about his father. Charming wanted people to think his father was a better man than he truly was.

"Um, no," Charming said, trying to be circumspect. "Henry's… um… other method of disposing of his wives."

She smiled. Her face softened, and he realized he was wrong. She wasn't just beautiful. She was the most beautiful woman he had ever seen. In either world. Which was saying a lot.

"Oh, my." Her voice lilted upward, as if she was suppressing a laugh. "He really is the tyrant, isn't he?"

Charming nodded, a bit uncomfortably. He didn't find his father amusing at all. He tried not to look at his father's deeds—or misdeeds. Not that they were illegal. Whatever the King did was legal; that was the law of the land. But Charming didn't have to like it.

"I prefer it here," Charming said. "In the Greater World."

With books, books, and more books being created all the time. Not to mention movies and television and games. He was even beginning to like Twitter novels, even though that panel at the last book fair had shaken him more than he wanted to admit. He didn't want the book to die. He wanted it to live, in its lovely hand-held form, for the rest of his (exceptionally long) life.

The woman's smile faded and her mouth twisted again. He was beginning to realize that was a physical sign of her bitterness.

"Of course you prefer it here," she said. "The Greater World loves you. You're an ideal. Everyone wants to be you or have you or marry you. You're not considered a bitter crone past her sell-by date who's jealous of younger women and can't come to terms with her lost potential."

Well, they had the bitterness spot on, he thought, but didn't say. Still, he suppressed a sigh. He thought she had seen him for who he was, but she hadn't. She had made up her mind about him on very little evidence—mostly on what she had heard (read?) about him, and on what other people thought.

Although, he couldn't prevent himself from saying, "Aren't you a little jealous of young women? I mean, you mentioned Ella's age right off. And you seem pretty focused on age."

Snow White's stepmother's eyes widened and her lovely mouth opened slightly. She wasn't frowning now. She seemed stunned. Hadn't anyone spoken to her like this before?

"Look," Charming said, opening his hands in what Ella always called his don't-blame-me gesture. "You're the one who made the comment about me marrying a girl who was 'thin, shapely, and oh, so young.' That sounds a little bitter and jealous to me."

The woman's mouth snapped shut. Her eyes narrowed. "Of course it would seem bitter and jealous to you. I suppose you think I tried to kill Snow White, like the fairy tales say."

It was his turn to lean back. Behind that bitterness was a lot of anger. A lot of anger. He could feel it radiating off her. And that intrigued him, although he didn't want it to.

Interesting that she thought he believed the fairy tales. He, of all people, knew how false they were. In any of the Kingdoms, if she had tried to murder Snow White, then she would either have been executed on Snow White's wedding day or at least have been imprisoned.

"People like you," she was saying, her voice getting even more strident, "believe in the fairy tales. Why shouldn't you? You live one."

He sighed. He didn't think divorce was part of the fairy tale, but he couldn't get a word in. She hadn't stopped talking.

"People like you," she said, "don't understand people like me. You have everything in life, and you don't understand people who have to fight for every scrap—"

"You're right," he said flatly.

She stopped, as if she was surprised at his words. Apparently, she didn't expect him to admit anything.

But he wasn't going to say what he really thought. He hated it when conversations veered in this direction. He was in a damned-if-he-did and damned-if-he-didn't situation. If he said he understood, he'd have to prove it, with life experience that she might or might not believe. And if he said he didn't understand, then she'd try to convince him. So he gave her his standard answer, the answer that allowed him to abandon the field.

"I don't understand people who like to fight," he said. "I never have. So have a good book fair, and I'll see you around."

He slipped past her into the hallway, feeling unsettled and somewhat disappointed. He liked her despite her anger, and it wasn't often that he found a woman attractive anymore. Most women his age had given up or had snared the right man and weren't interested in meeting anyone new.

But he didn't need the bitterness. He had enough of his own. He just tried not to think about it.

Just like he tried not to think about what the

world—his world—required of him. Technically, he should marry a younger woman and give his father the heir that his father was clamoring for. But Charming had already married a young woman, and that hadn't gotten him anywhere. And besides, he had children. Two lovely, intelligent daughters who he didn't see enough.

He found the stairs and took them two at a time, putting some distance between him and Snow's stepmother. He wondered what she would say if he told her he understood her bitterness, if he told her that he understood the weight of all those expectations.

Just because the expectations were good didn't mean they were harmless. He had been handsome and charming and where had it gotten him? Certainly not to a happily-ever-after.

He wasn't even sure he believed in happily-ever-afters.

The doors to the main exhibition hall were opening as he walked past, and his heart took a small leap. He was still unsettled—he really hadn't expected to find someone from the Kingdoms here—but he was getting past that. And considering how big this place was, he probably wouldn't see her again.

Which bothered him more than he wanted to admit.

Chapter 5

Mellie leaned the back of her head against the function room door, feeling unbelievably stupid. Charming had just shut her down. As if she were nothing.

I don't understand people who like to fight, he had said, as if she were one of them, as if she didn't have *a cause*.

She had cause to be angry, surely he could see that?

But she had been angry at him, partly—if she were truly honest with herself—because she was so attracted to him.

How clichéd was that? Being attracted to Prince Charming.

She shook her head and stood up. The worst thing she could do was go to the interview room right now and try to charm her way in. She could barely charm anyone on a good day, and at the moment, this wasn't a good day.

She had just embarrassed herself in front of a Charming.

A Charming she was attracted to, which had never happened before. She hadn't found a Charming attractive ever in her life (except this one, that day more than a hundred years ago). But then, she had blamed it on her exhaustion. Right now, she had no such excuse.

She headed back to the parking lot.

It was full now, cars stretching as far as the eye could see, glinting in the bright Los Angeles sun. It could be anywhere in Los Angeles—a huge parking lot filled with late-model cars, a warehouse-sized building filled with people doing something important, a few sickly trees, an unused sidewalk, and wide roads where the cars sped by too fast.

As she strode across the asphalt, she saw her people gathered around her minivan. They weren't in any order—it was hard to organize archetypes. And none of them were leaders. The leaders either remained in the Kingdoms or they had vanished to the winds here.

So she liked to think. Since it was clear, even from a distance, that only about half of the members of the California branch of PETA had shown up. Half of the ones who had RSVPed, that is. If Mellie had gotten half of the members of the California branch of PETA to show up, her people (if you could call them that) would have outnumbered the people in the book fair.

California had the largest number of archetypes in the United States, and in the top ten for archetypes in the Greater World. Most of the archetypes who had left the Kingdoms in the past fifty years had come to California. Most of the archetypes had to find work here because they needed money to survive. Kingdom money didn't translate, unless it was gold, and most of the archetypes couldn't get gold.

Mellie had had more gold than she knew what to do with, and she had sold a great deal of it in her first foray into the Greater World back in the nineteenth century. She had claimed she found it in California, in the so-called Gold Rush, but mostly she had brought it with her when she moved.

Mellie sighed and surveyed her troops, such as they were.

She had ended up with fifty-one protesters, fifty-two

if she counted herself. They gathered around her van, picking at the signs, and quarrelling amongst themselves.

Some had been in the Greater World for years, and had trouble finding work. The assorted woodland creatures—the birds that always seemed to guard Cinderella, the rabbits who had befriended Thumper in order to get close to Bambi, and of course, the poor deer hunter who got such a bad rap for murdering (murdering!) Bambi's mother—hung around the edges. A small grouping of tiny fairies—the ones who formed Tinker Bell's entourage before she decided to stalk Peter Pan—hovered in the center, dressed like Goth teenagers, and looking more like little girls trying to dress like their older sisters.

Those fairies had somehow divorced themselves from the Fairy Kingdom of Celtic lore. Or maybe they had never been part of it.

Mellie couldn't keep track of all of the archetypes in the Greater World. There were also the Greek Gods, whom she avoided whenever she could, and some really nasty magic users.

Two giants had joined her group, which was two more than last year, but only because they'd been cut by the NBA because they weren't agile enough. A few ogres stood to one side, wearing pirate scarves around their bald heads and rather ornate parachute pants with matching tops that somehow suited them. The little people were underrepresented for once—she'd heard that someone was filming *Return to Oz* all over again and needed Munchkins, realistic or not.

But the flying monkeys were here—or at least a few of them were. The ones who thought a movie like *Return to Oz* beneath them. The flying monkeys, a few trolls, one of the Billy Goats Gruff.

No real celebrities, however. No other stepmother, none of the witches, none of the crones (although, to be fair, most of them had moved to England and Canada, finding all kinds of work in the Shakespearean companies at the two different Stratford-upon-Avons). Mellie was the biggest archetypal celebrity at the fair, if you didn't count Charming (and why should she? He wasn't part of her group).

Rumpelstiltskin had shown up, but he never missed a protest. He loved creating havoc—and enticing beautiful women to bear his children. Mellie had never understood what attracted all those women to Rumpelstiltskin, but something did, because he'd fathered half-a-dozen children out of wedlock just since he moved to the Greater World. Fortunately for him, he was one of the best con men ever, and could spin metaphorical straw into very real gold.

He was a perfectly proportioned man who wore his clothes very well. His navy blue suit was silk and had to be too hot in this climate. His shirt was white silk, and he wore custom-made shoes. He leaned against the van as if he were posing for an automobile ad.

He could have led this group, but he knew better. The one time he had tried, Mellie had gotten furious and he hadn't liked that.

Not because he couldn't deal with furious women—it seemed furious women were his specialty, along with long cons—but because he really liked and respected her.

He wasn't a bad guy underneath that conniving

personality. In fact, he was one of the few archetypes who truly understood what she was trying to do.

He winked when he saw her approach. Then he inclined his head toward the back of the van and her heart sank.

The disheveled man sitting half in and half out of the van was trouble. He, too, wore a blue suit, but the suit looked like he'd been wearing it for weeks. His hair hadn't been combed in just that long. It had gotten tangled in his beard which was... blue.

Really and truly blue. Smurf blue.

When he cleaned up, that Smurf blue accented his eyes. He looked like he was made of sapphires. He was breathtakingly handsome underneath the mess, which was how he had married all those women, and he was, unlike the other archetypes, the only one who wasn't unjustly accused.

Bluebeard.

Mellie shuddered as she looked at him. He must have escaped again. No institution in the Kingdoms could hold him, partly because he was a very wealthy man, and partly because he was rumored to be a king's son—another Charming gone wrong, probably.

Badly, horribly, awfully wrong.

She sighed. She'd have to deal with him immediately. She couldn't let him inside the book fair. All the attention would be on him, and not on her cause.

As she walked up, she pulled one of the fairies aside. The fairy, blond and pale just like Disney's Tinker Bell, had gossamer wings and the most wicked tongue Mellie had heard on anyone, bar none.

The fairy kept her name secret like all fairies did, but

she was known as Cantankerous Belle—Tanker Belle for short.

"I know, I know," Tanker Belle said in her deep, gruff voice. She sounded like a full-size human chain-smoker—Bette Davis combined with James Earl Jones. "The minute I saw him, I knew you'd tap us."

"Sorry," Mellie said.

Tanker Belle shrugged. "What this time? Wrap him in some glamour and get him off the property?"

"I'd say yes, except this is a three-day affair."

"There's an upscale rehab center on the coast," Rumpelstiltskin said. He hadn't moved from his perch against the van. "I have his credit card. He can clearly afford it."

Mellie didn't want to know how Rumpelstiltskin had gotten Bluebeard's credit card, but she was grateful.

"A twenty-eight-day program?" she asked.

He nodded.

"Has he been drinking?" she asked.

"You want to go sniff him? He's either been sleeping in booze-soaked linens or he's been soaking it up himself." Tanker Belle hovered in front of Mellie like a giant hummingbird.

"Okay, then," Mellie said. "Get the address from Stilt over there."

"And the credit card," one of the other fairies said. "Last time, he didn't fork it over, and I paid."

She shook a tiny fist at Rumpelstiltskin.

"You still owe me," she said.

"I'll pay up," he said. "You just say when and how."

Then he grinned, and to Mellie's surprise, the fairy grinned back. Mellie shook her head, not fully comprehending the interaction—or, to be more accurate—not wanting to.

She made her way through the crowd of archetypes, heading for the signs. She needed to get the group organized. And she wanted to avoid Blue.

But that wasn't in the cards.

Tanker Belle was right—he smelled like he'd been bathing in whiskey. Whiskey and Aqua Velva. And vomit.

Not the best combination on a good day. And this was not—by any stretch of the imagination—a good day.

"I wanna help out," Blue said.

He had a lovely voice. Musical, deep, with enough of an accent to make him seem exotic. Or at least, he would seem exotic, if she hadn't heard it all before.

"You'll help out by going with Tanker Belle and the girls," Mellie said.

"Ah, Mel." Blue put his meaty fist on her shoulder. "I'm terribly misunderstood. I can talk to the press. I took classes in media relations at UCLA."

Somehow that didn't surprise her. She slipped out of his grasp and resisted the urge to wipe off her shoulder.

"Blue, you're not sober," she said. "Being sober is one of my rules, remember?"

He rolled those pretty blue eyes. "Hon, I don't do rules, except my own."

"Which is another reason I don't want you here," she said.

He leaned closer to her. A few of the woodland creatures gasped in disgust. It took all of Mellie's strength not to do the same.

"Everybody's got a story," he said. "You've never asked mine."

"I saw the heads," Mellie snapped. "I knew some of those girls."

He frowned and backed away, just like she knew he would. She'd said that to him five years ago, ten years ago, fifteen years ago. Each time, it made him walk away.

Only this time, he said, "You listen to everybody else. How come not me?"

"Sober up, Blue, and maybe I will," she said.

"I've talked to you sober before," he said.

"Sober up for more than a year," she said. "Then we can talk."

She snapped her fingers, and Tanker Belle flew over.

"C'mon, monster," Tanker Belle said. "We got a rehab facility to fly to."

"I told you before, Tank," Blue said. "I hate to fly."

"And I told you before, Blue," Candy said. "It's Tanker Belle to you."

She wrapped him in fairy dust and beckoned her companions. They attached little gossamer strings to the cocoon of fairy dust and raised him up, as if he were made of air.

Mellie looked around the parking lot. There were a few booksellers mingling about, a couple of authors arriving too late to get parking, and one or two of the union men who'd been carrying all that equipment. None of them looked over this way.

Even if they did, they wouldn't see anything. Just a bit of a heat shimmer or a glimmering caused—they'd think—by the sun. The more sensitive of them would see tiny birds, maybe even hummingbirds, flying in a circle, and they'd wonder why there were hummingbirds in the middle of a parking lot.

But they wouldn't wonder long. They'd return to whatever else they'd been doing and forget this entire incident had happened.

That was one of the neat things about fairy dust. It made people forget.

She'd had Tanker Belle and the fairies intervene more than once when a protest had gone bad.

But Mellie didn't have that option this time. Not with Tanker Belle and her gang funneling (literally) Blue off to rehab.

This protest had to go well.

She had to do everything right.

Chapter 6

CHARMING LOOKED LIKE A BOOK BAG TREE. HE HAD TWO stuffed book backpacks on his back, two equally stuffed book bags hanging off each shoulder, and four brimming book bags in each hand. Probably 150 pounds of books.

Not that 150 pounds hobbled him. After all he was one of the strongest booksellers here. (Okay, okay, truth be told, he *was* the strongest bookseller here.)

But 150 pounds draped off him in an awkward and badly packed manner made the weight seem at least double. He staggered as he walked, afraid he was going to leave a trail of books, the way that Hansel and Gretel supposedly left a trail of bread crumbs.

Only no birds would eat books.

Although booksellers would probably snap up some of the more exclusive advance reading copies.

He grinned to himself at the thought. He needed a grin, because he was already breathing hard by the time he reached the front door. The parking lot spread before him, a sea of glistening cars. His Mercedes was parked in the only remaining bit of shade—about two thousand miles away, as the crow flies. And he wouldn't be able to walk as the crow flies. He would have to stagger between the cars.

Which he did. He would have felt ridiculous if he were the only one doing this. But as he walked, he passed four other booksellers, stumbling under the weight of their treasures. Most of them had only four book bags full of material, but most of the booksellers were older than he was (Greater World years versus Kingdom years) and not as svelte.

Of course, they didn't have to maintain a kingly regimen either, just in case their Kingdom was invaded. Two days per week of jousting practice, three days of sword fighting practice, one day of archery practice, and one day of hand-to-hand combat practice (which he would replace with martial arts, if he ever became king), not to mention all the horseback riding.

When he came to the Greater World, he kept up his skills by running marathons (the most surreal being the ones sponsored by Disney. Sometimes he felt surrounded by the Greater World's inaccurate representations of his friends and family) and working on his black belt. He had a brown belt now. One day he'd use those skills in his hand-to-hand combat practice, just to let everyone in the Kingdoms know he wasn't some pushover bookish prince whose wife had walked all over him.

(Even if he was, to be truthful, a bookish prince whose wife *had* walked all over him.)

Sweat trickled down his brow as he passed yet another bookseller—this one smart enough to have brought one of those collapsible grocery carts that he had filled with his books.

"Good move," Charming said as he passed the bookseller.

"Saves my back," the bookseller said.

And his feet and his knees and his thumbs. Charming's thumbs had started to ache from the awkward angle he held them at.

He thought he'd never reach his car. But he finally did.

His hands were too tied up to activate the keyless entry, so he set all the book bags down, and fished for his keys. As his Mercedes chirruped at him, he let out a small sigh of relief.

He opened the passenger door, forced down the seat and filled the back seat with bags. Either he had to pack well or he had only two more trips ahead of him—which simply was not satisfactory.

He took the books out of their bags, arranged them in even stacks—biggest on the bottom, smallest on top. When he was done, he figured he had three more trips before he ran out of room.

By then, he'd probably be exhausted.

He locked the car and headed back. As he did, his gaze went to Snow White's stepmother's van. (What was that woman's name? Had he ever learned it? Or was she cursed with a stupid label, like he was?)

The back of the van was open and someone was rummaging inside.

Charming felt an unexpected urge to apologize, even though he hadn't done anything wrong. The woman had anger issues, but he understood those anger issues.

He also understood the bitterness. Bitterness and the feeling that no one else knew exactly what he was going through.

Especially when people expected him to be perfect. Prince Charming—as if he were an ideal. Apparently, he was an ideal. The beautiful stepmother was right; everyone wanted their own personal Prince Charming—especially if he looked like the Disney version that had once passed him in the Disney Marathon—thin, black-haired, stunningly handsome, flawless.

Charming wasn't flawless. He certainly wasn't thin anymore. Even with all the required exercise, he still had a paunch that wouldn't go away. For a while, Ella had called that paunch love handles. Then she'd pat that little roll of fat and tell him he wasn't working out hard enough. And finally she started pinching it, as if she could pull it off him with the force of her fingers.

Her sharp, little, pointy fingers.

He shook his head, tired of obsessing about that woman. But he couldn't help himself. Except for a few really unsatisfactory dates here in the Greater World, he hadn't been with anyone else since. And Ella had custody of the girls.

He really missed his daughters. Especially here, at the book fair. There had been a number of books he picked up just for them. When they'd lived at the palace, he would read to them every night.

Now he got to read to them for seven nights a month, when he had his one-week visitation.

He looked up in surprise. He had veered toward the PETA van, even though he hadn't wanted to. And, as he got close, he realized the person messing in the back of the van wasn't a person at all.

It was one of the flying monkeys.

He felt a surge of disappointment. He really wanted to see the beautiful stepmother again. He wanted to talk to her about something other than archetypes and being charming. He wanted to see if he could touch that soft skin of hers again, if maybe they could find common ground besides their uncommon background.

He'd never quite understood the flying monkeys. They weren't from his Kingdom. His Kingdom had a lot of inexplicable things—talking mice, magical birds—but they had counterparts in the Greater World. The Greater World had mice, they just didn't speak English. The Greater World had birds, they just didn't seem to care about the affairs of humans.

The flying monkeys were from one of the fringe Kingdoms, a Kingdom he'd never visited. Charming had met some flying monkeys and some tin men and some animated scarecrows. He'd also seen unicorns and dragons and all sorts of so-called mythical beasts. But only here in the Greater World. Never in the Kingdoms. As he got close to the van, he watched the monkey grab a loud, red 1960s Sergeant Pepper-y coat and pull it on, stuffing his wings into the back of it. The monkey put on a hat, a fake ZZ-Top beard, and sunglasses.

The disguise made him look human enough, until you peered and realized that greenish brown fur covered not only the skin around his eyes and his forehead, but also his hands and forearms.

With those hands, he grabbed two signs out of the van. He waved them a little, not because he was trying to get attention with them, but because he seemed to be having trouble controlling his wings.

It took him a moment to get the signs under control. As he did, he turned them toward Charming.

Book Unfair! Destroy the Lies!

Charming felt an odd flutter in his chest as he read those words. Book unfair? What book? What were they protesting exactly?

Had someone done an exposé?

The flying monkey closed the back of the van, sending a wave of fresh Magic Marker scent toward Charming. Then the monkey grabbed the signs, slung them over his shoulder, and marched toward the building.

Charming hurried to catch up.

"Excuse me," Charming said as he reached the monkey's side. "Are you with PETA?"

He said it the way the animal rights group did— pee-tah—and the monkey's mouth tightened into a little frown.

"I'm with PETA," he snapped, articulating each letter. "People for the Ethical Treatment—"

"Of Archetypes, I know," Charming said. "What's this about unfair books?"

The monkey stopped. Charming had to stop too. Up close, the monkey smelled vaguely rank. Something wild animally and sharp and somewhat unpleasant.

"You read these things?" the monkey asked as if there was something wrong with Charming.

Things. Charming frowned. "You mean books? Do I read books?"

The monkey nodded.

"Of course I do," Charming said. "Why else would I be here?"

The monkey's eyes widened and he took a step back, as if he had met an enemy worse than the Wicked Witch he had once supposedly worked for.

"You're being brainwashed, pal," the monkey said.

"By books?" Charming asked.

Books opened minds. Books expanded horizons. Books didn't brainwash. Books couldn't—at least in the Greater World.

In a few of the Kingdoms, books actually came to life and had powers that did make them dangerous. Charming had learned to avoid those Kingdoms, and so far, no one had traveled out of them bearing books.

Or if they had, the books lost their power once they reached the Greater World, which happened to a number of magical things. (Although it rarely happened to magical people.)

"Yes, brainwashed by books," the monkey said as if Charming were particularly dense. "You read those things, they warp you. You probably have no idea about the evil being perpetrated by those horrible fairy tales."

"Fairy tales," Charming repeated.

"That's right," the monkey said. "They're lies. Damn lies. And they've got to be stopped."

"The fairy tales have to be stopped," Charming repeated because he didn't entirely understand this. "Fairy tales have been around for hundreds of years."

"That's hundreds of years too long," the monkey said. "We've got to put an end to this madness."

"By protesting a book fair?" Charming couldn't keep the incredulousness out of his voice.

"We have to start somewhere," the monkey said. "Which reminds me. I have a meeting."

He tipped his hat to Charming, then loped away, his wings fluttering against the back of that red coat. The signs bobbed, mocking Charming.

Book Unfair.

Destroy the Lies.

Destroy…?

Oh good heavens. Did PETA want to destroy books? Was that why the organization was here? He was confused. They thought they could—what? Stop the spread of fairy tales? Make fantastic literature go away? To what end?

He needed to go back to the exhibition hall, but he found himself following the monkey instead.

Chapter 7

MELLIE WAS FIGHTING OFF A HEADACHE. SHE WAS HUNGRY, tired, and more discouraged than she wanted to admit. If she tallied up all the results of all the protests she had ever done, she could count fifteen newspaper articles (only three of them in "newspapers of record"), two rather snarky blog posts, some unflattering photographs, and one light piece at the end of a local newscast.

No one took her seriously. No one even tried.

Her effort to get the message out was failing, and she wasn't sure why.

Although she knew what her problem was here.

She couldn't find a foothold.

Five of her protestors were already marching through the hall, shouting *Death to Fairy Tales*! Another five were handing out flyers explaining PETA's position on fairy tales and why they were evil, along with the URL of the website she had started back when she first conceived of the protest idea.

No one really wanted to listen. Those who did stop did so reluctantly, looking longingly at the doors down the hallway, as if hoping for rescue. A few took the flyers and tossed them when they thought they were out of sight.

She really did need a new strategy. She just didn't know what it was.

She tried to think about it as she carried her sign — *Not All Stepmothers Are Wicked!* — and marched in her circle, keeping her eyes out for those pasty rent-a-cops. This time, she wouldn't let them move her out of the way. This time, she would hold her ground.

She was halfway around when she saw a familiar, elegant figure come through the door leading to the service entrance. That Charming got around. He still looked marvelous, even if he was frowning.

She wasn't sure she had ever seen a Charming in a full-on snit before, but he clearly was. Had someone stolen his precious name badge? Or had they refused to give him books?

As she rounded the circle, she had to turn her back on him, which was disappointing. At least he was wonderful to look at. And she was curious to see where he was going.

Suddenly a hand clamped tightly on her shoulder, pulling her backwards, away from her chanting line.

She normally took a swing at anyone who touched her unnecessarily—she'd learned that because of all the gropey people in the palace (particularly the knights)—but this time, she thought about it before she beaned the grabber with her sign. It could be one of the security people—and such an action was guaranteed to get her thrown out—or worse (better?) it could be a reporter.

She glanced down at the hand warming her skin, and saw it was beautifully shaped, with long elegant fingers. Only two kinds of people had hands like that—famous people and beautiful people.

She turned her head even farther, and saw Charming's face dangerously close to hers. His eyes, behind those glasses, were sky blue fringed by long dark lashes, his skin even more flawless up close (except for the flush building in his cheeks), and his beautifully shaped lips were pulled back in a thin line.

He wasn't in a full-on snit. He was angry.

She had no idea that Charmings even got angry. Was it allowed?

He grabbed her sign and tossed it to the floor. Then he pulled her to the bend in the hallway, away from the marchers. She signaled them with her hand to continue walking, not that any of them had come to her defense.

"Tell me you're kidding," he said, as if they'd been having a conversation.

His grip on her shoulder was firm, but not painful. Still, she slipped her hand under his wrist and lifted his fingers off her skin. She felt an ache where they had been.

"I'm perfectly serious," she said, not sure at all what he was referring to. So she got to choose the topic. "Not all stepmothers are wicked."

She turned toward him as she said that, and realized that she was a half an inch away from pressing her entire body against his. For a second, she was tempted. Then she took a step back to put a proper distance between them.

"I *know* that about stepmothers," he said. "I happen to like mine."

She raised her eyebrows. "Your father remarried?"

He shook his head, the look of annoyance on his face growing. "My stepmother-*in-law*," he said. "Ella's stepmother. I like her. She's a strong woman, who had a few bad breaks."

"See?" Mellie said, forcing herself to smile. "My sign is right."

"I'm not talking about your damn sign!" he snapped. "You want to ban books. Don't you?"

The fury in his voice startled her. She had rarely seen any man that angry, let alone a Charming. (Well, she had never seen a Charming angry at all, but she had seen a lot of angry men—some of whom had some real magic behind the anger. Charming didn't need magic. He had strength of personality. His anger was... formidable.)

"I don't want to ban books, exactly," she said, forcing herself to remain calm. "I just want to reduce the lies a bit."

"By banning books," he said.

"Not all of them," she said. "Just the ones that lie."

"Just the ones that lie," he repeated. "You mean fiction?"

She shrugged. "I suppose. It's—"

"Fiction is very, very important," he said, his voice rising. "Storytelling is how people learn. You get people to understand new cultures and other lives through *stories*. Made-up stories. Fiction."

"Yes, exactly," she said. "Which is why it can't lie."

He rolled his eyes. "Fiction lies for the truth."

"Then tell me," she said, "what truth do fairy tales tell?"

"Fairy tales?" he asked. "This is all about *fairy tales*?"

"Yes," she said. "They misrepresent us."

Then she shrugged, feeling a bit angry herself.

"Well, they misrepresent some of us. You, for example, have nothing to fear from them. They don't attack you and call you evil and wicked and—"

"Don't start with that 'people like you' crap again," he snapped. "People like me know that happily-ever-after is a crock. I'm divorced, remember?"

She bit her lower lip. She really hadn't put that together.

"I'm divorced, I don't see my kids enough, for heaven's sake, and I'm not perfect." His voice was rising.

"Do you know how hard it is to go through life when everyone expects you to be perfect?"

She almost said, *Obviously not*, but thought the better of it. He was angry enough.

"Do you know what your problem is?" he said, leaning close to her. "You don't know how lucky you are."

His arrogance took her breath away. "Lucky?"

"Lucky," he said. "You're beautiful, you're smart, you're successful enough to travel the Greater World, for heaven's sake, and all you care about is what people think of you."

"I do not," she said.

"You do too." He swept an arm toward the protestors. "Are you really an Archetype? Nowadays? Maybe a century ago, when women didn't have as many opportunities. And maybe when you couldn't choose your own identity. But who in this world knows who you are unless you point it out to them? And when you do, they think you're crazy."

"You don't know—"

"I do know!" He was yelling now. "Of course I know. Do you know what some officious little American government prick did when I told him my real name after I passed my driving test? Do you?"

She swallowed. "No."

"He laughed." Charming lowered his voice. "He laughed and said my parents ought to be shot."

She smiled. She couldn't help herself. She could picture that. She, at least, didn't have to go around introducing herself as the Evil Stepmother because that wasn't her real name. Never had been.

"Go ahead," he said, with some heat. "Laugh. But

it's not fun. I actually prefer Dave. No one laughs when I say my name is Dave."

"Hey!" A door opened near Mellie. A man peered out. "Can you people pipe down? We're taping in here."

One of the ogres—whose name she always forgot—raised his sign and waved it in the man's face. "This book fair is unfair!" the ogre growled. "It's—"

"Yeah, yeah, yeah," the man said. "Someone is always publishing something someone else objects to. Whoop dee ding dong do."

Then he slammed the door closed.

Mellie stared at it for a moment. Her heart sank. *Whoop dee ding dong do. Whoop dee ding dong do?*

That man, a man she didn't know, had just dismissed all of her hard work with a single *whoop dee ding dong do*.

And don't forget his other comment, some small voice said inside her head. *That someone is always publishing something someone else objects to.* Like it's normal.

Charming was watching her. He looked at the closed door, then looked at her, as if he realized that man's comment had made some kind of impression—although he clearly wasn't sure what kind.

The protestors had stopped marching and shouting.

"What do you want us to do, Mellie?" the selkie asked.

She didn't know. She had no idea anymore.

So she shrugged. "Take a lunch break."

They set their signs down and bolted out of the hallway. She wondered if she'd ever see them again.

She didn't want to look at Charming. He would be laughing. He would gloat. Or he would be gone already.

But she couldn't help herself.

She looked.

He had an expression of compassion on his face. "It really bothers you what they think, doesn't it?"

Her lower lip trembled, and she bit it. Hard. Evil stepmothers weren't supposed to cry. Nor were they supposed to care about the opinion of a Charming.

But here she was, on the verge of tears, in front of a Charming who actually appealed to her.

"Back when I was thin and shapely and beautiful and oh, so young, I didn't care," she said. "But then more thin and shapely and beautiful and oh, so young things showed up and I stopped being important, and I would say something a little sarcastic, and I suddenly got called old and bitter and jealous, and it just went downhill, no matter what I did. Words hurt, Charming. Words hurt."

He nodded. "So you thought you could control the words."

"Isn't that what you do with that golden voice of yours and that marvelously soothing manner? Don't you control the words?"

He gave her a rueful smile. "If I did, don't you think I would have ended up with custody of my daughters?"

Mellie looked at him, really looked at him, for the first time. He was very handsome. Elegant, not quite as trim as he could be, and just a hint of a bald spot that he might not even know about. A few lines around the eyes.

Not as young as he used to be either.

Seasoned.

Like her.

Only no one called him old and bitter and jealous.

But, back when she first met him (all of a few hours ago), he had called himself a nerd.

"What are you really doing here in the Greater World?" she asked.

"Me?" his voice squeaked just a little. "Getting books. I told you. I read a lot."

She picked up his badge. It was purple, not for royalty, like she'd initially thought, but for booksellers. "You got an illegal badge?"

"No," he said. "I sell books back home."

"You're a merchant?" She couldn't quite keep the incredulousness from her tone.

He straightened his shoulders as if by making himself taller he would become more powerful. "It's an honorable profession."

He was being defensive. That surprised her. "I just thought being prince was profession enough."

"Maybe in the Greater World," he said. "Here princes have to give speeches and do good works and have meetings with other princes. Back home, all I do is wait for my father to die."

He flushed a dark red.

"I didn't mean that the way it sounded," he said.

"I know what you mean," she said. "You like it better here."

He nodded.

"Why?"

He waved his badge at her. "People don't have any expectations of Dave the Bookseller. Except one."

"What's that?" she asked, actually curious.

"They expect him to know a lot about books."

———

As he said that, he suddenly knew how to solve her problem. Charming held out his hand.

"Come with me," he said.

The hallway was quiet, now that her people weren't shouting. The signs still lined the corridor. Her small team had left them behind. Fliers littered the floor. She had made a mess.

She wasn't looking at the mess. She was looking at his hand as if she expected him to be holding a dagger. "Why should I come with you?"

"Because you're going about this all wrong," he said.

She frowned, turning her head slightly in that way people had when they were considering something they hadn't thought of before. Or maybe she just wasn't sure if she should walk away with a crazy man who had been angry with her a moment before, and who now believed he had the solution to all her problems.

Because he did. He did have the solution to all her problems.

Or at least, to what she thought her problems were.

"I'm going about what all wrong?" she asked.

"Getting them to think better of you," he said. Although he wasn't exactly sure who "they" were—the folks in the Greater World? Clearly, or she wouldn't be here protesting. What about the folks back home? Did she want them to think better of her too? Because that would be harder.

She said, "They need to know that we're not evil. We're just people, doing the best we could with a bad hand—"

"I know," he said. "I know what the perception is, and I know how wrong it is. But you can't change it by telling people they're wrong. That whole 'people like you' thing—"

"I'm sorry I said that," she said. "It's rude."

"So are these placards," he said. "They insult book people."

"They do?" she asked.

She clearly didn't understand.

He sighed and let his hand drop. "Book people love books. Most book people love books more than anything in the whole world."

His voice shook. He was talking about himself. He knew that. He wondered if she did.

"When you tell book people that they should change books or censor them or ban them, you're taking away the one thing that makes books so wonderful."

"There would be other books," she said.

He shook his head. "You miss the point. The point isn't that there would be other books. Or even that there would be more appropriate books. The point is that books themselves are an adventure. They challenge us, change our perceptions, make us more than we are."

There it was: the first person plural. Right after he had sworn to avoid it. He was revealing himself, but he didn't know how to do this any other way.

"We need to know that all kinds of books exist. Books that make us fall in love. Books that scare us. Books that are so full of lies they make us angry."

"Why would you want that?" she asked.

"Why would you not want it?" he asked.

"Because they're lying about us," she said.

"Do they ever call you by name?" he asked. Then he

frowned. "What is your name, by the way? I only know the Disney name, and that can't be right—"

"It's Mellie," she said.

"So Disney had it right?" he asked, trying to remember. Was it Millificent? Millicent? Mill—

"Melvina," she said. "My name is Melvina. Which is actually a good name. It means—"

"The female form of Melvin," he said. "It means 'chieftain.'"

Her mouth was open just slightly. "How did you know that?"

He smiled, happy to give her the answer. "Books," he said. "I have an eidetic memory. So I remember everything I read."

"Good heavens," she said. "Doesn't that clutter up your brain?"

Which was a fairy tale character's answer if he had ever heard one. But he didn't say that to her. He didn't want to insult her.

Instead, he said gently, "I don't have much more to clutter it up with. My whole life is about—"

"Waiting for your father to die, I know," she said, not without a bit of compassion.

He didn't want to talk about that. He was sorry he had said it earlier. Something about this woman made him more honest than he usually was.

Mellie. It suited her. Just like Melvina did. Only Melvina was one of those formal names, the name that a person used when they needed the dignity of their full name. Like David. The Biblical King wasn't King Dave. He was King David. But Charming would have wagered that all his friends called him Dave.

"What I was asking," Charming said, keeping his voice gentle, "before I sidetracked us, was do any of these fairy tales mention you by name?"

She looked away from him, as if the door behind them—the door that got slammed a few moments ago—had suddenly become very interesting.

"No," she said sullenly, rather like one of his daughters when he caught them in a lie.

"Do these fairy tales describe you accurately?" he asked.

Her gaze snapped back to his. "That's the whole point. Of course they don't. Why else would I be—"

"No, no," he said. "I mean, do they describe you accurately physically? From that lovely dark hair of yours to those emerald eyes."

He took her hand. It was soft. Her skin was as smooth as he remembered it from a few hours ago, and he didn't need to know that. He didn't need reminding about how attractive he found her.

He wanted to kiss her, and wouldn't that startle her? Just the urge startled him.

He leaned toward her, traced the side of her face with his thumb. She watched him, her mouth open just slightly.

"Do those fairy tales you hate describe the way that your cheeks flush just slightly when you're feeling passionate about something?" he asked quietly. "Or the rich, almost musical timbre of your voice?"

That flush he had mentioned had grown in her cheeks. He had unnerved her.

He was beginning to unnerve himself. He knew he could pour on the charm. He had just never done it unintentionally before.

His thumb had a mind of its own, touching that soft skin of hers. And if he got any closer, he would kiss her, and wouldn't that just scare her to death?

It scared him.

So he talked. He talked instead of kissing her because he didn't want her to run away.

But he kept his voice soft and gentle, as if he were talking to a frightened rabbit.

"I mean," he said, "do those fairy tales mention any identifying marks, anything about you that's unique to you, something that someone—when they first meet you—would say, 'Why look, Gladys! That's the Evil Stepmother from the Snow White tale.'"

She let out a reluctant bark of a laugh. "No, of course not."

"Then what angers you so?" he asked.

She sighed. Her hand moved in his, as if she thought of taking it out of his grasp, but she didn't.

Instead, she leaned into his caressing thumb, just a little, as if she didn't realize that she had done so.

"It affects all of us stepmothers," she said as if she were confiding in him. Maybe she was. "We've become a cultural stereotype, especially here, in the Greater World. We're expected to be hateful and evil, to try to kill our husbands' children, and to try to destroy his family when in reality, most of us do our best to become part of the family—sometimes to heal it. It's a destructive, horrible myth. Think about it. Children read stories about horrible stepmothers, and then their mother dies or leaves in a divorce, and suddenly they have a stepmother. Whom they're programmed to hate. We have not just the difficulties of blending families. We have to fight this horrible perception all the time."

Charming sighed. Ella had hated her stepmother. Lavinia had come into Ella's house with her father, already married (which Charming blamed on the father) and with two daughters of her own, and, Ella said, seemed nice enough. Then Ella's father died, and everything changed. Ella got treated poorly. (*She ran wild*, Lavinia said. *I just imposed some discipline; not well, because I was in terrible, horrible grief.*)

"You don't agree, do you?" Mellie said. He had been silent too long, lost in his own thoughts, a problem he'd had his whole life.

She moved that beautiful head away from his thumb. Then she pulled her hand back.

"You don't think this is a problem at all," she said, her tone becoming strident again.

Maybe that was how she dealt with embarrassment. She used her anger, her power, to keep people from seeing how vulnerable she was.

He couldn't grab her hand again; that would be wrong. But he felt like he had missed an important moment—and he didn't want to. He didn't want that closeness to go away.

"Actually, I do think this is a problem," he said. "It's a serious one, and no amount of picketing will change it."

She blinked hard, looking away from him. He could sense her frustration. Unless he missed his guess, she was very close to tears.

"So tell me, Mr. Perfectly Charming? What *am* I doing wrong? I suppose I'm not nice enough or *charming* enough to make my point properly."

She did have a wicked tongue, he would give that to the storytellers. But she only seemed to wield it when she was frustrated.

"You can make your point any way you want," he said. "But you need to use the right vehicle."

"I'm trying to get on television. I'm trying to get interviews—"

"I know," he said. "But that's ephemeral. You need to try it my way."

"The Charming way?" she asked. "Oh, good. Because I'm clearly the most charming person in the room."

He smiled. "You don't need to be charming to follow the Charming way," he said. "Come with me."

He held out his hand again.

She looked at it one more time.

"You don't quit, do you?" she asked.

He didn't answer that, because he wasn't sure he would like the answer. He just kept his hand extended.

She rolled her eyes, then put her hand in his. Her touch was soft, her skin warm and smooth, and this time, sent a tingle through him.

"Oh, all right," she said. "Show me the way, Obi-Wan."

He tucked her hand in the crook of his arm, then put his other hand over it.

"I don't think of myself as Obi-Wan," he said. "I'm more Luke than anyone."

"Oh, goody," she said with that tart tone. "The milquetoast character."

He shook his head. "The hero," he said softly. "I always like to think of myself as the hero."

And he hoped, in this case, that he wasn't wrong.

Chapter 8

IF SHE WANTED TO SHOW CHARMING THAT SHE WASN'T anything like her stereotype—bitter, frustrated, angry— she was certainly doing a good job.

Not.

Mellie let him lead her to the stairs. It felt right to walk beside him, his big hand clasped gently over hers. He had tucked her hand in the crook of his arm, royal style, as if they were heading to a ball.

Yeah, right. Like she would ever go to the ball with Prince Charming. If anything, she would stand in the corner (in a truly lovely dress) and diss the people going by. Ostensibly for amusement, but really because she wished she were one of them.

Even now, she wasn't one of the beautiful people. She was just walking with one, one who had happened to take pity on her.

He eased her up the stairs. What was it about his princeliness that made her feel like she was floating? The way that he maneuvered her forward? The gentleness of his touch? That endearing sense of shyness that he gave off?

Or maybe that was fake shyness. Maybe he knew how to make people feel comfortable, needed and wanted. And maybe he knew that she was a sucker for a shy man. Maybe knowing how to be what other people wanted was part of his charm. His magic.

Because everyone from the Kingdoms had a bit of magic. His clearly was the power to charm. Hers wasn't that subtle. Once upon a time, she had had the ability to use magic for really big things. But then she had used it all in one of those once-in-a-lifetime spells, and the magic hadn't come back.

She hadn't missed it.

Much.

Although she thought if she still had magic, she'd use it here, to repair all that damage the fairy tales had done.

She swallowed hard as they reached the top of the stairs, feeling nervous, looking for the rent-a-cops and the burly union guys. They would toss her out if they found her here again.

Normally that wouldn't bother her, but she wasn't feeling very normal at the moment. Charming had already seen her bad side. He didn't need to see anything worse.

He smiled at her and patted her hand, as if he could sense her nervousness. Great. He was sensitive too. Just what she needed.

Another overburdened bookseller staggered out of the exhibition hall, carrying two heavily laden book bags in each hand, red-faced already. No one offered to help him, not even Charming, who watched with—

Well, she would have said compassion, but that wasn't right. He was watching with envy.

He wanted to be doing *that*?

"I'm getting in your way, aren't I?" she asked.

It took a moment for him to look at her, as if he hadn't quite realized that she had spoken, and when he had realized it, he had to take another moment to comprehend it.

"No, no," he said. "Come on."

He led her to the exhibition doors.

"Do you have a badge?" he asked.

She had one. She had tucked it into one of her pockets when one of the burly union guys threatened to take it away from her and bar her from the premises.

She pulled out the badge, the lanyard crinkled, and the plastic holder creased.

Charming raised his eyebrows at the mess—didn't he ever accidentally destroy something?—but didn't say a word.

She put the badge around her neck.

"Orange," he said softly. "That means you don't have book privileges. And I didn't think to ask for an extra badge. So you can't take anything out of here."

She almost said, *Why would I want to?*, but then she saw the look of distress on his face. He thought she would want to carry books out. He thought she would be disappointed.

"That's okay," she said, hoping she put the right bit of edge of dismay in her voice.

He glanced at her sideways, smiled slightly as if he didn't believe her, and pulled open the doors.

A cacophony of light and sound greeted her. Voices, indistinguishable from one another, blended together. She didn't hear words, just the rise and fall of conversations. Hundreds of conversations.

The air smelled of ink and glue and perfume and hair spray and mildew from the overworked air conditioning. The lights were very bright, aided by displays that had mirrors, displays that had flashing lights, displays that had pinwheels of color. Product everywhere—book product—also reflected the light, and people milled about, mostly wearing red or black power suits, although more than a few of them opted for corduroy blazers with patches on the elbows and pressed blue jeans.

Occasionally, someone short with a purple badge—the males almost indistinguishable from the females (at least at a distance)—staggered out the front door with armloads of book bags. She finally understood why people who left carrying swag had red faces.

The exhibition hall seemed to go on forever. She couldn't see the back end of it. She couldn't even see the middle. The aisles were crammed with people, displays, books, and tchotchkes.

No wonder everyone ignored her protests. They were so overstimulated by this place they didn't have the capacity to notice anything else.

"Mellie." Charming's voice penetrated the noise. He said her name with just enough warmth that she tingled. She wished she hadn't heard that. Or, to be more accurate, she wished she hadn't heard it while paying attention to something else.

Because she could get used to a man saying her name that way.

She could get used to *this* man saying her name that way.

She looked over at him. He was talking to a man behind a table. The table had laptops and lists and more badges on it, as well as more lanyards and some stickers.

"This man wants to put a sticker on your name tag," Charming said.

She felt a twinge of alarm. A sticker? "For what?" she asked.

"I get one guest. I've never taken the guest, but they'll let you change your status. You okay with that?"

She didn't know if she was okay with that, but Charming wanted it and he seemed to know his way around.

"Just hold out your badge, miss," the man said.

Miss. She looked at him in surprise. The man was balding, but pleasant enough, and he certainly couldn't be as old as she was. Yet he had called her *miss*, not *ma'am*. Maybe she would like this place after all.

She held out her badge and he stuck a big purple splotch across the bottom. She had been expecting something small. That splotch covered everything but her name. And written in magic marker along the splotch were the words, *The Charming Way*.

"Enjoy," the man said with a smile.

She nodded, too stunned to say anything to him.

As she let Charming lead her into the main part of the exhibition hall, she said, "What's the Charming Way?"

"I thought we had that discussion," he said.

"No," she said, indicating her badge with her free hand. "He wrote that on my splotch."

Charming gave her a funny look. "Your what?"

She suddenly realized how that sounded. "My sticker. He wrote that on my sticker."

"It's the name of my bookstore," Charming said. She wasn't sure, but she thought he sounded reluctant to say that. "Back home."

"Oh," she said. "I hadn't realized I was making a pun earlier."

"It's okay," he said. "You weren't. You can only pun intentionally."

She hadn't known that was a rule. She shrugged and let him lead her down the main aisle. As they passed a young, thin woman with too much makeup, she handed them both book bags. Mellie, remembering what Charming had told her, was about to turn hers down, when he said, "It's okay. That's why you're on my store. So you can take samples from here."

A book bag was a sample? How bizarre. She took the bag, wrapping the cloth handle over her free wrist.

Charming pulled her to one side, near one of the booths, but not directly in front of it. They stood just outside the traffic flow which was, she noted, considerable. People moving back and forth, most of whom carried packed book bags. A few people were trying to shove more books into a bag, while a few others carried only one or two books under one arm.

"What do you think about vampires?" Charming asked.

"Excuse me?" Mellie said. She looked over at him. She wasn't sure, in all the noise and activity, that she had heard him correctly.

"Vampires," he said. "What do you think of them?"

"Personally?" she asked.

He nodded, watching her as if her answer made all the difference in the world.

"I don't like them," she said.

"Why not?" he asked.

"Have you ever met one?" she asked.

He smiled, but didn't answer. "I asked you your opinion. Just tell me. What do you think of them?"

"Why?" she asked.

"Indulge me," he said.

"You're not going to introduce me to one, are you?"

she asked, her skin crawling. She had no idea how a vampire could be in this well-lit place, but there might be some magic that would make it possible, some magic she didn't know.

"No," he said. "I'm not going to introduce you to one. Just tell me why you don't like them."

"They smell," she said, and then bit her lower lip. She hadn't expected *that* to come out of her mouth.

But they did smell. If they just walked by, they smelled faintly of dried blood and graveyard dust. If one spoke, however, the stench of rotting flesh was overwhelming.

Her eyes watered just thinking about it.

"They do," Charming said. "What else?"

"Why would I like one?" she asked. "Every vampire I meet wants to kill me. And you, for that matter, and anything else that is flesh and blood."

She shuddered as she spoke. She'd had a few too many run-ins with vampires, particularly in the dark days after Snow's wedding, and she really didn't want to see another vampire ever again.

"Come with me," Charming said, and without waiting for her response, led her to a gigantic booth filled with books. As she looked at the nearest display, she saw pictures of men dressed as vampires, standing in sexy poses, wind blowing back their capes.

"What's this?" she asked.

"This," he said, "is the modern vampire."

"No, it's not," she said. "Vampires aren't even human. They're an entirely different species, one that preys on flesh and blood, like jackals. They'll even go for the dead if they have no other choice, like hyenas. They're—"

"I know that," Charming said gently. "But vampires

care about their reputation too. About the time we started dealing with those Grimm people, they had to deal with someone named Stoker. He let the Great World know about them—"

"So?" she said.

"And the Greater World heard how evil they are," Charming said.

"And you think that's bad?" she asked.

"What I think doesn't matter," he said. "What matters is what the Greater World thinks. And right now, the Greater World thinks vampires are sexy."

She shuddered. The very thought was horrifying. Had no one in the Greater World seen a vampire? Not only did they smell, but they had huge bat wings that looked—yes, indeed—like capes, arching over them. They had gray skin—truly gray, gunmetal gray—and pale red eyes that could see movement in darkness, just like cats could. They had long fangs that sometimes cut their black lips. They were pure predators, who ripped through flesh looking for fresh blood.

There was nothing sexy about them.

Nothing.

At least from a human perspective. Other vampires might differ, since they did procreate—with each other. She didn't know a lot about vampire reproduction, except that it happened like it happened most other places in nature—when a male and a female of the same species had some form of sex.

She shuddered again. Even that was more than she wanted to think about.

"Why would anyone write this?" she asked. "It's all lies."

More lies. Everywhere in this room—lies.

"Think about it, Mellie," Charming said. "Who benefits?"

No one, so far as she could tell. No one benefited at all. Vampires didn't look like this, and no one would want to have a close-up encounter with a real vampire. It was just... disgusting.

"How could anyone benefit from this?" she asked him.

He smiled. "When the barriers between our worlds eased," he said, "and members of the Kingdoms came into the Greater World in larger numbers, someone named Polidori saw a vampire and wrote a story about him. As a predator. Vampires became a staple of fiction."

"As heroes?" she couldn't keep the contempt from her voice.

"No," Charming said. "As villains. These were warning stories, made all the more powerful by a book you've probably heard of. *Dracula* by a fellow named Bram Stoker. He made vampires loathsome but powerful things to be avoided. And it worked for a very long time."

"Worked?" she asked.

"To those in the Greater World who believe that fantasy and fairy tales have no basis in fact," Charming said, "Stoker's tales still served as a warning to stay away from that shadowy individual walking down a dark alley. Vampires had a tough time finding prey here."

"Which is a good thing," Mellie said.

Charming nodded. "Unless you're a vampire."

She looked at him sharply, then back at the books. Dozens—no, hundreds of them. Sexy human males with fangs and a bit of danger. Posters, clearly aimed at teenage girls, of a pasty boy with bright red lips and fangs. Statues of these boy/men, hats with vampire logos, and even some fake fangs sat on makeshift shelves.

"Vampires did this?" she whispered.

She thought she had spoken to herself, but Charming nodded.

"They went on a PR offensive in the last few years," he said. "They decided they needed a public relations make-over. Vampires are all the rage now. Teenagers dress up like them. Prince Charming is passé. Now they all want to fall in love with Edward."

"Edward?" she asked.

"Long story," he said. "Suffice to say that the vampires used to be as angry about their own image as you are."

She felt a bit dizzy. She had forgotten to breathe. She wasn't sure she wanted to emulate vampires, but she was curious about this. After all, vampires had a bad reputation and unlike hers, theirs was deserved.

"So how did they do this?" she asked.

"They started writing."

She blinked at him. Writing? Seriously?

He must have seen her shock, because he said, "You can't defeat the power of the book. But you can make it work for you."

"You think I should write about being an evil stepmother?"

"Why not? It worked for the Wicked Witch of the West." He grabbed a book with a green witch on the cover off the shelf. "She's got her own sympathetic Broadway play now and it's going to be a movie or so I hear, and she has her own soundtrack, not that horrible thing from *The Wizard of Oz*, and—"

"You're kidding," Mellie said. She'd met the so-called Wicked Witch of the West and she was a difficult person at best, and not all that bright.

Besides, she was green. Vivid, unpleasant puke-green.

People in the Greater World found her sympathetic? Because of a book?

Mellie took the novel out of Charming's hand. She looked at the tastefully designed cover, with a witch on a broomstick overlaid with some green, and she read the back cover copy.

The book claimed to tell the real story about the Wicked Witch of the West. The poor, misunderstood woman.

But she wasn't that misunderstood. She had a lot of very powerful magic, a terrible temper, and a willingness to take her anger out on anyone who got in her way.

Mellie read the reviews in the front pages of the book. All positive. All talking about the lovely take on the old story, one that put everything in a new light.

Then she handed Charming the book back. He tucked it in her bag.

She picked up one of the vampire books—also with a black cover and an apple, of all things. She read the promotion copy. It was about high school. Vampires in high school? Misunderstood, *polite* vampires in high school?

What?

She grabbed other books, read some more. Vampires in night clubs, vampire detectives, vampires with thousand-year-old loves, vampires—sexy, handsome, and oh, so mysterious.

And heroes.

Mostly, they were the misunderstood heroes of these books. The only person who understood them was the heroine, who could see past the darkness and into the goodness of this poor creature trying to fight his very nature.

Mellie shook her head. "You've got to be kidding me."

"I'm not," Charming said. "If you want, I can show you the same kind of thing for werewolves, and zombies, and—"

"Zombies?" she asked. "Why zombies? They don't even exist."

Thank heavens. The very idea of zombies creeped her out.

"Trends are trends are trends," Charming said. "Sometimes writers want to put a new spin on the trope."

"Trope," Mellie said. "What am I supposed to do? Write about the misunderstood stepmother?"

"Yes," Charming said.

Her breath caught. He was serious.

"You could write a nonfiction book," he said, reaching into a display in a nearby booth, pulling out some drivel about the power of human relationships. "But I worry about that."

"Why?" she asked.

"Because what's true for you and me—nonfiction, if you will—sounds fantastic to most folks in the Greater World. Plus you'd have to do talk shows, and guest appearances and interviews, and if you started talking about your relationship with Snow White, you'd undercut your credibility. And no one can research your background—not completely. At least, not here in the Greater World."

Mellie frowned, her head spinning.

"So what do you want me to write?"

He shrugged one shoulder. "Women's fiction, maybe," he said.

"What?"

"Something very Jodi Picoult," he said, grabbing a book. "Or Barbara Delinsky."

She didn't know what he meant. He grabbed yet another book and tucked it in her bag.

"Or," he said, "better yet, romance novels with wicked stepmothers as the heroines."

"The poor misunderstood stepmother who finally ends up with Prince Charming?" She couldn't resist. She added so much venom to her tone that he let his hand drop from her arm.

"Something like that," he said.

At least he managed to keep the look of disgust off his face, even though the idea repelled him enough to make him realize he'd been touching her.

She shook her head. "I don't write."

"You can't write?" he asked.

She glanced at him, realized he thought she was illiterate, like so many in the Kingdoms.

"I can read and write, thank you," she said, keeping that bite in her voice. "I just have never written anything longer than a letter."

"You don't have to if you don't want to," he said.

"I don't have enough magic to conjure one of these things," she said.

"That's not what I mean," he said.

"Then what do you mean?" she asked.

"There are a lot of writers here who'll write the book for you," he said.

"They'd do that?" she asked.

"For the right amount of money," he said.

"You're playing some kind of joke on me, right?"

"No," he said. "Ask anyone."

So she did. Without Charming hanging on her. She went to any booth that had signs reading "author signing" and talked to the author. The poor person usually looked grateful for someone to make conversation, although there was always a moment of terror (or barely disguised greed) when she mentioned that she wanted help writing a book.

By the time she was done, she found out that the process was called "ghost writing" (she wondered if ghosts had started it all—they had had pretty good press over the years) and a lot of people would do the work, for a fee.

She had tucked nearly a novel's worth of business cards into her book bag. Charming had stayed close by, although he'd been filling his book bag too—as well as other bags. He looked almost as heavily laden as the booksellers she'd seen earlier.

"This is unbelievable," she said as she got closer to him.

"If you can't beat them, join them," he said.

"But I know nothing about this world," she said. "It would take a lot of effort."

"You know the Greater World," he said. "You've been in and out of it for more than a century."

"I mean the book world," she said. "I know nothing."

"There are a lot of places that will help you learn about it," he said.

She felt a thread of disappointment. She had hoped he would help. But of course he wouldn't. He just wanted her to stop yelling about banning books.

He said, "I'm sure we can find some writing books here, and I know some folks who'll help with marketing. Then I'll read whatever you write."

She looked at him in astonishment. "You'd do that?"

He mirrored her astonishment right back at her. "Why wouldn't I?"

"Well, I thought…" She let her voice trail off. She wasn't going to tell him what she thought.

She stammered for a moment, groping for the right word. Finally she said, "Thank you. I'd love to take you up on this."

He grinned. "Then come with me, Mellie. We have to find you some books on writing and marketing, not to mention some current vampire novels, and some cutting-edge paranormal romance. You ready to do some research?"

"Yes," she said. Her heart lifted. She wasn't sure if he caused it or his idea caused it.

But she felt hopeful for the first time in years.

Finally she had something to try that felt positive—like she was doing something besides screaming at people.

And she had help.

Beautiful, charming, princely help.

He was so kind.

Before she could stop herself, she kissed him. She meant it as a thank-you on the cheek, but somehow she missed and hit his lips.

And he stood very still, his eyes open, the surprise clear.

She immediately stepped back. "I'm sorry," she said. "I'm sorry. I'm just so…"

Her voice trailed off when she realized that his cheeks were red. He was blushing, and the blush made him more handsome than ever.

"It's all right," he said.

For a brief, almost surreal moment, she thought he

was going to put his hand against her face again, pull her close and kiss her.

Then one of the stout booksellers, dripping book bags from all of his limbs, slammed into Charming, and sent him stumbling backwards.

Mellie reached for him, but he held up a hand, signaling he wasn't hurt.

"This is quite the place," she said, trying to cover up her mistake.

"Yes," he said, the flush still on his cheeks, making his eyes seem bright.

"You promised to help me research," she said.

"Yes," he said, then seemed to gather himself. "I did."

He took her book bag, then put a hand on the small of her back, sending another tingle through her. Only this time, she didn't impulsively act on it.

She'd already made a fool of herself in front of this man, letting her emotions run wild. She'd been angry at him, nasty to him, and then when he was nice, she kissed him.

Women probably did that to him all the time.

Which explained why he had stood so still. He was *charming*. Charming. And charming people didn't tell you when you'd overstepped a boundary. They just pretended like it hadn't happened.

Like he was doing now, leading her through the crowd, pointing out books. He was helping her, even though he didn't have to. He had so many other things to do.

But she would enjoy each moment while she could.

And she would promise him that she would never ever try to ban books again.

The Rough
Draft

Chapter 9

HE COULDN'T STOP THINKING ABOUT HER. THAT WAS THE strangest thing of all.

Charming couldn't stop thinking about Mellie, and that sudden, unexpected kiss. In fact, that kiss had become his refuge, the way her soft skin felt under his hands had become his escape.

And he needed escapes.

Charming pulled his silver Mercedes into the parking lot of the most exclusive private school in Beverly Hills. There were countless other cars already parked, as well as a few limos. Some had drivers. Most of the rest weren't being driven by parents, but by nannies and au pairs.

He eased down the windows and shut off the engine—not that it made much difference to the interior noise. The car purred when it was on, so soft that it seemed less annoying than a background hum.

Then he rested his head against the back of the leather seat and closed his eyes, just for a moment.

If anyone had asked him how he expected his future to go after that book fair, he would have smiled. He would have said that he had an excuse to call the most beautiful woman he had ever met. He would invite her to his condo, or maybe out for coffee. He would talk books to her, talk writing with her, and gradually, talk about the Kingdoms and how hurt they both were.

Then he would kiss her, instead of pulling away.

He regretted that—his lack of response. He played that kiss over and over in his mind. He had been so stunned that he couldn't bring his arms up, couldn't quite lean in. He hadn't realized she was attracted too, and by the time he understood that one important fact, she had stepped away, acting embarrassed.

No matter what he did, he couldn't rekindle the moment. So he had exchanged phone numbers with her, and talked to her about writing, and set up their first meeting for the very next day.

Who knew he would have to cancel?

He pulled out his cell phone and looked at the time emblazoned across the screen. Ten minutes. Ten minutes of quiet. Ten minutes before he had to make decisions again.

He got home from the book fair—and his life immediately turned into chaos.

His mother had called him on his other cell phone, the magical one, the one that could contact anyone in the Kingdom at any time. She had snuck away from his father and gave Charming the scoop:

Ella had decided she didn't want to be a mother any longer. So she dumped the girls on the castle doorstep. Charming's father, the King, took the girls back in, so long as they remained quiet and didn't appear in public until it was time to make an "advantageous" marriage. Charming's mother had contacted him, quietly, without her husband's knowledge, saying she didn't like what was happening with the girls.

Neither did Ella's stepmother, Lavinia. She had called moments later and said (among other things): *You have no idea what they're learning here. With your*

father's negative attitudes, the Kingdom's reaction to
the divorce, and the way women are still second-class
citizens, your daughters are getting the wrong message.

Lavinia was the one who urged Charming to sue for
full custody. She said Ella wouldn't fight him. She also
stressed that things had turned dire.

She wouldn't say why, and neither would Charming's
mother.

But anything that concerned his girls and the word
"dire" made him run to the Kingdoms immediately.

Although he had found a moment to call Mellie. And
once again, he had sounded like an idiot.

He'd told her he had an emergency in the Kingdoms
with his girls. She had made some kind of protest, but he
didn't hear it all because his Kingdom phone was ring-
ing again. So he had said something stupid about being
back within a month and helping her then.

He had no idea why he had chosen a month, but he
had been right to do so. It had taken forever to get the
new custody decree, even though Ella didn't fight it.
Ella hadn't even shown up in court, forfeiting her rights
to the girls by that move alone.

Charming's girls were a mess, grateful to see him, but
more uncertain of themselves than they had ever been.
He had made a decision then and there to bring them
back to the Greater World with him. The Kingdoms
were destroying them, taking their strong personalities
and molding them into simpering things.

He liked strong women, even though his father didn't.
And whenever his father started talking to him about the
way he was encouraging the girls toward bad behavior,
Charming let his mind wander to Mellie—and that kiss.

That kiss. It had sustained him through the transition to the Greater World. Through the purchase of a house appropriate for raising children, not a condo for bachelors. Through the hiring of staff, particularly since he had left his most trusted valet and his closest friend in charge of the bookstore in the Kingdom. No matter how much Charming's father pushed, Charming wouldn't give up the Charming Way.

Although he thought about it. Then he realized he had enough money to start a bookstore in the Greater World. Enough money. He shook his head.

He had money. That wasn't an issue. He'd learned long ago that gold bought a lot in the Greater World. He wasn't as rich as he was in the Kingdoms, but he was better off than almost anyone else in the Greater Los Angeles Area, which was saying something.

He could just spend his days managing his money, reading, and parenting his girls, but he knew that wouldn't be enough. So he was looking for a storefront, and trying to figure out how he could build a place that wouldn't lose money. Independent bookstores seemed to be an iffy proposition in the Greater World, which was proving to be a shock.

But first, he had had to deal with his daughters and their transition. He had spent most of his time searching for a school, one that would tolerate his daughters' quirks. He hoped he found it.

Today would tell. They had just experienced their first day at a Greater World School.

And he'd been worried all day. Worried, and thinking of Mellie. Thinking he should call her.

Of course, he had thought that ever since he got back,

but he wasn't sure what he would say. He would need to apologize for failing to call. (He could have called from the Kingdoms, but he kept putting that off. Truth be told, he didn't like the phone.) He wanted to see her, and he kept making excuses to himself that he wouldn't call her until he *could* see her.

Which meant a lot of time went by, more time than he had planned.

He glanced at his phone again. Nine minutes until school ended. Nine minutes to worry about his daughters. Nine minutes to think of a way to approach Mellie.

He scrolled through the contacts list, saw her name, and stared at it, like he had done countless times before. He was scared. Not of women, but of relationships. Things had gotten so bad with Ella that he didn't even want to try.

That was the bottom of it all. His marriage had left him so badly injured that he—a man who had fought three separate wars—was afraid to contact a woman.

So his thumb did it for him. It pressed her number, and the phone dialed.

His breath caught. He had to hang up. He needed to hang up.

But before he could, Mellie answered.

She said hello.

Chapter 10

MELLIE SAT IN HER THIRD COFFEE SHOP OF THE DAY. THIS ONE was large and crowded, with some kind of jazzy music playing in the background. It had a large counter and efficient baristas, who worked like a well-planned team.

She was becoming a coffee shop connoisseur. The coffee shop closest to the Malibu beach house she had rented had a lot of "aw-shucks-whatever" employees who couldn't seem to make a simple latte.

She could make a simple latte these days. She had bought a laptop—her fourth since she had begun this project—and had started lugging it to coffee shops where—she'd read—writers spent their days, able to concentrate on their work and yet feeling as if the people around them were—what? Companions? Co-workers?

Mellie didn't know, but she was beginning to think they were all more interesting than she was. And here, with all the tables filled by scruffy-looking people tapping contentedly on their laptops (or talking about deal points on the phone—loudly, so everyone else heard), she was beginning to think they were all more successful than she was too.

They were more successful at writing. Or at least, at typing.

She was no longer sure why she was trying this. She had been so inspired by Charming. His solution to her problems seemed so elegant, so simple.

Write a book, he said, as if anyone could do it.

Write a book.

She was trying. At first, it seemed easy. She rented a house in Malibu—writers all lived in Malibu or in New York. She'd set up her computer in her fancy office overlooking the ocean, and for the first week, she reclined on the deck, reading all those books she'd gotten for free at the book fair.

And trying not to feel abandoned by Charming.

Those moments in the book fair had seemed magical. He was so handsome, and he seemed to know everyone. He walked her through the place, her hand tucked in his arm, his other hand occasionally covering hers. Some of his glamour trickled down on her, making her feel beautiful.

People smiled at her. They talked to her. They explained things to her.

They didn't call security guards on her.

If only she hadn't kissed him.

Not that the kiss had been a bad one. He hadn't felt it, of course, but she had—that tingle when their lips touched, that moment of *yes, this is right*. Followed immediately by panic when she realized he hadn't participated, had in fact just stood there, staring at her, waiting for her to get done.

At least, that's how she interpreted it. How many other women had kissed him like that, drawn by his looks, his charm, his amazingly warm personality.

And to his credit, he didn't say anything. Just smiled ruefully, blushed, and tucked her hand in his arm again as if nothing had happened.

For him, nothing had.

For her, her entire perspective had changed. Two

husbands—and never had she felt like that during a chaste kiss. She had finally found a man she was completely attracted to, and he viewed her as a mildly crazy woman in need of his help.

She made herself sip her latte and stare at the screen. Around her, conversation echoed. The jazz seemed more mellow than it had a moment before.

She had such dreams, leaving that book fair. Not only would people start taking her seriously, not only would she strike a blow for stepmothers everywhere, but she would be able to spend some time with Charming. They had exchanged email addresses and cell phone numbers, and he had promised to help her write the book, giving her advice and guiding her in what he called "the right direction."

It didn't matter that he hadn't felt the spark. She would talk to him, and maybe befriend him, and maybe he was the kind of man that valued friendships with women, understood that friendships were the building blocks to a true, long-lasting solid relationship.

And pigs would fly.

Or, rather, pigs would fly here, in the Greater World, since some pigs did fly in the Kingdoms.

Instead, Charming had called her the morning after the book fair, and told her he was leaving immediately for the Kingdoms. She felt betrayed. He had completely destroyed her vision of the future. She'd even said, "I thought we were going to work on the book," sounding like a needy girl after her first date.

He said, "Something's come up with my girls," and it took Mellie a moment to realize that he meant his daughters, not all the women who were interested in him.

He promised to be back within the month and, he promised, he would go over her book as soon as he got back. "So," he admonished her, "get me as much of it as you can."

He'd sounded like a man who fully intended to work with her on this book. She caught herself before she said anything else negative, asked him if there was anything she could do, and he had said that she needed to be ready to talk with him when he got back.

More than a month had passed.

He hadn't called.

He wasn't going to.

He'd blown her off.

Somewhere in the middle of it, she decided she would write the book anyway. But, while it was easy to read a book, turned out it wasn't so easy to write one.

She only had twenty pages, and she suspected they were twenty crappy pages. Lately, she had been toying with just writing a screenplay. She loved movies. She had loved them long before Disney eviscerated her in his "classic" *Snow White and the Seven Dwarfs*. Even he couldn't put her off movies forever, although that was when she had realized that she needed to fight the perception he had made people form.

Screenplays turned into movies, she was learning, was even harder than the novel form. Still, she had brought a screenwriting program for her latest laptop, and she kept a second screen open with the screenwriting software working. She had a variety of scenes there, more than she had in the novel itself.

She was trying to decide which to work on, screenplay or novel, when her cell phone rang.

She groped for her purse, found the phone, and glanced at the caller ID.

Charming.

He called.

Her breath caught, and her heart started to pound. She was reacting like a lovesick teenager and she didn't care.

Before she could even think, she had put the phone to her ear and said hello.

"Mellie?" His voice was just as rich and warm as she remembered.

"Yes," she said, sounding breathless even to her own ears.

"It's Charming."

She didn't want to say *I know*, because then he'd know that she was sounding breathless because of him, so she said, "Oh, hello," and as the words came out, she realized just how lame they sounded.

"I was wondering how the book is coming," he said.

"Slower than I want." She looked around. A few people were watching her surreptitiously, like she watched other people when they were on the phone in the coffee shop, wondering who they were talking to and if the call was important.

This call was important.

"I promised I'd look it over." He sounded business-like. She didn't want him to sound businesslike. She wanted him to be interested in her, not in the book.

But she had to remember who she was. She was a wicked stepmother. He was Prince Charming. He was helping her, and he didn't have to.

And he had called—despite the kiss.

"Are you ready for feedback?" he asked.

Yes. No. She wanted feedback immediately. She didn't want feedback at all.

Especially on this dreck.

But if she didn't get feedback, she wouldn't see him.

The man at the next table over was staring at her. She turned toward the wall, decorated with multi-colored mugs, and hunched over.

She wondered if Charming could hear her heart pounding.

"It would be nice to know if I'm going in the right direction," she said, and realized that was the truth. But she wasn't talking so much about the book as about the whole idea of the book. She wasn't sure she was capable of doing this.

It was the first time she had ever thought herself incapable of anything.

"Do you want to email me some pages?" he said. "Then we could get together to talk, if you'd like."

She imagined him, reading this drivel on his computer, deciding he didn't want to see her after all.

"It might be easier if you just read it when we get together," she said.

"I'd like to spend some time on it," he said.

There wasn't much to spend time on. But she didn't want to say that. She had been a diplomat once, and she finally called on those skills.

"I only have twenty pages I'm even happy with," she said.

"Oh," he said, sounding disappointed. "Still, that'll take me some time. Why don't you email them along with a few paragraphs about where the novel is heading?"

Where it was heading? If she had to answer that

question honestly, she would say this: It was heading off a cliff.

She wasn't going to win the no-email battle. "Okay," she said. "How's tomorrow? I know this great coffee shop…"

She let her voice trail off. She had practiced the coffee shop line during the first two weeks he was gone because she didn't want to scare him off by inviting him to the house. Men always thought women had designs on them, particularly when the women invited the men home.

So she was going to pretend she didn't have designs. Not that she had unrealistic designs. She wanted to be friends—if she could control that spontaneous urge to kiss him.

"Coffee shop it is," he said, and asked for directions.

"See you tomorrow then," he said, sounding awkward and reluctant and not charming at all. Did telephones negate his magic? Was it all in his look and his smile and his eyes?

Wouldn't that be strange if it was.

"Tomorrow," she said, and hung up before he could.

She tucked the phone back into her purse, her hands shaking. She closed her eyes for a moment. She was giddy as a school girl. She felt young and frivolous and goofy.

And she felt like a fraud.

She wasn't a writer.

He was expecting a novel.

She barely had the beginning of one. If it was fair to call what she had written a novel. If it were fair to call those letters on those digital pages writing.

He made her nervous. No one had made her nervous in more than two hundred years.

She made herself take a deep breath. Time to go home, and get to work.

Chapter 11

SHE SOUNDED CALM. THAT CALL HAD ONLY TAKEN TWO minutes, and yet it felt like a lifetime.

Charming gripped the phone tightly in his right hand and looked out the window of his Mercedes. The school doors—reinforced steel against fake brick—remained firmly closed. School hadn't let out yet. Some of the other parents and the nannies, limo drivers, and au pairs were standing outside their cars talking.

Mellie had sounded calm, as if nothing had happened. She made an appointment with him, nothing more.

She'd probably forgotten the kiss.

She probably was one of those people who spontaneously kissed people who pleased her. Or she hugged them. Or she put her arm around them.

She hadn't looked like a hugger when he met her, but she had been tense. When he helped her, she had probably reverted to type.

And he had imbued that moment with great significance, when it meant no more than a casual thank you.

He would have to adjust his priorities for that meeting. He would have to focus on her book, and nothing else.

Certainly not that kiss.

Inside the school, some kind of bell rang and everyone moved back to their vehicles. He tucked his phone in the breast pocket of his shirt and watched the door.

Children of all ages poured out, wearing the school

uniform, black and gray with white shirts and black shoes. A little ornate logo decorated the shoulders of the suit coat, like a glued-on epaulette. The uniforms were ugly, but everyone had to wear them.

The children talked to each other, slowly separating, some walking down the street, others heading to their various vehicles.

He didn't see his daughters.

He got out of the car, his breath catching in his throat. Were they all right? Had something gone wrong?

He was about to pull his phone out of his pocket again to see if he'd missed a call or a text when his oldest daughter peered out the school door.

Imperia was stunning, just like her mother. Blond, blond hair, bright blue eyes, all on a peaches-and-cream complexion that not even bright sunlight could destroy. Even though Imperia was only twelve, she had a way of holding herself that matched her full name. She was imperial and imperious. Haughty, regal, and oh, so majestic.

His eldest daughter always made him feel somewhat inadequate.

Maybe that was why his nickname for her had brought her down a peg, even though it suited her as well. He called her Imp. And she could be impish, but only around the people she loved the most.

Everyone else called her Imi, which he didn't like any more than Imperia. But Imperia was a family name, given to oldest daughters for generations. He didn't have to like it, his father told him. He just had to give the name to his daughter.

Imperia gave the outdoors her most haughty

expression, mouth pursed, chin up, eyes blazing, then she softened as she turned toward the door. She extended her right hand, and a smaller hand took it.

Charming hadn't realized he was holding his breath until that moment.

Grace was all right, then.

Grace, all of eight, the accidental child and, if he were honest, his favorite person in all of the worlds he'd ever been in. He and Ella hadn't had much of a relationship by the time she got pregnant with Grace. He would never tell his youngest daughter she was the result of one drunken night after one extremely excruciating ball.

As surprising as she had been, she had never been unwanted. Charming put all of his hopes and dreams into her. Imperia was the female heir, the family baby, but Grace was all his.

Until Ella took both girls away, with his father's blessing.

Charming walked toward the curb. Imperia had warned him to stay away from the school doors ("The kids'll think you're controlling, Dad," she said, as if that were a bad thing) but he was torn. Something was wrong. He could tell just from Imperia's posture.

Grace stepped out of the school. Her round face was red and tear-streaked. Her white-blond hair was mussed, and her uniform was torn.

He couldn't help himself now. He ran up the sidewalk, only to stop as his eldest daughter glared at him.

She hadn't learned that look from her mother. She had learned that one from her great-grandmother—Charming's grandmother, also named Imperia. That look could freeze anyone in place, even a concerned father heading toward his beloved baby daughter.

Imperia leaned over, whispered to Grace, and then stood up straight. Imperia raised her chin. Grace looked at her, mouth trembling. Imperia elbowed her. Grace took a deep breath—it seemed to hitch going in—and then raised her chin too. The look didn't have any of the haughtiness and grandeur that Imperia's had. But Grace's look had a certain wounded dignity.

Until she saw Charming.

Then she burst into tears and ran down the stairs, slamming into him so hard that he had to put one foot back so that he wouldn't fall over.

"I'm not coming back," she said. "I'm not, I'm not. They're mean."

He cupped his hand around her small head and held her close. She was sobbing.

"Mean?" he asked, looking at Imperia.

Imperia's mouth formed a thin line. "They called her names."

"Did anyone pick on you?" he asked, knowing the answer already.

"Of course not," Imperia said. "But they seem to dislike Grace."

He held Grace for a long time. Finally she brought her head back. Her cheek was indented with red marks made by the buttons on his shirt.

"They called me Princess Grace," she said.

"You are Princess Grace," he said.

"They said everyone named Princess Grace dies in car accidents. They said the real Princess Grace did."

He let out a small breath. Of course. This was Los

Angeles. Even kids knew who the old movie stars were, and there had been one named Grace Kelly who had married the Prince of Monaco, and twenty years later, died in a serious car accident.

"The car accident part is mean," he said, "but the rest isn't. Have you ever seen the Princess Grace from the Greater World?"

"No-o." Grace's voice hitched.

"She was one of the most beautiful women who ever lived," he said, then kissed the top of her head. "Like you."

"I'm not a woman, Daddy," Grace said with a giggle in her voice.

"Not yet," he said, and thanked whatever gods heard him. He still had his little girl. "Come on to the car, girls. We can talk all the way home."

"We're going home?" Grace asked, her voice rising.

He heard the hope, and hated it. She meant the Kingdoms. She meant the palace.

"We're going to our new home," he said.

"Like our new school," Imperia said, not quite under her breath. "It all sucks."

The comment made him ache. He wanted to ask her if she thought being with him sucked, but he was afraid of the answer. So he pretended he hadn't heard her.

He led his girls back to the Mercedes, one of the few cars left in the lot, and then slowly, carefully, drove them home, suddenly afraid of car accidents, and losing his little precious princesses all over again.

Chapter 12

MELLIE SAW HIM THROUGH THE WINDOW OF THE COFFEE shop. She tried to pretend she wasn't looking for him. She had her laptop open and she typed—albeit comments on someone else's blog—but she really kept an eye on the window.

She positioned herself at a table in the center of the room. She took the seat that enabled her to see both sets of windows and the door. She could only see the counter and the barista if she turned slightly. But she could watch the windows without raising her head from the computer screen.

Charming looked frazzled. He drove his silver Mercedes past the door, then around the block, and into the parking lot. He got out, ran a hand through that thick, black hair, and took a deep breath.

Mellie wasn't sure if he was nervous about seeing her or if he didn't want to see or if he was nervous about both seeing her *and* telling her that her book was crap.

Which it was.

She should have thought of that before making it be her excuse to see him again.

Only it hadn't really been exactly an excuse. It had felt like salvation at the time.

He pointed his remote at the car, and the headlights winked on and off. If the jazz overhead wasn't so loud or the conversations so obnoxious, she could've heard the little chirrup of acknowledgement most cars gave as well.

Oh, she was obsessing. (And who wouldn't? He was the most gorgeous man she had ever seen.)

Once he started walking toward the front door, she put her head down and typed rapidly. She wasn't going to send the comment; she barely knew what she was writing. But she had to look busy. Legitimately busy.

She didn't want him to know how she felt. She hated being a cliché—whether it was an evil stepmother cliché or a lusting-after-the-handsome-unattainable-prince cliché.

She typed and waited, and tried very hard not to look at the door.

———————

Charming had a heck of a time finding the coffee shop. There had to be eight hundred billion coffee shops in the greater Los Angeles area, most of them centered around the major studios. He went into five coffee shops, none of which looked quite right and none of which had Mellie inside.

He almost left the folder with printed copies of the twenty pages and Mellie's notes in the car. But he carried it to one last coffee shop before giving up.

And then he saw her, sitting near the fake fireplace in the back. The fake fireplace was off, which made it seem almost regal. Mellie looked beautiful sitting there, softer somehow. At the book fair, he had seen her as all angles—not quite the angular beauty portrayed by Disney, but a tad too thin, a bit harsh around the edges.

That harshness was gone now. She looked younger, her black hair down around her shoulders. Her clothing wasn't as harsh either. She wore a black sweater that accented her fair skin, and black pants that had a small flare around some stylish boots. She didn't look like a fairy tale creature at all or, as she seemed to prefer, an archetype.

She looked like a trendy, beautiful Southern California businesswoman working her afternoon away in a coffee shop.

He suppressed a sigh. He felt dumpy and awkward. He'd been up for hours, soothing Grace who hadn't wanted to go back to school, then walking her to class, meeting with the principal. Charming hadn't lost his temper in that meeting, but he had channeled his father. He had told the principal that, with the prices Charming had paid to get his daughters into the school, his daughters deserved to be treated with respect from everyone.

The implied threat seemed to get through.

He hoped.

He did feel the strain. Being forceful was not his normal style, and it exhausted him.

Mellie looked up from her computer and smiled. She had seen him. The smile had worry in it, as if she knew he was uncertain about being here.

More forcefulness—or was he going to be charming? He didn't know. All he knew was that he had read her first twenty pages, and wished that he hadn't.

Maybe today was his confrontation day. Once he got through all of this, he would be done with confrontation for the entire year. Or at least, he wished he would be.

He made himself smile in return, then he held up one finger, and walked to the counter. He ordered one of the fancier drinks—chocolate, espresso, and lots of cream—and didn't even try to sound like a native.

He was too tired to pretend to be anything other than what he was.

Dave the bookseller, who was meeting a woman he barely knew to talk about a terrible book he had told her to write, a woman he was attracted to, a woman who would probably balk when she learned that in the past month he had become a full-time single father to two rather lost little girls.

He paid for his drink, then walked over to the table, and made himself smile as he sat down.

"Mellie," he said, using his warmest voice.

He was pouring on the charm—he knew it, and he wished he wasn't. But he didn't see any other way to do this.

"It sucks, doesn't it?" she said, putting the same emphasis on the word "sucks" that Imperia had used the day before. Was that something girls got taught when they came to the Greater World? Or did they just feel free enough to use the word here, when they wouldn't have used the word at home?

Mellie opened the door. But he wasn't going to walk through it. After all, she had worked on this project for a month. And he really didn't want to hurt her feelings. He wanted her to kiss him again.

She probably wouldn't, even if he was particularly gentle about this book. He had to keep reminding himself that their one kiss was not really a kiss at all.

It had been a spontaneous thank you, one she probably forgot in an instant.

He needed to charm her. He needed to take the

attention off that damn book. He needed her to realize that he liked her.

"You're looking particularly beautiful today," he said with a smile.

She smiled in return, but the smile was reluctant, as if she couldn't help it. The smile made her seem young and vulnerable.

"How are you?" he asked. "Well, I'm fine. Gee, it's been a while since we've seen each other. Is everything working out well for you?"

Her smile grew and became sincere. She clearly understood what he was doing, and it made her eyes twinkle.

"How are you, Charming?" she said. "Or do I call you Dave here?"

She didn't put that snide emphasis on the name, and he appreciated that.

"No one notices Dave," he said. Usually he liked that. Just not with her.

"Everyone notices Dave," she said. "You should've seen the look that the barista gave you as you came through the door."

He flushed. Mellie had been watching him, then, from the moment he arrived.

"Yes," she said, "I saw you come in. And I saw you hesitate. Is it that you don't want to see me or you don't want to tell me about the book?"

She wasn't going to let it go. He had hoped they might have a few minutes of flirting before he had to talk about the book.

Although, if he was really honest with himself, he would say that he never wanted to talk about the book.

She shrugged one delicate shoulder in response to his silence. "I don't mean to push you. I'm just the kind of person who likes to get the bad news out of the way first."

He bit his lower lip. They had a moment—just a moment—before he had to sound like a jerk. He could lie to her, he supposed, but he wouldn't feel right about that either.

After all, she really wanted to change her image—rather, the image of Evil Stepmothers—and he had come up with the perfect way to do it.

Just not the perfect writer.

"And you," she said, "are clearly the kind of person who doesn't like dealing with bad news at all."

She got that in one. Ella had accused him of going passively through life, letting things happen to him. While that wasn't completely accurate, it took a lot for him to demand something he wanted, at least for himself.

"Look," Mellie said. "You can go if you want. I release you from your promise, if that's what it takes. I know that you were just being kind at the book fair."

Charming looked at her. She had a pleasant expression, but a slight frown creased her brow. She believed that? She believed he was just being kind?

Hadn't she figured out how much she attracted him?

He sighed. Probably not. When he had been surprised by that kiss, he had probably communicated disinterest. Even though he hadn't meant to.

"I'm sorry," he said before he could stop himself. "It's already been a rough day."

"And I'm about to make it rougher," she said with compassion.

He shook his head. "No. I'm just tired. I yelled at someone this morning, and I don't do that very well."

Now her pencil thin eyebrows went up. "You yelled at me at the book fair. Have you met someone else who tried to ban books?"

He smiled in spite of himself. "No. Nothing like that."

"Then what was it like?" she asked.

He shook his head. She didn't need to hear about his personal woes. He grabbed the folder and opened it.

"How about we talk about the book instead?" he asked.

"Yeah," she said, looking at the pages before him with trepidation. "How about it? It'll be such fun."

And he could tell, just from the tone of her voice, that no matter what he said, he would disappoint her.

He hated disappointing anyone.

But he had no choice here.

Because she was right: her twenty pages really did suck.

Chapter 13

CHARMING HADN'T SEEMED THIS DISTANT, NOT EVEN AT THE book fair when he was yelling at her. Then Mellie had felt a connection. Maybe it had only been because they were both from the Kingdoms, or maybe it had been because they both felt a little out of place. But they had seemed like similar people.

Even if he was handsome and charming and obviously beloved, and she was the scourge of the Earth.

Now, however, he didn't seem to want to be with her. He was charming, but it had a fakeness to it—or maybe the kind of charming that he delivered to everyone else.

That was it. He was charming to everyone else.

At the book fair, he had been honest with her.

He wasn't going to be honest now.

Although there was that moment, when he told her about his rough day. She had actually seen pain in his eyes.

What could cause a man like him pain?

She wasn't sure how to ask him. Or if she should ask him.

He wanted to divert the conversation from him to her book. She'd let him tell her about how horrible it all was, then she would offer to buy him another coffee, and let him talk about his own life.

People did talk to her, and tell her their woes. She knew how to listen. It was one of her best skills.

He looked like he needed a shoulder. She'd provide

it—and, she promised herself, she wouldn't scare him off by kissing him.

"I'm ready," she said. She folded her hands on the cool cover of her laptop, and braced herself for the bad news.

"Do you read for pleasure?" he asked.

Read for pleasure? She blinked at him. Read what for pleasure?

"What do you mean?" she asked.

He had smoothed his hands over the manuscript. She couldn't see if he had made any markings on it. "People read books for enjoyment. Do you?"

But she could tell from his tone that he already knew the answer. She didn't. It hadn't even occurred to her.

She supposed she knew that people read for pleasure. After all, why would all the various books exist? But she hadn't really thought about it, any more than she had thought about those games and comic books that seemed all over the Greater World culture now. She didn't even shop for pleasure, although she had a greater understanding of that than she did of reading.

"Sometimes I enjoy what I read," she said, wanting to give him the answer he wanted.

He smiled. The smile was as gentle as his tone, and very sad. "That's good. But reading for pleasure is something else, something you do because you enjoy it, not because you enjoy it when someone else tells you to do it."

"Like you," she said.

"Yes," he said, as if she were a particularly good student.

"Then, no, I'm sorry," she said. "I don't read for pleasure."

He nodded and looked down.

"That's a problem, isn't it?" she said.

He continued nodding. He didn't meet her gaze.

She glanced at all the other people staring at their laptops. Were those people all online? Or were they all writing?

And if they were writing, did that mean that they liked reading for pleasure?

"Are my pages that bad?" she asked.

Charming ran a hand over the lower half of his face. Then he sighed. His gaze met hers, and she was struck again by how handsome he was. His glasses didn't magnify his eyes, like so many people's glasses did. Instead, they accented the startling blue.

Her cheeks warmed. She wanted him to think well of her, and she had blown even that by trying something she had no business trying.

"It's not so much that the pages are bad," he said, and she could tell just from the words he chose that he was lying. "It's the proposal you wrote."

"Proposal?" she asked.

"The part telling me what the rest of the book would be like," he said. "Books, novels, they all tell stories. You have no story here."

"I said that people would learn they were wrong about stepmothers, and my heroine would have a good life," Mellie said.

"But 'people' aren't who the story is about. The story is about Mally—which, I'm sorry, is a name you'll have to change—and she doesn't change. She just educates people as to who she is, and then they like her, and that's the end."

Mellie frowned. Her heart was pounding. She really didn't understand any of this stuff. "So?"

"Characters change, Mellie," he said. "Because people change. You've changed over your lifetime, haven't you?"

She shrugged a shoulder. In some ways she had. In other ways, she felt like the same person she had always been.

"I certainly have changed." He glanced at the door—because he wanted to escape? "I'm not even the same person I was a month ago."

Uh-oh. He'd met a woman who didn't want him here. Mellie could understand that. No woman would want to share this man.

"How have you changed?" she asked and braced herself for an I'm-in-love-it's-great saga.

His face seemed to collapse in on itself. He suddenly looked nothing like Prince Charming, and everything like Dave the bookseller—a middle-aged, overburdened man who wasn't getting enough sleep.

"You don't want to hear this," he said.

"Oh, but I do," she said, and she did, because she suddenly realized she was wrong. It wasn't about another woman. Something had happened to him. Something that bothered him.

The something he had mentioned that was "rough." The something she had thought she would have to pry out of him.

Apparently, she didn't have to pry. Apparently, he wanted—make that *needed*—to talk.

"You just want me to tell you about me so that I don't talk about your book any more," he said.

"No," she said. "I want to know. What's changed?"

He looked at her again, and this time, she saw the man from the book fair. He wasn't distant. He wasn't trying to charm her. He had returned to his eyes.

He flipped the manuscript pages, as if he didn't even realize what he was doing, and said, "My wife abandoned my daughters."

Chapter 14

THAT WASN'T HOW HE MEANT TO SAY IT. HE HAD MEANT TO say something innocuous like *I have my daughters with me right now* or *My living situation had changed* or *I'm going to be a single parent for a while*.

Not *My wife abandoned my daughters*.

"What?" Mellie asked. She looked shocked.

So did the doughy guy the next table over, who had been watching them all along. Charming glared at him and the man bent his head and started typing on his laptop again.

"I mean," Charming said, trying to repair the verbal damage a little, "she's not my wife anymore, but—"

"Are they all right?" Mellie asked. There was concern in her voice and in her eyes. She meant it, and that made his breath catch.

She actually cared about his daughters, whom she hadn't met.

No one had asked that before, at least not as the first question. They always asked about him—how was he doing?—not about his girls.

"Ella didn't hurt them or anything," he said. "I mean, she didn't literally abandon them, leaving them alone at the house or anything. She dropped them with my parents, and then told me that she didn't want them anymore."

Again, blunter than he had planned. Blunt in a way

he never was. He didn't use the diplomatic phrase. He had told the truth.

What was it about this woman that made him want to tell the truth?

"Did she tell the girls that?" Mellie asked with concern.

He nodded and glared at the doughy man who was still watching them. Charming wanted to slam the doughy man's laptop down on his fingers. Charming was angry. Good heavens, he hadn't realized how angry he truly was until this very moment.

How dare Ella tell his girls that they were unwanted?

"How old are they?" Mellie asked.

Charming looked at her, saw fury in her green eyes. If Ella came in here right now, Mellie would go after her, yelling with that passion he had seen at the book fair.

She was angry—not for him, but for his girls.

And she didn't even know them.

"Twelve and eight," he said.

"That's the worst time for girls," Mellie said. "Twelve, not eight. Your twelve-year-old needs her mother right now. She needs to learn how to be a woman. Your ex isn't giving her a good example right now."

Then Mellie clapped her hand over her mouth.

"I'm sorry. I'm so sorry," she said through her fingers. "It's none of my business. I shouldn't have said that. I'm sorry."

He reached over and hooked his fingers through hers, bringing her hand down. He thought he remembered how soft her skin was. But he had forgotten. He had forgotten how wonderful it was to touch her.

"It's okay," he said. "You're the only person who has said what I've been thinking."

"I mean, how selfish can a woman get?" Mellie said, then looked like she wanted to clamp her hand over her mouth all over again.

He twined his fingers through hers. He should let go of her hand. That would be best, letting go of her hand. But he couldn't bring himself to do it. That simple touch was holding him up, calming him.

And she wasn't pulling away.

"I suppose they're still with your parents?" she asked.

"Good heavens, *no*," he said. "That would be worse than leaving them alone."

Again, honesty. He never would have said such a thing about his parents—at least not in the Kingdoms.

"I brought my daughters here," he said.

He tried not to look at their clasped hands, but he couldn't help himself. Her fingers were long and slender, the nails coated with a red polish that matched her lips.

Even her hands were lovely.

He wanted to put his other hand over hers, but he didn't let himself.

He didn't want to scare her off.

"Your daughters are here? In the Greater World?" she asked.

He nodded. "I brought them here a few weeks ago. We've been trying to get settled. But it's not working."

"I should say not," Mellie said. "Not only do they have to deal with their mother's perfidy, they have to deal with a new life in a new culture."

"I've brought them here to visit before," he said, feeling worried. "Did I do something wrong?"

He shouldn't have asked that. He *never* asked that.

Princes weren't allowed to ask that. Royalty was always right.

If his father had heard that question, he'd be screaming right now.

Charming suppressed a shudder. His father would think all of this terrible—the coffee shop, the school, Charming's hand holding the hand of a woman who was an actual adult, and not some nubile eighteen-year-old suitable for breeding.

"Under the circumstances, you didn't do anything wrong," Mellie said. "It's probably better for your daughters here. They don't have to deal with the whole inheritance thing, and I assume the whole family is back in the Kingdoms…?"

He nodded.

"That's probably for the best too."

Had she met his family? Probably. People went between Kingdoms all the time.

Her hand held his, her fingers wrapped loosely around his, her thumb rubbing gently against his forefinger. That simple movement made his heart beat faster.

What was wrong with him? Was he so lonely that he found a soft and compassionate touch erotic?

He made himself concentrate on the conversation.

"I enrolled the girls in the best school," he said, "and already people are picking on Grace."

"That's the oldest?" Mellie asked.

"The youngest." His voice broke, just a little.

"Your favorite," Mellie said.

"You're not supposed to have favorites," he said, and realized that was honest too. He had just said yes in the only way he could.

Poor Imperia. Her mother had abandoned her, her father loved her sister better, and she was about to hit puberty in a strange world.

"I don't know what to do," he said. "I've never raised children before."

"I have," Mellie said.

He must have given her a startled look because she added, rather defensively, "I don't just mean Snow and her brother. I had my own children with my first husband and you never hear about them. They're doing just fine and they gave me grandchildren, and they're here in the Greater World and are quite successful. Snow was nearly grown when I met her. And I didn't do everything right there. But I do know children and I like them and I like to spend time with them."

He stared at her. She seemed nervous suddenly. Her thumb had stopped moving, and he missed that. Her fingers had tensed. Her entire body had tensed.

Did she expect him to judge her? To hate her for having a life?

Had she thought he believed all that crap about her history with Snow White?

"Look," Mellie said with a bit of a sigh. "I can't write, right?"

He opened his mouth, not sure what to say, because he was in a truthful mode, and the truth would be really painful.

"You don't have to answer that," she said. "It's all over your face. I can't write, and I need to because your idea about the books is a great one. I did all the research and I think you're right. I think your idea is the way to go."

His mouth was still open. He started to speak when she added, "But I know children. I know how to build a household. I have references even here in the Greater World. I've helped some of the PETA folk when they came over, baby-sitting the children while the adults looked for work. I even started a day care center for a while, although I sold it. But what I'm saying is this. I would be happy to help you. And you don't have to help me. Maybe you can teach me how to read for enjoyment or something. I mean, I'm not in any hurry on my quest, but your daughters grow a little bit every day. So you teach me how to read for pleasure, and I'll help you ease your girls into their new life. If-if-if you want me to."

And she looked at him expectantly, as if she expected him to make a decision right then and there.

She had startled him. He didn't do well when he was startled.

She startled him a lot, and he froze, and that was bad. He had to somehow overcome that reaction because he didn't want her to think he wasn't interested, and he didn't want her to think he was a doofus, even though he acted like one.

"I can't teach you how to love reading," he said. "The theory is that once you read one book, you like reading and you'll continue to do it. But that doesn't seem to be true for you, so I wouldn't know what to do…"

She nodded, as if she expected that. He could tell, just from her body language that she now expected him to blow her off, tell her he wasn't interested in her at all.

But he was interested. In her, in her advice, even in her damn book. He had only one problem: He wasn't sure how deeply he could let another woman into his life right now. His girls had been badly hurt. They needed some time to heal, and introducing them to a new woman, particularly one who might not stay, would be a bad idea.

"It's okay," she said into his silence. "You don't have to teach me how to like reading. It's not a big deal."

"It is a big deal," he said. "It's important to you."

Her gaze met his, her green eyes filled with compassion. The compassion almost undid him.

"Your daughters are important to you," she said softly.

He nodded.

"And you don't want me to meet them," she said. There was so much meaning in that sentence. She thought he didn't want her to meet them because of her reputation.

"It's not that," he said. "It's that their mother left them, and they're so lost, and I'm afraid they won't know how to react to someone new."

"You're afraid they'll attach to someone, and then she'll leave, and they'll be hurt again," Mellie said.

"Yes," he whispered, half expecting her to say she would never do that.

Instead, she said, "That's really wise," and took his breath away.

No one had called him wise before.

"I'd… um… still like your advice," he said. "I think I need it. Can we meet here for coffee tomorrow? I'll find out what kind of stories you like and you can tell me how to handle my daughters."

"Right here?" she said, clearly stunned.

He nodded. "My treat."

"Um, sure, yeah," she said. "That would be great."

It would be good for him, too. It would be better than good. It would be spectacular.

He brought her hand forward, bent over, and kissed it. He wanted to nibble his way up her arm and nuzzle her neck, and—

He stopped himself before he embarrassed himself. He had just told her that he wanted some distance because of his daughters, and then he starts kissing her.

He kissed her hand again, then gently let it go. She held it up for a moment, as if she wasn't sure what to do with it. She looked surprised, and a little confused.

He stood. He couldn't stay any longer, not and have a rational conversation, one good for her and good for the girls.

"I'll see you tomorrow, then," he said, and hurried out the door.

Chapter 15

MELLIE WATCHED HIM GO. SHE WAS ALWAYS WATCHING this man coming and going. She couldn't keep her eyes off him.

Even if he had just bolted. He grabbed her twenty pages, and hurried out of the coffee shop as if she was going to chase him. All the other women in the place watched him go—they couldn't keep their eyes off him either.

And they hadn't just been kissed.

Not that it was a real kiss. It was a buss on the hand. A little more than a buss, actually. A kiss on the hand. The back of the hand. Something he had been trained to do from childhood, a way of honoring women.

There was no flirting in that kiss. Mellie had had men kiss her hand and flirt with her at the same time. They looked up at her over their clasped hands, and kept eye contact as they kissed her.

But Charming had just kissed her hand, ever so politely. She liked to imagine that he had lingered for just a moment, but he hadn't. He had kissed her hand properly, then let go, and left her, clearly a bit embarrassed that he had revealed so much of his life.

Poor man. His wife sounded horrible. His *ex*-wife. Cinderella.

Imagine if Mellie had tried to tell all those little girls who believed in the glass slippers, the gowns, the fairy tale, what Ella was really like.

Mellie would have been run out of town.

She shut off her laptop, and tucked it into the bag she used to tote it all over town. Then she left the coffee shop.

She was unsettled. She hadn't expected the meeting to go the way it had. But she would see him again.

And that was a small victory. Maybe then he would have an idea about what she should do with her own writing project—her own image problems.

But she also needed some advice from an outsider, someone who knew the Kingdoms, and someone who understood her.

That left only one option. That left Selda.

———

Selda spent her days managing the Archetype Place in Anaheim. Anaheim was a heck of a drive from the coffee shop, but Mellie made it in record time.

The Archetype Place had been Mellie's idea. She had founded it decades ago, when this part of Anaheim was an absolute wasteland.

Disney had started hiring people from the Kingdoms (unbeknownst to him) for his new theme park, Disneyland, which was considered revolutionary nearly sixty years ago. Mellie had found a building not too far from the theme park and bought it for a song. She expanded over the years, so now the Archetype Place took up an entire city block.

The Archetype Place brought the Kingdoms folk together. It provided day care for both magical and non-magical youngsters, counseling for those who had trouble making the transition from the Kingdoms to the Greater World, and helped the less fortunate in the group find homes and jobs.

One small wing of the super large building housed PETA. It had started one night (about the time Mellie opened the Archetype Place) when a discussion turned into a bitch session about fairy tales, the Greater World's misunderstanding of magic and magical beings, and of, course, the great Walt Disney himself.

Initially, Mellie had tried to have meetings with Disney. In fact, her first attempt had been before the Disney *Snow White and the Seven Dwarfs* came out. She talked to Disney about doing fairy tales right, about making sure that he jettisoned those horrible Grimm brothers and told the truth.

All she had gotten for her pains was a caricature in the movie, and an image of an evil queen/stepmother who looked enough like Mellie to make all of her friends cringe.

Still, over the years, she had tried to talk to him, and he hadn't ever taken another meeting. One of his under-lings later told her that he was afraid she would ask for a piece of the film because her image was in it.

But she wasn't going to make money off that drivel. She just wanted to be heard.

She had turned to picketing in the years before Disney's death, inspired by the protest movements of the 1960s. She occasionally tried to have meetings with the Disney brass, but no one ever took her calls.

Eventually, she stopped picketing the studios and went to the source materials. The books. She figured if the books changed, the movies would change.

Or at least, she had hoped that would happen.

So far, none of her dreams had come true. Maybe she should have wished upon a star.

She had her own parking space in the lot behind The Archetype Place. No one had taken her spot, even though she hadn't been there in almost a month. Driving from Malibu to Anaheim took hours, especially in bad traffic, and she hadn't seen the need before today.

All she had done was put the protests on hold, telling everyone she had another plan.

The building looked like one giant warehouse, with the front decorated brightly, to look like a series of fake storefronts à la Disney. The rest of the building was painted white and had no windows on the sides and back, so that the folk could be themselves. Magic happened inside—not Disney magic, but real magic. Not a lot of it, and none of it evil.

In fact, the only rule Mellie initially had for the Archetype Place was No Evil Allowed. Sometimes that meant banning folk, and sometimes it just meant banning their behavior.

The main doors were made of magic-reinforced smoked glass. No one from outside could see inside. In fact, if you stopped in front of the glass, you couldn't even see your own reflection—something she relished, because for years, anytime she stopped anywhere near a mirror, someone would mutter, *Mirror, Mirror on the wall, who is the fairest one of all?*, pissing her off.

This morning, the Frog Prince manned the front desk. He was in his frog form. His beloved wife had died some years ago, and ever since, he seemed to prefer his frog form. He once told Mellie that his princely form reminded him how the woman he loved had helped him regain it. Now that she was dead, he had no one to look beautiful for.

He certainly did not look beautiful now. His skin was mottled and dry. He needed to either change back into human form or get into some water for a while. He sat on top of a lily pad that served as a desk blotter, and peered at her out of the corner of one bulging eye.

"Well, you finally decided to grace us with your presence," he said.

"No need to be snide," she said. "I've been busy."

"Drinking coffee and surfing the net, I hear."

She frowned at him. "Have you been spying on me?"

He shook his broad froggy head. "I haven't left this place in a week. But you've been seen everywhere but here."

"I was trying something," she said.

"Trying to snare a prince?"

She glared at him. "Are you jealous?"

"No," he said and hopped off the lily pad. He put one long toe on the intercom, and said into it, "Guess what the cat dragged in."

"I'm assuming that was Selda you spoke to," Mellie said. "I take it she's in?"

"What else does she have to do?" the Frog Prince said. Then he hopped to the front of the desk. "Say, when are you bringing your prince in here? I hear he's been wandering the Greater World without any idea that we exist."

She ignored the question and went through the double blond doors leading into the back. She hadn't told Charming about this place, despite ample opportunity. Before she met him, she had no idea he was wandering the Greater World without any help. She hadn't said anything at the book fair, mostly because she felt like Charming didn't need any help transitioning into the Greater World—he was doing better than anyone else at The Archetype Place except maybe Selda.

But today, today Mellie should have told him, if only to give him some help with his daughters.

She walked down the hall, past her office, which was locked tight. It looked abandoned and forlorn. She wasn't used to seeing it dark. But she hadn't wanted to come here, not while she was trying to write, not while she was trying something new.

She rounded the corner. The door to Griselda's office was open. Mellie felt relieved. Selda had completely adapted to life in the Greater World. She didn't look like any of the stereotyped wicked stepmothers. She wasn't angularly beautiful like Mellie nor did she dress like a middle-aged fashion model. She didn't exude malevolent intelligence either.

Instead, if she had to fit any stereotype at all, it was that of Earth Mother. She had been the model for several 1970s drawings in alternative publications of women who had gone back to nature, women who no longer cared about what was then called Madison Avenue and its opinions of how women should behave.

She was the first of Mellie's friends to let her hair go natural, the first to stop wearing any make-up at all, and the first to wear sweats in public.

Selda had decorated her office in the Archetype Place in brown tones, accented with bright orange and green, and instead of looking dated, the office felt warm and comfortable. Selda had placed overstuffed chairs

in the corners, and let stuffed animals and pillows litter
the floor.

Which meant at any given moment, there was usually
a cat or two sleeping on one of the pillows, a child or
two cuddling one of the toys, and a dog or two snoring
on a chair.

The office smelled of pet dander and coffee, which
Mellie also found soothing. She stepped inside. Selda
was at her desk, almost impossible to see behind the
potted palms on the floor around it, and the spider plants
hanging from the ceiling above.

"When Froggy told me you were coming," Selda
said, "I didn't believe it. How's the famous author?"

She had put on weight in the last month. Selda gained
twenty pounds and then lost them with startling regular-
ity, never ever regaining the thin form she'd had in her
Hansel and Gretel days.

"Unable to get words onto the page," Mellie said. She
sank into a nearby chair. A puff of cat hair (or was it dog
hair?) rose in the air around her, and then settled like
snow on a windless day.

"I never thought of you as a writer," Selda said.

"Oh, jeez," Mellie said. "Not you too."

"Well, if not me, then who?" Selda asked. "I'm the
one who always gets to correct your signs."

Mellie frowned. "Correct my signs?"

"You can't spell, dear," Selda said. "Haven't I told
you that?"

"You keep harping on the difference between 'it is'
and 'its' possessive," Mellie said, "but you've never
said anything about spelling."

"What do you think that is?" Selda said.

"A detail," Mellie said.

"So your handsome charming prince told you that you can't write," Selda said.

Mellie's eyes narrowed. "Have you been spying on me?"

"No, it's just that you told me you'd meet with him in a month or so after that book fair. It's been a month or so, and you're here, looking very sad."

Mellie shrugged. "He didn't say anything bad. But he didn't have to. I only got twenty pages in a month."

"I'm sure you wrote more than that."

Mellie smiled at her good friend. Selda knew her well.

"All right," Mellie said, "I wrote more than twenty pages. But twenty pages were the only thing resembling some kind of story. Everything else I wrote was a rant."

"And that surprises you how?" Selda asked.

Mellie shook her head. "I don't know. I just figured I could do this."

"Mel, dear," Selda said. "Your entire life is a rant. You're one of the great crusaders against injustice wherever you find it. And you make a difference. You're just not a very reflective personality."

"So?" Mellie asked.

"So writing really isn't your thing," Selda said.

"Tell me about it." Mellie flicked a big wad of dog hair (or was it cat hair?) off the arm of the chair. "Still, I think the idea is a good one."

"It is," Selda said. "So why don't you just hire someone to do it?"

Mellie sank farther into the chair. "Like you?"

"I can't write," Selda said.

"You just said you corrected my writing," Mellie said.

"I corrected your *grammar* and your *spelling*," Selda said. "That's not writing."

"But—"

"No buts," Selda said. "I hate writing. I'm one of the few of us who went to college here—"

In the 1970s, which was when she first went all Earth Mothery. Mellie remembered how traumatic that change had been.

"—and I hated writing even then. I once paid a guy to write one of my papers, and it was the only paper I got an A on."

Mellie wasn't sure what an A was, but obviously an A was desirable.

"Well, I assume your guy's from the Greater World," Mellie said, "and I can't hire him. Charming already introduced me to some of those ghosty people, and they're all grounded firmly in this world. They wouldn't like or believe anything I say."

"So hire one of us," Selda said.

"None of us can write," Mellie said.

"What about your prince?"

Mellie's eyes narrowed. "He's not *my* prince."

"He's bookish," Selda said.

Mellie sat up. "You know him?"

Selda leaned back in her chair and put her Birkenstock-covered feet on top of her messy desk. "I've met him a few times. He's much too introverted for my tastes."

Mellie rather liked how quiet and thoughtful he was. So different from the other Charmings that she'd met.

"He doesn't have time to help me," Mellie said. "He's dealing with his daughters."

"His daughters?"

Mellie nodded. "He has full custody now, and he just brought them to the Greater World."

"Well, that's no surprise," Selda said, folding her hands across her ample belly.

"That he brought them here?" Mellie asked.

"That he got full custody. Ella was never suited to parenthood."

Mellie raised her eyebrows. "You seem to know a lot about this family."

"I remember the marriage," Selda said. "It was clear it would never work."

Mellie leaned forward. "How do you know that?"

"Anyone with a brain could've figured that out," Selda said. "They got married for all the wrong reasons. He married her because his father decreed that he had to marry right away, and she married him because he was a prince."

"Other relationships have had less to build on," Mellie said.

"I suppose," Selda said. "But Ella was a rebellion for Charming. His father wanted some kind of politically advantageous marriage, and Charming wanted something romantic. So he picked the prettiest, most downtrodden girl he could find and elevated her to a princess. How much more romantic can you get?"

Mellie shrugged a shoulder. Put that way, it did sound romantic.

"But marriage isn't about pretty or rebellion or rising up. It's about love and companionship and children and better and worse, and neither Charming nor Ella were ready for that."

"How do you know this?" Mellie asked again.

"I keep my ear to the ground," Selda said.

Mellie leaned back and sighed. She liked Charming, but that wasn't any reason to involve him in her life or her problems.

"He's too busy to help me," she said.

"Why don't you let him make that choice?" Selda asked. "He's already helped you a lot. Give him another chance."

"But his daughters…"

"He can't parent all the time, Mel," Selda said. "You know that."

She did know that.

"You're just afraid he's going to say no," Selda said.

Mellie looked at her oldest and dearest friend. Selda had a point—which was annoying. Sometimes it wasn't nice to have someone know you that well.

Selda's grin widened when she realized she'd hit her mark.

"But," she said, "have you ever thought about how you'd feel if he said yes?"

Mellie's heart skipped. "He won't."

"What if he does?"

Mellie flushed. "He'll learn how difficult I am."

"He lived with Ella. I have a hunch he won't find you difficult at all."

"Why are you pushing this?" Mellie said.

"Because," Selda said, "I've never seen you so interested in a man before."

"I'm not interested," Mellie lied.

"And," Selda added, "you said it yourself. This book idea is a good one. Much better than all that stupid protesting. This thing might actually work."

"Which thing?" Mellie asked. "The writing, the book, or the friendship with Charming?"

"Which one do you want to work?" Selda asked.

Mellie didn't answer. She didn't have to. They both knew that she wanted all three.

Chapter 16

CHARMING WAS SHAKING AS HE DROVE HIS MERCEDES. Honesty and charm didn't go well together. He wasn't used to saying what he thought. *Blurting* what he thought.

No wonder people got embarrassed so easily. When you blurted, you said things you could regret.

My wife abandoned my daughters.

It was true—more or less (he wasn't sure why he had thought of Ella as his wife at that moment, although she was the only wife he'd ever had)—but it wasn't diplomatic. Or charming. Or really, any of Mellie's business.

But who else could he tell?

No one here in the Greater World would understand exactly what he was saying. Not only did people marry for life in the Kingdoms (although that had been changing for a while now [even if some people (like his father) disapproved]), they never, ever, ever gave up life at the palace. Especially when they had wanted it as much as Ella had.

But times were changing. Divorce had become more prevalent, the respect for the monarchy was declining, and celebrity was on the rise. The fairy tales had made for a lot of changes, in the Kingdoms as well as outside them.

Some people felt that if they didn't have a fairy tale written about them, they didn't really and truly exist.

He drove to the new house. He couldn't call it home yet, even though he liked the place. It was a faux Tudor, built to earthquake standards, with a lovely, curving brick walkway that went to an arched front door. The mullioned windows gave the place an authentic feel, and the outside looked like something that belonged in one of the forests in the Kingdoms.

He had thought the girls would feel at home here, but they hardly noticed the place. Although they did notice the garden in the back, filled with flowers they had never seen before. The winters in the Kingdoms were cold, so the plants there were hardy. Even in the summer, only the hardiest survived.

Here, anything that could handle the summer heat thrived. Desert plants and tropical plants—big leaves, bright colors. Things he didn't know the names of. Whoever had owned the house before him had clearly loved plants and the outdoors and had made this one spectacular.

So spectacular he hadn't been able to answer most of the girls' questions about the plants. He didn't know what they were or how long they bloomed. He didn't even know if they were annual or perennial.

And he was a bookish guy. He should know anything.

Just like he should know whether Mellie, famous for being Snow White's (murderous) stepmother, had actually raised children on her own.

He wasn't even sure how to research that, although he knew he should. Fairy tales—hell, life—was full of mistakes people made when they trusted the wrong person.

Although she felt very trustworthy.

And very beautiful.

And if he hadn't controlled himself, he would have
been all over her in that coffee shop. He *never* acted like
that, not once in his whole life.

What was wrong with him? Was he that lonely?

Or was he that attracted to her?

He parked on the driveway, knowing he only had a
few hours before he had to pick the girls up. Then he
went inside the house.

It was quiet. It didn't smell like home yet. It smelled
of cleaning chemicals, as if no one had lived here in a
long time. He wasn't sure what he could do to make this
house feel like a home.

He set the folder down on a nearby occasional table,
glad he remembered to bring Mellie's writing home. He
didn't want her to see the red marks he had made all
over the interior pages. No sense in hurting her feelings
worse than he already had.

Somehow he had thought that writing books would
be easy. Or at least, writing would be easy for anyone
with magic in their background. He had no trouble writing. He'd even sold some things—a few essays, and a
handful of short stories.

But he didn't blame that on talent. He figured his
charm had extended to the page.

Besides, he thought, it didn't take much to sell.
After all, those Grimm brothers had taken stories from
people's real lives and made a series of "tales" that got
retold for generations. He'd read the original tales and
they weren't very well written.

But they were compelling.

Maybe compelling was hard.

He went down the hallway to the back of the house

to his favorite room. The house had a library, which he was also using as a study.

The library overlooked the garden. If he had to be honest, he would have said that this was the room that convinced him to buy the house. Floor-to-ceiling mahogany shelves, an extra-high ceiling, and a librarian's moving ladder so he could put things on the top of ten-foot-high shelves.

The garden wall was covered with windows. They came outfitted with blackout curtains to keep the light out or sheers which theoretically kept out the worst of the light. And whoever had built the house had tinted the glass so that the UV didn't pour in either.

He didn't really care, although he probably should have. He just loved the light and the view—so fresh and bright and not Kingdomy. He was surrounded by books, but overlooking the garden. The world couldn't get more perfect than that.

Except…

He needed his daughters to be happy.

He sank into the chair behind his desk. He had a laptop folded behind the desk and a very elaborate desktop computer pushed to one side. He didn't use either at the moment.

Instead, he picked up his Kingdom phone.

He set the Kingdom phone in the center of his desk, tapped the phone's surface, and murmured the name of Ella's stepmother, Lavinia.

The phone didn't ring. Instead it just connected. An image of Lavinia appeared on the phone's screen.

Lavinia looked nothing like the stepmother in Disney's *Cinderella*. She was slight and blond. He had heard rumors that she was of mixed race—her mother had been a fairy of the Tinker/Tanker Belle variety, and her father had been a smaller than average human being. But Charming couldn't (or wouldn't) imagine that.

Still, Lavinia had an ethereal beauty. Instead of being the wizened creature of the fairy tales, she was one of the greatest beauties in the Kingdom—certainly more beautiful than Ella had ever been.

"Charming," Lavinia said, her voice rich and musical, even through the phone's magic. "I trust all is well."

"We're adjusting." He didn't want to lie to her, but he also didn't want to tell her how difficult things had become.

"There's a story in those two words," Lavinia said.

"No," he said with a sigh, "just everyday life."

"Then to what do I owe this call?" Lavinia asked.

"Did I tell you that I met Snow White's stepmother, Mellie, a month or so ago?" he asked.

"Mellie," Lavinia said. "Now that woman has gotten a raw deal."

He smiled ever so softly. This was why he called Lavinia. The one thing that some of the films about her had depicted correctly was her love of gossip.

"Didn't all of you stepmothers get a raw deal?" he asked, knowing that was a better response than a direct question about Mellie herself.

"In the fairy tales, yes we did," Lavinia said. "Not in life, necessarily."

He forgot: she had always been kind about her fortunes. She had loved Ella's father, and figured that the year or so she spent with him was the best year of her life.

"But Mellie, she was the target of some particularly malicious lies," Lavinia said.

"The poisoning," he said.

"Yes, that," Lavinia said. "To be fair, she brought some of it on herself."

That took him aback. He had thought she was completely innocent. "How so?" he asked.

"She was so insecure," Lavinia said. "You know what insecure people are like. They always care about what other people think."

Of course, Lavinia hadn't cared enough about what other people thought. If she had actually put herself in other people's shoes, she might have avoided some of the mistakes she made with Ella.

"And," Lavinia was saying, "when you're that kind of insecure, people take advantage of you."

"I'm confused," Charming said. "What does that have to do with the poisoning?"

"She was trying so hard to be everything to everyone, she wasn't succeeding at anything," Lavinia said. "She made herself beautiful for her husband, and tried to be the perfect mother to Snow, who was nearly a grown woman at the time, and she was trying to be the perfect royal in her little section of the Kingdoms, when she hadn't had a clue how to do it. She insulted so many people, and they wanted to see her lose her position."

He remained silent. Lavinia had been accused of some of the same things, but she hadn't married royalty, and she had a small circle of friends who protected her. It sounded like Mellie did not.

"Snow wasn't very popular either," Lavinia said. "In fact, that girl was a terror. She ran away from home—you know that, right? She ran away after her father died, saying she wasn't going to live with that thing he had married. She expected Mellie to come after her, but Mellie didn't. She figured Snow was a grown woman who could make her own choices. And that was her greatest mistake."

"Snow wasn't grown?"

"Oh, in years perhaps," Lavinia said. "But not emotionally. She was very pampered, very catered to, and quite selfish. She learned how to be a better person."

"With the Dwarfs," he said.

"Before that," Lavinia said. "She got lost in the woods and almost starved. The Dwarfs saved her life, but at a cost. She had to pay them back, and since she wouldn't go to Mellie for money, Snow had to work off her debt."

"All that 'Whistle While You Work' crap?" he asked. "That's true?"

"Except that it wasn't Snow's idea," Lavinia said, "and she didn't participate happily. But she learned how to scrub floors and cook meals. She grew up."

Fairy tales never dealt in nuance. Charming leaned back in his chair.

"Okay," he said, not needing the rest of that story. "So what about the poison?"

"Well, that's where it gets interesting," Lavinia said.

He waited. Lavinia always loved to make dramatic pauses.

"You have to remember that we got the story from Snow after she recovered," Lavinia said.

He hadn't known that. "So she could have said anything she wanted."

"Well, there really was no proof of anything," Lavinia said, "except that she bought a poisoned comb from a peddler woman. Snow lost all of her hair and was furious, but she couldn't do anything. The poison certainly wouldn't have killed her."

"Everyone thought that peddler woman was Mellie?" Charming asked.

"Using magic to disguise herself as an old crone," Lavinia said. "But what no one remembers is that there was a rash of comb-attacks around that period."

"There was?" Charming hadn't heard anything about it.

"If you were vain enough to buy one of these elaborate combs, you lost hair. It was one of two things," Lavinia said. "It was either someone after all the women with lovely hair or it was an inept peddler trying to make a good product and screwing it all up. I vote for the latter, by the way."

"Wow," Charming said. He had had no idea. "So the peddler woman didn't come back and give Snow an apple."

"Have you met Snow White?" Lavinia asked, and then continued, not waiting for his answer. "Does she seem stupid enough to buy poison from the same old peddler woman *twice*?"

He'd often wondered about that part of the story. "Not really," he said, mostly because Lavinia expected a response from him.

"Precisely," Lavinia said. "Personally, I think what happened was a bit darker."

"Darker how?" he asked.

She sighed. "This isn't the stuff of children's stories anymore."

He waited through another dramatic pause.

"You've heard the rumors about Snow's ex-husband, right?" Lavinia asked.

"One of the other Charmings," Charming said.

"Who changed his name when he became king, but that's another story," Lavinia said. "Unlike you, he was always misnamed."

"Thank you, I think," Charming said.

She laughed. "Seriously, Charming. Your name suits you."

"But didn't suit him," Charming said.

"Well maybe as a young man," Lavinia said. "But he got progressively creepier as he got older. There was a reason he wanted that coffin, you know."

"Snow White's coffin," Charming said, just to be clear.

"With Snow in it," Lavinia said, in that tone she used when the gossip got particularly good.

"Okay," Charming said. "Obviously, I haven't heard the rumors. Why would he want a glass coffin with a beautiful but supposedly dead woman inside of it?"

Lavinia sighed. "Oh, Charming, you are so naïve."

"All right, I'm naïve," he said. "Spell it out for me."

"He's not fond of living women," Lavinia said.

Charming waited for the dramatic pause to end. But she didn't say anything else. So he thought about it, then shuddered. She couldn't mean…?

"Necrophilia?" he said.

"In the worst possible way," Lavinia said. "Rumor has it when he was furious when his aides dropped the coffin and the poison apple dislodged from her throat."

"I thought she hadn't had any poison," Charming said.

"That's the other version of the story," Lavinia said. "The substantially ickier version. He pried open the coffin, found out she wasn't really dead, and she blackmailed him into marriage. They made up the story together."

"That would mean she had to plan the whole thing," Charming said.

"Yes," Lavinia said. "And you can't tell me that you haven't met some crazy girls who would do anything to marry you."

He closed his eyes. "Oh, I didn't need that image."

"You asked," Lavinia said.

He wasn't sure he had asked for that much information. "So you think Mellie never tried to harm Snow."

"Honestly, I think Mellie did everything she could to help Snow. I've always wondered why Mellie doesn't have magic anymore," Lavinia said.

Charming frowned. "What do you think she did?"

"I don't know," Lavinia said. "But her magic disappeared right around the time Snow married her handsome prince. You can't seriously think if Mellie had magic, she would have let the rumors about her continue to thrive."

He hadn't thought of that. "But you don't know what happened to her magic."

"Nope. I haven't even heard speculation," she said. "And, surprisingly enough, I don't have any either."

He took off his glasses and rubbed his eyes. "She does have other children, though, right?"

"Snow has a brother," Lavinia said, "who considers Mellie his mom. He's a good kid. I like him."

Charming nodded. "What about her own children?"

"They're older than Snow," Lavinia said, "and all but one lives in the Greater World. Nice kids, nicer than mine, and I like mine."

He laughed. "So she likes children."

"She's good with them," Lavinia said. "I heard she wanted to open some kind of day care in the Kingdoms before this whole Snow thing broke. Have you been to the Archetype Place?"

"The what?" he asked.

"Clearly you haven't then," Lavinia said. "The place Mellie started to help Archetypes deal with the Greater World. She had started the day care center in there, but the Place is much bigger than day care."

"She never told me about it," Charming said, wondering why.

"She probably figured you didn't need it," Lavinia said. "It's really for Kingdoms folk who have trouble adjusting to the Greater World, and that's clearly not you."

He sighed. That wasn't him, until he brought his daughters here to live.

"So now, Charming," Lavinia said, "you have to tell me what this is all about. Is this about my granddaughters?"

He thought about it for a moment, decided that full honesty wasn't the best here, and said, "Yes. I feel like they need a bit of contact with the Kingdoms, someone who understands the differences, but not someone who is family, you know?"

"You don't want me there, in other words," Lavinia said.

"Or my folks or your daughters," he said, adding his stepsisters-in-law. "I was just thinking of some casual contact so that girls could know that people from the Kingdoms do well in the Greater Worlds."

"Mellie would be a good choice, then," Lavinia said.

"She hasn't come home in decades. She feels like she isn't welcome here, and she's probably right."

He smiled. That made him feel much better.

"Of course you realize that my giving you permission to spend time with Mellie would just send Ella over the edge," Lavinia added.

"Then let's not tell her about this," Charming said. They could add it to all the other things they didn't tell Ella.

"I won't if you won't," Lavinia said. "So long as you bring my granddaughters home sometime soon."

"I will," he said, hoping her definition of soon and his were very different. "Thanks, Lavinia."

"Anytime," she said, and then her image vanished in a haze of stars.

He stared at the Kingdom phone for a long moment.

He had a few other people to check with, from his valet to the most foul-mouthed fairy of all, Tanker Belle. But he felt a lot better than he had a little while ago.

He could safely talk to Mellie.

Finally, someone who might help him with his daughters.

And heaven knew, he needed a lot of help.

Chapter 17

MELLIE SAT IN THE COFFEE SHOP, FEELING STUPID. SHE HAD felt all fired up after talking with Selda the day before, but upon reflection, she realized that she had been right in the first place. Charming wouldn't help her. He had too much to do, too much to consider.

And just because she was attracted to him didn't mean he was attracted to her. She'd lived long enough to realize that life didn't work that way.

She arrived early, even though she hadn't planned on doing so. It seemed like everyone except Charming was already here. The pudgy guy who had been typing madly on his keyboard yesterday was typing madly today. Other familiar people sat around the room, usually at the same tables they'd occupied the day before.

She had her laptop open, even though she wasn't writing. She had logged onto the Net but she hadn't even Googled "evil stepmother" like she usually did. In fact, she hadn't Googled "evil stepmother" in a long time, not since she started the book.

She sighed and stared at her home screen, which was the Archetype Place. The web design was lovely, and had all kinds of positive images of fairy tale characters going in and out of ornate doorways. She had an email account there, but she hadn't checked that in a while either.

Only her private account, which was on a different server.

Only the account that Charming knew.

She almost closed her laptop when she thought of that. She was going crazy over a man, something she never thought she would do. Well, that wasn't entirely true. She had done it before, with her first marriage. She had really fallen for her first husband, even though the marriage was arranged. She had met him on their wedding day, and had felt great relief at his warmth and friendliness.

He hadn't been a handsome man, although she had heard he had been in his youth. But he wasn't young, nearly fifty years older than she was, and childless. But he was kind and he was funny and he was smart, and he taught her how to survive in the world.

But when he died, he had left his entire estate to their children, not to her. Her children had taken care of her, but she was still young and vibrant and she didn't want to be beholden to her children for the rest of her life.

So she had married again, but the marriage hadn't been a love match. More a marriage of convenience. Her second husband had paid a bride's price, but since her parents were gone and her children didn't need the money, he had given the entire amount to her. And she had saved it, which had turned out to be the most prudent thing she had done with that marriage.

He had wanted someone to raise his children. His son, still ten, had been wonderful, but his daughter—Snow—was a handful. Mellie thought, since Snow was nearly grown, that the children part of the arrangement would be easy.

Of course she had been wrong.

She picked up her coffee mug. The ceramic was warm against her fingers. Maybe she deserved a muffin.

Or a cupcake. Or one of those really yummy lemon bars in the case.

Anything to take her mind off Charming.

Who probably wouldn't show.

———— ∿∿ ————

He wasn't going to ask for help, even though he hadn't slept at all the night before.

Charming stood outside the coffee shop, just to the left of the main windows. As he parked his car, he saw Mellie go inside, laptop under one arm. She looked so put together, so efficient.

So lovely.

She would probably think him a fool for the situation he had gotten himself into.

He had gotten his girls into.

He sat in the car for nearly fifteen minutes, waiting so that he wouldn't seem too early or too eager. When he finally got out, he couldn't quite bring himself to go inside.

What could Mellie do anyway? Tell him to calm down? Tell him to put his daughters in a different school? Tell him to move to a new community?

Tell him to give all the bullies who were picking on Grace poisoned apples?

He bit the inside of his cheek as a punishment for that thought. He couldn't say anything like that, not even as a joke. It wasn't respectful for one thing, and it was wrong for another. If she had any magic at all, she would tell him to try something more direct.

Like change all those bullies into frogs.

Heck, he'd change them all into bowling balls if he could. Or racquetballs. And then he'd make sure they could still feel pain. That way when they hit a racket or a bowling pin, they'd bruise.

With the knuckle of his forefinger, he pushed his glasses up. It was probably a good thing that he didn't have any real magic. He wouldn't use it well.

In fact, he was beginning to think he was more likely to create poisoned apples than Mellie ever would have been.

He squared his shoulders and pulled open the door to the coffee shop. It smelled of ground coffee beans and cinnamon rolls. His stomach growled. He hadn't eaten breakfast.

Heck, he had barely finished dinner the night be-fore—only managing a few bites because he needed to set an example for the girls.

This time, however, he had learned his lesson. He walked over to the table, set his briefcase down beside it, and smiled at Mellie. She was so beautiful. He wanted to kiss her in greeting, but of course, he wouldn't.

He didn't want to alarm her.

She closed her laptop and smiled back at him.

"I'm getting one of the cinnamon rolls," he said. "You want one?"

"Sure," she said and reached for her purse, probably to give him enough money to pay for the thing.

He turned away quickly and headed for the counter, ordering a regular coffee and cinnamon rolls. He hadn't asked her if she wanted something else to drink. But it was too late. He paid for the food, had the rolls warmed and a heap of butter put on the side, and carried them back to the table.

Then he went back for his coffee, forks, and a pile of napkins.

He managed to set it all down on the table without spilling a drop. Mellie had put her laptop away. The two cinnamon rolls sat in the center like the prize for a contest.

"So," she said, "when was the last time you got any sleep?"

He started. "Is it that obvious?"

She nodded.

He ran a hand through his hair, feeling how thin it got on top. If he looked at his hand as he brought it down, he would probably find a few strands between the fingers.

Strands he couldn't afford to lose.

He had to look awful. Here he sat with the most beautiful woman he had ever met, and she could tell he wasn't sleeping and he was a wreck. Not so charming now, as Ella would say.

Not charming at all.

"More problems with the girls?" Mellie asked.

"I'm not sure it qualifies as more," he said. "It just continues."

Grace in tears after school. Imperia looking like an avenging angel.

He had gone in that morning and spoken to the principal again, explaining that his daughters had lived with his wife out of state, and weren't adjusting well. The principal had promised, just like she had the day before, that his daughters would be just fine.

He was scared to death that they weren't.

"The same thing?" Mellie asked. "Someone is picking on your youngest?"

He nodded. "And it makes no sense. Grace is sweet and sensitive and shy. She wouldn't bother anyone.

I'm not even sure why she'd being noticed. She's lovely, but she always tries to disappear into a corner whenever she's in a new situation."

Just like her father. He had no advice to give her, because he didn't know how to behave in those circumstances.

He didn't even know how to talk to a beautiful woman.

Mellie used her fork to spread butter across her cinnamon roll. He had forgotten to get knives. He didn't know what that meant. There was probably some symbolism in there somewhere.

"What about your oldest daughter?" Mellie asked. "Is anyone picking on her?"

"No, but they wouldn't." He followed her lead and spread the butter with his fork. It took more coordination than he expected, and gave him something to focus on besides the sympathetic look on her face.

"Why wouldn't they?" Mellie asked as if she were really interested.

"Because," he said, looking up. She was watching him closely, hanging on each word. "No one would ever pick on Imperia. They wouldn't dare."

Mellie's eyebrows met in the middle. The doughy guy at the next table glanced over at Charming, clearly startled.

What had he said? He didn't know.

"You named your daughter Imperia?" Mellie asked.

"Well, I…" he let his voice trail off. Then he glared at the doughy guy, who bent over his computer as if it had suddenly gotten much more fascinating. "I, um, didn't."

"You didn't name her?" Mellie asked.

Charming shrugged. "My father said it's tradition to name the oldest girl Imperia."

"Is it?" Mellie asked.

"Yes," Charming said, feeling defensive.

"And you agreed to this name?" Mellie asked.

He bristled. Imperia had been born twelve years ago. "What was I supposed to do?"

"Name her something decent," said the doughy guy from the next table. "Jeez, buddy. Talk about dooming a kid for life."

Charming stood.

"This is none of your business," he said. He sounded angry. He never sounded angry. But he was. And he was smart enough to know it was easier to attack a guy he had never met than it was to deal with the conversation he was having.

And the memories that it brought up.

"You're right, you're right." The doughy guy held up a hand as if he actually expected Charming to assault him. "I'm not going to listen anymore. See?"

He dug into the pocket of his coat and removed an iPod. He ostentatiously pulled out earbuds as well and put them in place. Charming continued to stand. Charming had daughters. He knew that just because the earbuds were in place that the music probably wasn't on.

The guy punched the flywheel in the middle and suddenly tinny sound screeched out of his ears. The doughy guy was going to go deaf within five minutes if he kept the volume that loud.

But Charming didn't care about the doughy guy's hearing. Charming just wanted some privacy so that he could talk to Mellie.

He sat back down.

"He has a point," Mellie said softly. "Imperia is really not the best name for a child."

"What can I do about it now?" Charming stabbed his fork into the cinnamon roll. "Change it on her? It suits her."

"It does?" Mellie asked.

He nodded.

"She's imperial?"

He nodded.

"Haughty?"

He nodded.

"Demanding?"

He nodded.

"Beautiful?"

"Oh, yeah," he said, and sighed. That would be another problem in a few years. She was stunning. "And intelligent and articulate and strong. You can tell from the moment you meet her how powerful she is. I don't know where she got that personality, but not from me or Ella. Imp is a force of nature."

"That's what you call her? Imp?"

He picked at the roll. He wasn't looking up. He didn't want to see the expression on Mellie's face.

"Yeah." He didn't want to say that he thought the nickname would keep his daughter humble. "Everyone else who knows her calls her Imi."

"That's a little better," Mellie said. "Imp is interesting. Does that fit?"

"Sometimes," he said with a bit of a smile. At home, when she was comfortable. Certainly not lately. Lately she had wrapped herself in her Imperia persona and raised her royal chin against the world.

"Imperia," Mellie mused. "Haughty, demanding, beautiful, strong… and threatening?"

He frowned. He was getting annoyed. Couldn't she leave Imperia's name alone? "Why?"

"Is she threatening?" Mellie wasn't going to let this go.

"To whom?" He wasn't going to give in any farther on the name.

"To anyone who meets her," Mellie said.

"She probably wouldn't seem threatening to you," he said. Mellie was powerful in ways he never could be. He couldn't imagine anyone threatening her. Angering her, yes. Disappointing her, surely. But threatening her? Never.

"But is she threatening to children her age?" Mellie asked.

He thought of that royal chin, raised in defiance; of those beautiful features accented by his father's piercing blue eyes; of that tone she could get in her voice when she didn't like something.

"Yeah," he said softly. "I'm sure that's why those children haven't picked on her."

"But they are picking on her," Mellie said.

He shook his head. "That's what I've been telling you. They've been picking on Grace."

"Because Grace is an easy target. And picking on her probably makes her sister mad."

Mad? It made Imperia furious. He leaned back in his chair. He had clenched a fist without realizing it. Frosting stuck to one of his fingers, making it sticky.

"They're picking on Grace to get at Imperia?" he asked.

"Probably," Mellie said. "That's what I would do."

He thought about that a moment longer, rubbing his

sticky fingers against each other. Imperia would never get mad if someone came after her. Imperia would merely look down her nose at them and cow them into submission.

She was more articulate that most children her age, both in and out of the Kingdoms. She was prettier. And she was smarter.

How did you go after an immovable force? Figure out what made it move.

He felt an odd surge of pride that his oldest daughter loved the youngest enough to cause this crisis. Then he looked at Mellie, who was watching him with compassion.

He was grateful he had spoken to Lavinia, grateful he had learned a bit about Mellie. Because her advice was good. And it seemed like her heart was good too.

Which just made her all the more desirable.

He cleared his throat before he trusted himself to speak. "Are you sure about this?"

"Of course not," she said. "I haven't met your daughters. But I believe what you say. The youngest is sweet and shy. There's no reason to go after her—for her own sake. But there's a reason to go after your oldest daughter. Power struggles start young, particularly among girls."

He frowned. "This means the other girls are smart enough to figure out what bothers Imperia."

"Of course they are," Mellie said. "They're prepubescent girls."

He blinked hard, thinking about that.

"That is assuming," Mellie said, "that it's the older girls going after Grace."

"Yes, it is," he said. "That's why the principal said it would stop. The older girls would give up once they found a new target."

Mellie shook her head. "They have their target and it's Imperia. Grace is collateral damage. I'll wager that Imperia just comforts her sister and tells her to buck up, doesn't she?"

"I taught my girls to solve their own problems," he said.

"Well, tell Imperia to solve this one," Mellie said. "If she can intimidate those other girls, then she needs to do so now."

He thought about that for a moment. He had always told the girls to keep their problems separate. That one won't be around to help the other when they get older. Not that Grace helped Imperia much—except on girl things, things Charming didn't entirely understand.

He smiled almost involuntarily. This felt right. This felt completely right. And Mellie even had the solution.

He had to get to his girls, and tell them how to solve this. He stood. "I don't know how to thank you," he said.

"Just let me know if it works," she said.

He felt so relieved that he wanted to hug her. He bent over to hug her, and thank her, and tell her how grateful he was.

Somehow he kissed her instead.

His lips met hers and hers opened. She tasted like coffee and sunshine and something wonderful, something he had never ever tasted before, something he couldn't taste enough. His hands slid onto her shoulders and were about to slide down when he remembered where he was.

A coffee shop.

Public.

He never kissed a woman in public except that one time with Ella, and look where that had gotten him.

He stopped, and took a step backwards. He was old enough—and Charming enough—to know better than to apologize. He didn't say anything at all, because he wasn't sure what the best thing to say was. He would either grab her and kiss her everywhere or he would shut down and apologize.

He didn't dare do either.

Mellie looked up at him, her emerald eyes open wide. She looked young and vulnerable. Color touched her cheeks—a rose color that matched that faint rose scent she had.

She looked as stunned as he felt.

And that thought made his brain start to work again.

"Thank you," he said. "You have no idea how much this is going to help."

Then he grabbed his briefcase and fled the coffee shop, before he did something they both would regret.

Chapter 18

MELLIE HAD NEVER BEEN STRUCK DUMBFOUNDED BY A KISS before. It was a hell of a kiss. A no-holds-barred-oh-my-heavens kind of kiss. The best kiss ever.

And it was her fault, because she had tilted her head upward just a little, meeting his lips—lips that were probably going to brush her cheek—with her own open mouth. She had forced the kiss, and lonely man that he was, he had enjoyed it.

Until he remembered how she was.

She pressed her hands against her hot cheeks. It had taken all of her strength to keep from grabbing him and forcing him backwards over the table. And when he stepped back, it took even more strength to keep her arms at her side so that she didn't grab him, pull him forward, and kiss him until someone kicked them out of the coffee shop for lewd and lascivious conduct.

He was a Charming. Hell, he was *the* Charming. How many people thought of Snow White's Charming when they thought of Prince Charming or of Sleeping Beauty's Charming? They all thought of Cinderella's Charming. *This* Charming.

Mellie's Charming.

Her cheeks grew even warmer.

She knew she had looked at him like a silly little fan girl when he stepped back. And that look had caused him to grab his briefcase and flee.

Of course, he'd said something polite—a nice, tame thank-you, with a calm voice and such a warm smile. But he was a Charming, he was *the* Charming, and of course he was nice about it. He saw that he had rattled her and he couldn't deal with it (after all, he was a *shy* Charming), and he fled before the situation got worse.

She was still in her chair, two unfinished cinnamon rolls in front of her (neither of those would last long), but she was staring at the door now, probably with a wistful look.

How many women launched themselves at him? How many females had done so—females of all ages? And what about gay men? Charming probably had to dodge admirers everywhere he went, all of whom looked at him with that same combination of wistful and longing.

The same way most people from the Kingdoms looked at her when they met her—with terror and utter loathing. Then they got to know her and they realized she wasn't so bad after all.

She wondered if anyone ever completely got past Charming's charm. Which made her wonder if anyone ever completely got past their loathing of her—and that thought made her cringe.

"That was weird," said the pudgy guy.

She looked over at him, about to make some kind of comment about the pudgy guy's nosiness, but she stopped herself in time.

Besides, the pudgy guy wasn't done talking.

"I mean, you gave him the answer, then he kisses you, and runs away as if whatever he had to do was more important. Weird."

Her cheeks warmed even more. She shrugged, uncertain what to say.

"I didn't mean to listen in," the guy said. "But he named his daughter Imperia. I didn't even know that was a name."

"Anything's a name," Mellie said, "if you use it that way."

"I guess," the guy said. "He's kind of a piece of work, isn't he?"

"Charming?" she asked. Who would describe Charming as a piece of work?

"Oh, hell, no," the pudgy guy said. "He's not charming at all. What kind of charming guy leaves without a proper good-bye?"

It took Mellie a moment to realize the guy thought she had said that Charming was charming, which he was—except, apparently, to the pudgy guy. Although Charming had gotten mad at him after all. She wouldn't have thought that a Charming could get mad. Or at least, this Charming.

"Look," the pudgy guy said, "you're a pretty lady and awfully smart, and you deserve someone better than that guy. I mean, he can't even sit still."

"He's not that bad," Mellie said, her cheeks so warm that they actually hurt. The pudgy guy had called her pretty.

"I don't mean to be talking about him," the pudgy guy said. "It's just that I don't want you to think I'm creepy or anything, but I couldn't help noticing you the last few days. And that guy aside, I'd like to get to know you better. How about lunch?"

She didn't recognize him, and he didn't have that sparkle that indicated he was from the Kingdoms.

He was from the Greater World and he had just asked her to lunch.

Normally, she would have gone. Then she would have regaled him with her stories of downtrodden archetypes, after she quizzed him on his knowledge of fairy tales, of course.

But she didn't want to do either today. She didn't care what he thought of evil stepmothers. She didn't even care that he had a mind open to change. She used to think she could conquer the fairy tale myths, one open mind at a time.

"Thanks," she said, "but—"

"But you're holding out for that guy," the pudgy guy said.

"No," she said quietly. "He's nice, but we're such opposites. And besides, I don't hold out for anyone."

The pudgy guy smiled. He wasn't bad-looking when he smiled. "There was still a *but* after you thanked me for the invitation."

"Yeah," she said. "I'm not really up for lunch."

She looked at the cinnamon rolls.

"But you could save me from one of these."

He patted his stomach. "Like I need more cinnamon rolls," he said, and grinned. "However, I'm not the kind of man to turn one down."

She laughed. "I'm Mellie," she said, pushing a chair back.

"Dave," he said, and she actually flinched.

"Seriously?" she asked.

"Seriously, I'm David. But to people I like, I'm Dave."

"And you hope to be someone's prince charming someday," she said softly.

"Oh, no," he said. "I've been someone's prince charming. I don't like being an illusion. I want to be someone's Dave someday."

She smiled. "That seems like a reasonable ambition," she said as he joined her at her table.

"I don't know about reasonable," he said. "But it's practical. And I've learned the hard way that we should be practical in relationships."

"Yeah," she said, feeling more than a little sad for both of them. "Practical always works best."

Chapter 19

IT WORKED!

Mellie's suggestion had worked!

Charming had never been so startled by anything in his life. That wasn't true, of course. He'd been startled by Ella's abandonment of their daughters, constantly startled by his father's self-centeredness, startled by Mellie's protest at the book fair. But this startlement had been so much better than those.

Charming actually could do something for his daughters. Something good.

He had told Imperia to defend her sister before comforting her. He had even implied that it was okay to get physical. (He implied it because his contract with the school stated that physical arguments between students [fistfights, in other words] could result in expulsion.)

Imperia had looked relieved. So had Grace.

He bundled them off to school the very next day, and they had come home laughing. *Laughing*. His daughters, happy because of school.

Not that he had to worry about any untoward magic. The Charming family didn't have conventional magic. (That's what real witches were for.) They had unconventional magic—charisma, power absorption, charm, and grace. So his daughters couldn't turn anyone into toads or bowling balls.

But Imperia could make people feel very small without

casting a spell, and make them regret they ever picked on Grace. And Grace would forgive them which would make them feel better. Because that's how Grace worked.

He was so happy he actually cooked them an aged mutton dinner, the Kingdoms' equivalent of pizza. Then he watched and waited for the next few days, hoping that the change in his girls wasn't a fluke.

He also hoped that he wouldn't hear from the school. He didn't want to discover that he had been wrong about his girls—that they actually had real magic after all. (He had been afraid that some real magic lurked in Ella's family; something neither of them knew about.)

But no calls, and no change in mood. After nearly a week, Grace wanted to go to school. She was starting to make friends.

And Imperia actually smiled a few times on her way to school.

Charming saw both responses as the most positive thing that had happened to him since he got full custody of the girls.

That, and the kiss.

The second kiss. The one he had initiated.

The real kiss.

He wondered what Mellie thought of it. He wasn't sure he wanted to find out.

He wasn't the suave, debonair man of the fairy tales. As a young man, he had looked suave and debonair, and he had seemed mysterious because he was so shy. All he had to do was smile at a girl and people talked for weeks.

But that never taught him social skills, and he really never had to court anyone before.

Although he was hesitant about courting Mellie. He had his girls to think about. He needed to give them time to settle.

Still, he couldn't stop thinking about Mellie. Every evening, he thought about calling her, and every evening, he didn't. He didn't quite know what to say.

He would surprise her instead, and show up at the coffee shop. He had promised he would teach her how to enjoy reading. He wasn't sure how to do that.

He also wasn't sure whether or not it would make a difference once he did teach her how to read for enjoyment. Not everyone who read for enjoyment wrote good books. If that were the case, then the numbers of writers and readers would be roughly equivalent.

As a bookstore owner, he could attest that was not true.

He found some books that had appealed to him, and guessed as to whether or not they'd appeal to Mellie. He packed them into his briefcase.

Then he drove his daughters to school, looked at some properties for his bookstore, and finally, finally drove back to the coffee shop to see Mellie.

He didn't call ahead.

He didn't want to scare her off.

—∿∿—

So far, Mellie had had three lunches, one dinner, and more coffee than she wanted to contemplate with Dave. He was a nice man, although not all that physically attractive. Still, he had a sense of humor, and he was smart.

More importantly, he was a writer. A real writer. He was a script writer for a television show she had never heard of—one that involved terrorists, violence, and one heroic man who could save the world. She didn't entirely understand. It sounded like pure fantasy to her—particularly when Dave told her what this man went through.

Apparently, all the writers worked in the same room. They came up with the plots together, and then they assigned who would write what. He came to the coffee shop to do his writing because otherwise, he said, people would look over his shoulder and make him nervous.

She didn't make him nervous—or so he said. But he did get serious about his work. Toward the end of the afternoon, he pounded out the pages rather than converse with her.

She didn't mind. She was surreptitiously observing his method, trying to copy it. He wouldn't let her see what he was writing, day in and day out, because he couldn't, he said. His work was embargoed, whatever that meant.

But he was sharing other screenplays with her, the ones he wrote "on spec" which he explained, over their only dinner, meant "on speculation" which meant that he was writing for free, hoping that someone would buy the screenplay.

Rather like she was trying to do with the novel.

She thought about telling him her idea, and then having him write her a screenplay "on spec." Or maybe she could get him to outline a novel for her, so that all she had to do was fill in the rants.

But she hadn't asked yet.

She read Dave's spec screenplays and they made her nervous.

They were filled with nuclear bombs going off in cities, mass murder, the rise of dictators, and one man (always one *man*, never one *woman*) who was the only person who could hold back the threat.

There was no romance. There was no magic.

And mostly, there were no women.

She disliked that the most.

The one thing she knew about her book—if she ever got a chance to write it (or got someone to write it)—was that it had to be woman-friendly. Women would understand all the pressures stepmothers went through. Women knew how hard mothering was. Women knew what it was like to feel less and less attractive as they aged.

Women were her target audience.

And the more she talked to Dave, the more she realized he was not her target writer.

He hadn't arrived yet this morning at the coffee shop. He had warned her he would be late. There was some kind of writer's strategy meeting at his television show, and he didn't dare miss it.

In fact, he had warned her it might take all day.

She understood.

What surprised her, as the morning wore on, was that she didn't miss him. In fact, she was a bit relieved he hadn't shown up.

Which meant she probably couldn't keep coming to this coffee shop. He was making her uncomfortable, and she would have to break that to him gently. She liked him. He was nice enough. But he wasn't that interesting as he talked about this show she never watched, and then talking about his two ex-wives.

She never talked about her husbands. She did say she'd been widowed twice, and he had raised an eyebrow and said jokingly, "Black widow, huh?"

She had looked up the term later and even though he had been joking, it really, really bothered her.

Her husbands had died of natural causes. What was it about this world and the Kingdoms that kept wanting to cast her as a murderer?

So she sat in the coffee shop and goofed around with the screenplay she had started before she met Dave Bourke. His screenplays flowed, and they had a lot of speakers per page. It looked like:

STAR: *speaking, speaking, speaking*
MINION: *answering, answering, answering*
STAR: *speaking some more*
MINION: *answering some more*

Hers looked very different. It looked like:

EVIL STEPMOTHER: *rant, rant, rant, ranting, ranting, ranting, even more ranting, and more ranting than that, ranting, ranting, ranting, making cogent points, but still on a soapbox, telling the world exactly what she thought all the time without taking a breath without even thinking ofbreathingsometimeswithoutanyspacesbetweenwords at all as if she didn't have spaces between thoughts like Selda once said it was as if she breathed out and breathed in while talking just to make her point before anyone else could get a word in edgewise now that was a magical*

*talent albeit one most people did not have and
the people who did have it were people you didn't
want to have it which was why Mellie knew her
screenplay wasn't working.*

But it wasn't just the dialogue in the screenplay that
didn't work. It was also the lack of story. She found that
very, very, very frustrating. Because she liked movies,
and she understood storytelling. Or at least, she understood the necessity for it. And if what Charming had
said was true—that someone had to enjoy something to
write about it, then she had the prerequisites to write
screenplays. Because she did enjoy movies.

She had just never thought about what made them
work before.

And she was having trouble thinking about it now.

Someone set a briefcase on her table. She looked up,
startled. She hadn't heard anyone come in. She'd been
so engrossed in her screenplay thoughts that she had lost
track of the time.

The briefcase looked new. It was wide and trimmed
in gold. She had to move slightly so that she could see
past her laptop and the briefcase.

There, standing at the other end of her table, was
Charming.

"You want some more coffee?" he asked. "And a cinnamon roll? I could do with a cinnamon roll."

And before she could answer, he walked over to the
barista. Mellie watched him go. He sounded nervous. He
didn't look nervous (did Charmings ever look nervous?)
but he sounded very nervous, speaking five times faster
than he had before. As he walked to the counter to order,

he wiped his hands on his beautifully tailored slacks, as if his palms were moist.

Mellie didn't like the way her heart rate increased when she realized he was back. She didn't want to be thrilled (but she was). She wanted to be calm and collected and completely uninterested.

She could pretend she was all of those things, but she wasn't. She couldn't stop herself from watching him as he ordered, gesturing with his right hand, and then smiling at the barista.

The barista, who wore black, and was tattooed and pierced everywhere, and had to be all of twenty-five, watched him as if she were entranced.

He even moved elegantly, as if he had been a dancer in a previous life. Maybe he had been. After all, dance was required of royalty in all of the Kingdoms. Just like fencing and jousting and horseback riding. He moved like an athlete because he was an athlete.

He just wasn't the kind of athlete she had become accustomed to in the Greater World, the skinny, entitled guys who filled the evening news or the famous, puffy guys bulked up on steroids or the average, everyday guys who were so full of themselves because they started their day by running five miles.

Charming made it all look easy—of course he did. That was part of being charming, making everything look easy.

The way he bought cinnamon rolls (she had yet to see him finish one), he should have weighed an extra hundred pounds or so. But he didn't. He looked perfect, the way that men looked in advertising—with that triangular shape—the broad shoulders tapering to narrow hips and a really, really, really nice butt.

He started to turn and she made herself look away before he finished the movement. She didn't want him to see her. She really didn't want him to know what she was thinking. The very idea made her blush.

She braced her cheek on one fist. How much had she blushed since she met this man? Nearly every day (except in the last week, when she hadn't seen him at all). Sometimes more than once per day. She was blushing like a new bride.

A new bride whom no one had told the facts of life.

A new bride who had no inkling that there even were facts of life.

"I'm sorry," he said and she jumped again. He took the briefcase off the table. "I forgot to set that on the floor."

"It's okay." She smiled at him, hoping the color in her cheeks had receded somewhat.

He set both cinnamon rolls down, just like he had a week ago. Only this time, he remembered the butter, the napkins and the silverware—including the knives.

Then the barista said, "Dave!" and Mellie started for a third time, glancing at the door. But there was no Dave. It took her a half second to remember that the Dave she knew as Dave and the Dave the barista had just called were different people.

Of course, Charming couldn't go around telling people his name was Charming. That would get more of a reaction than telling people his daughter was named Imperia.

He went back to get the coffees. Mellie slid her cinnamon roll closer. She wasn't going to pretend she lacked an appetite. She was going to need all the sugar and fat she could get to make it through this conversation without making a fool of herself.

In fact, she wasn't even going to start the discussion, because she was too afraid she would demand to know where he had been.

He came back, sat down (slowly and elegantly, without spilling anything on those perfectly creased pants), and said, "I owe you."

She set her fork down. She hadn't expected him to say that. She had expected something witty or just a little bewildered, like *I wasn't sure you'd still be here*.

In fact, if he had come a day or two later, she wouldn't have been here at all.

"You owe me?" Mellie couldn't for the life of her imagine why.

"My daughters love school," he said as he stirred sugar into his coffee. "They love it."

Mellie frowned ever so slightly. Did he think she'd magicked them somehow? Because she certainly hadn't done that, nor had she done anything else.

"That's good, isn't it?" she asked, trying not to sound as confused as she felt. "That they love school. It's good, right?"

"It's better than I ever could have expected," he said. "I think we'll make it here now. I was afraid we'd have to go back to the Kingdoms."

He sounded relieved and happy. She'd never really heard him sound happy before—except when he was showing her the books at the book fair.

"I'm glad it went well," she said politely, still not sure what it had to do with her.

"You did it," he said. "You made all the difference."

She took a sip of her coffee, even though it was still a bit too hot to drink comfortably.

"I didn't do anything." How could she have done anything? She hadn't even met his daughters.

"But you did," he said. "You figured out why the kids in that school were picking on my Grace. You solved the whole problem."

"So they were going after Imperia?" Mellie still didn't like that name.

He nodded. "And I gave Imp permission to defend her sister."

"I'm so glad it worked out," Mellie said.

"It wouldn't have without you," Charming said and grinned. "I'm in your debt."

"No." She shook her head. In the Kingdoms, being in someone's debt was a great responsibility. She didn't want that obligation from him. She wanted him near her because he wanted to be near her, not because he was obliged to.

"I brought books," he said, pulling his briefcase on top of his thighs. He clicked it open and pulled out book after book after book, most of them paperbacks, most of them with attractive, shiny covers.

"Charming, I—"

"These aren't vampire romances," he said. "Or vampire YA novels. Or vampire urban fantasies. They're books I think you might like from all different time periods. There are a few vampire books, but nothing like you've read before—"

"Charming," she said. "Really, it's not necessary."

He was stacking the books on the table. "But I think it is. I promised I'd teach you to enjoy reading, and I think something in this mess might just do it. I've included a lot of women's fiction. I think you'll like some of these books. They're—"

"You read women's fiction?" The voice beside Mellie was dry.

She looked up. Dave stood beside her, arms crossed, with a supercilious expression on his face. He seemed possessive and contemptuous at the same time. He was glaring at Charming.

Mellie felt her heart sink. This was not going to go well. This was not going to go well at all.

Chapter 20

"I READ EVERYTHING," CHARMING SAID, WITHOUT LOOKING up. He was still grabbing books from the briefcase. "Books are books are books, as far as I'm concerned."

Then he realized he wasn't answering a question from Mellie. He was answering a question posed in a contemptuous male voice.

He raised his head.

The doughy guy who had been eavesdropping on their conversations the week before stood next to Mellie as if he owned her.

Charming pulled the last of the books from his briefcase and closed it. Then, very slowly, he set it on the floor.

"Don't you read women's fiction?" Charming asked the doughy guy.

"Why would I?" the doughy guy said. "It's for *women*."

Mellie's mouth opened slightly. The color in her cheeks rose again.

"Well, that's where you're wrong," Charming said. "Women's fiction is just a marketing category, designed to appeal more to women than to men. But there are stories in that category that any human being would like."

"I'll take your word for it," the doughy guy said. He hadn't moved. If anything, he looked even more planted against Mellie's side.

She wasn't asking him to move.

Had Charming missed something here?

"Now that you've given Mel your little presents, why don't you just run away, like you did last week," the doughy guy said.

Charming frowned. The doughy guy thought Charming had run away? Well, maybe he had, but not because he was scared. Or rather, scared too badly. He had to deal with his girls. And in no way was he going to tell this doughy guy that. He wasn't going to tell the doughy guy anything.

What Charming wanted to do was wipe that supercilious smile off the doughy guy's face. And it wouldn't be hard. He obviously never got out much, and he certainly didn't get much exercise. Charming could flatten him with a single blow.

But Mellie had become a modern woman, a woman of the Greater World. A punch to the doughy guy's face probably wouldn't impress her.

She hadn't said anything. She was watching Charming. Charming's heart started to pound. Were they a couple now?

"That's right," the doughy guy said. "You can skedaddle now. Mellie and I have a lunch date."

Mellie shook her head slightly. Her gaze met Charming's.

"Actually, Dave," she said, and Charming heard apology in her tone. She was going to tell him to leave. Using the name he used in the Greater World because calling him Charming would sound stupid. "We don't have a lunch date."

Charming knew that. What was she playing at?

"I know," he said, standing slowly.

"We do too," the doughy guy said. "I told you I'd be back this afternoon."

Charming blinked. He wasn't quite sure what was going on. Neither was the doughy guy. He frowned at Mellie.

"That doesn't mean we have a date," Mellie said to the doughy guy.

She stood as well, moving slightly away from the doughy guy.

"Dave Encanto," she said to Charming, "meet Dave Bourke."

Charming felt his mouth drop open. It took him half a second to recover, and when he did, he realized he had three options. He could bluster his way out of here, he could challenge the other Dave, or he could charm the man.

It didn't take much thought to realize which option was best.

Charming leaned forward—he was taller than Dave Bourke—and extended his hand. "It's a pleasure to meet you."

Bourke didn't move. His arms remained crossed. "You're the doofus who named your daughter Imperia. Imperia Encanto. That's a really stupid name."

The comment was designed to make him angry. Charming knew that. But it didn't make any difference. He *was* angry.

Once again, someone was attacking one of his daughters.

Only this time, that someone didn't even know his daughters.

"Perhaps you would like to reconsider your attack on my child?" Charming asked quietly.

"I wasn't attacking your poor kid," Bourke said. "I was going after you for saddling her with such a wretched name."

"Dave," Mellie said with a warning in her voice. But Charming couldn't tell if the warning was for him or for Bourke.

And honestly, Charming didn't care.

"Really?" Charming said. "Because I would think that someone named Bourke has no grounds to stand on."

"Dave," Mellie said, only this time she was looking at him.

"Bourke isn't such a bad name," Bourke said. "And it's certainly better than Imperia."

"Dave!" Mellie turned toward Bourke. "Stop. Now. Both of you."

"My daughter has no place in this discussion," Charming said, taking a step forward. He had wanted to hurt this guy from the man's first interruption a week ago. Now he had an excuse. He would pick up the doughy son of a bitch and slam him against the ceiling, and see how he liked that. Charming could do it. He'd done it before — in tournaments, to be sure, but those men, at least, were in fighting shape. This man hadn't been in a physical altercation in decades, if at all.

"As I said," Bourke said, "I really can't go after you. You have the perfectly pleasant name, Dave. Even though you're not one of the most pleasant men I've ever met."

"I'm *charming*," Charming said, although he wasn't sure if he was objecting to the insult or if he was introducing himself. He took another step forward.

Then Mellie barged between them. She put a hand on

each of their chests like the referee in a wrestling match. She had to use force to keep them apart too. Charming could see her arms straining with the effort.

"Enough," she said again. "You will both listen to me now."

"You get 'em, lady," someone yelled from another table, and laughter sounded all around.

Charming finally noticed everyone else. The usual group of regulars sat in their chairs. The barista clutched a cell phone, but didn't hold it to her ear. One man near the back stood as if he had been about to get involved.

"First you, Dave," she said looking at Charming. "I thought you were supposed to be charming. Charming people do not menace other people. Didn't you learn that in Charm school?"

He bristled. "They didn't have charm—"

"And you," she said turning toward Bourke. "I spent some time with you this week, and put up with your occasional insensitive comments. I realize you don't even understand that you're making them half the time. But for your information, if you want a woman to date you, you don't call her a black widow."

"Unless you got money," that same voice yelled.

Mellie looked over Bourke's shoulder at the source of the yelling. So did Charming. He saw a young, laptop-toting guy who wore a ball cap with the name of a popular sitcom blazed across the front.

"And you," she said to the yeller before Charming could say anything. "Butt out."

The yeller leaned against the wall, but kept a small smile on his face.

"When I called you a black widow, it was a joke," Bourke said.

"Some joke," she said. "It was offensive."

"You should've said something," Bourke said.

The color in Mellie's cheeks had moved down her neck. She looked like she was going to explode. Charming wanted to step in, but Mellie kept her hand on his chest. He couldn't move forward without using force.

"I've been meaning to tell you," she was saying to Bourke, "that we're really not suited. But I was going to do it in private. However, since you've decided to make a scene—"

"I didn't decide to make a scene," Bourke said. "It's your charming friend here who started it."

"I didn't malign a good book," Charming said.

Mellie glared at him. "You can shut up too. You stop being charming when someone attacks your choice of reading material. And that's just strange."

Charming frowned. That wasn't true. It wasn't strange at all. Books were personal, and attacking someone's choice of reading material was like attacking someone's clothing or his looks.

He started to say that, then realized that Mellie had turned back to Bourke.

"Anyway," she said, "you're a nice man, but you're not right for me."

"Ah, c'mon, Mellie," Bourke said. "So I can be rude sometimes. I'm a successful writer. I make a load of dough, and we've had fun times."

Charming straightened his shoulders. She *dated* this man? She *slept* with this man?

"We have a lot in common," Bourke was saying.

"We're both adults, we're interested in writing, we both work in Hollywood—"

"We have nothing in common," Mellie said. "You don't even know what an adult is. I'm interested in writing only because Charming here—"

And she took a breath, clearly catching herself.

"I mean, Dave here," she said.

Bourke laughed. "Charming," he said over Mellie. "That suits you, doofus."

"Better me than you," Charming said stiffly.

"Dave here," Mellie said louder, "is the one who said I should put my experiences into a novel. He has a point. You see, Dave—"

And this time, she made it clear she was speaking to Bourke.

"—I want to write women's fiction about step-mothers. *Evil* stepmothers, and how they're really not evil at all. Just like the way a woman who is unfortunate enough to be twice-widowed is not a black widow."

Bourke's pasty skin got even paler. He finally understood that things weren't going well for him.

"Mellie," he said. "I can teach you how to write. This guy can't. He's just a reader. He's not a real writer. He doesn't know anything—"

"He knows more about women's fiction than you do," Mellie said. "He at least appreciates women. And he's never said anything bad about me, although I've given him cause to."

Charming suppressed a smile. He leaned into her hand just a little, liking the pressure against his chest.

He wondered if she could feel his heart beat.

"So, Dave," Mellie said, without looking at Charming, "why don't you go back to your explosions and your manly men and the famous people you write for and leave me alone?"

"You don't mean that, Mellie," Bourke said.

"Oh, for…" She let her arm drop away from Charming's chest. He nearly fell forward due to the lack of pressure.

"I *hate* it when men tell me I don't mean something," she said. "I *hate* it when someone dismisses me, like you have over and over and over. I *hate* it when—"

"I think he gets the point, Mellie," Charming said, putting his arm around her. Unlike his family, Mellie had once had magic. But there was nothing like anger to revive dormant magic. And when someone used magic in anger, there was no telling what would happen.

"You have no place in this discussion," she snapped at Charming.

"Actually, I do," he said to her. "Technically, *you* don't have any place in this fight."

She made a face, one his girls made when they were very small. It was a cross between a grimace and a pout.

"I do too," she said.

"No, you don't," Bourke said, sounding relieved. "Your 'charming' friend here and I were having a discussion about literature before you butted in."

"I butted in to tell you that I don't want to spend any more time with you," Mellie said, sounding indignant.

"Well, honestly," Bourke said, "that discussion should be held in private."

"Too late," Charming said. "She already broke up with you."

He tried not to sound cheerful about it.

"We weren't dating," Mellie said. "So I can't really break up with him."

"We were too dating." Bourke's face was getting red. "What do you call all those meals?"

"I paid for my own food," Mellie said. "And you paid for yours. So that doesn't qualify as a date."

"What is this, high school?" Bourke asked. "We're two adults. We talked about our lives, our passions, our interests—"

"The lady told you that she didn't want to spend time with you anymore." Charming used a tone he often used with his daughters. The tone hid his jubilance. Mellie hadn't slept with Bourke. She hadn't even considered the time they spent together dating. And Bourke had pissed her off. So Bourke wasn't a rival.

"You stay out of this," Bourke said to Charming.

"I thought this was our discussion," Charming said. "I thought I had just had that argument with Mellie."

"It *was* our discussion." Bourke's agreement sounded begrudging. "It was about your girly interest in reading material."

"My what?" Charming asked. He wasn't quite sure what to take offense at, although he knew he should take offense at something.

"What's wrong with girls?" Mellie asked at the same time.

"Dude," the baseball cap kibitzer said in a stage whisper to Bourke, "you're not going to get anywhere insulting the woman."

"Shut up!" Charming, Mellie, and Bourke said to the kibitzer in unison.

The kibitzer raised his eyebrows, grinned, and glanced at everyone around, as if he were proud of getting that reaction.

"You insulted my daughter," Charming said to Bourke.

"I insulted *you*," Bourke said. "*You* gave your daughter a stupid name."

Mellie put her hand on Charming's chest again. He hadn't even realized he moved forward menacingly until she had made that move.

"I think you should stop talking now," Mellie said to Bourke.

Charming recognized that tone. It was a warning tone, one that the magical used in the Kingdoms as fair notice that magic was about to occur.

"Don't, Mellie," Charming said softly.

She ignored him.

"You think I should stop talking, do you, your highness?" Bourke asked.

Charming started. He wasn't used to hearing anyone called "your highness" except members of his family. It took Charming a second to realize that Bourke was using the phrase sarcastically.

"You think you can break up with me," Bourke was saying, "because I am occasionally rude?"

"I didn't break up with you," Mellie said. "To say that we broke up would imply that we were dating, which we were not."

"Why the hell else do you think I was spending time with you, woman?" Bourke asked. "I don't have lunch with just anyone. We were dating. In fact, I was going to work on getting into your pants this weekend."

Charming put his hand over the hand Mellie had

pushed against his chest. He did that to hold her in place because her eyes had just flared dark green.

"You were going to get into my what?" she asked.

Charming shook his head. Sometimes she seemed very naïve about the Greater World. "Don't go there, Mellie."

"He wanted to get into my pants," Mellie said.

"He's male," the kibitzer yelled.

This time half the coffee shop shouted, "Shut up!"

They didn't see the problem. Mellie was getting very mad.

"Look, Bourke," Charming said, "you're not making friends here. You should probably pack up your things and go."

"I'm not the one who's leaving," Bourke said. "You're not a regular here. I come here every damn day. I spend my hard-earned money on their crap coffee because it's near the studio. I am staying. *You* are going."

"Oh, for God's sake." The barista held up the cell phone. "You're all going to leave in a minute if you don't shut up."

"What are you going to do, honey?" Bourke asked. "Goth me to death?"

She shook the phone at him. "I've got the cops on speed dial. So get out."

"All of us?" Bourke asked.

She looked at Mellie and Charming. "You two going to keep on shouting?"

Charming wanted to say *He started it* just like any ten-year-old in trouble, but he didn't. Instead he gave the barista his warmest smile.

"My friend and I have some business to discuss," he said. "We never intended this to be a shouting match.

Mr. Bourke here interrupted us, and he angered me. I'm so sorry about that. The disruption won't happen again."

The barista blinked at him. She looked a little flushed. "Okay," she said. "If you two sit down and don't bother anyone else, you can stay."

"Good," Bourke said and headed to his table.

"Not so fast, asswipe," she said to Bourke. "You're leaving."

"Hey!" he said. "You're not the boss. You don't have the right to toss me out."

She waved the phone at him again. "For a screenwriter, you're pretty dense. You know what I have here?"

"911 on speed dial," he said tiredly.

"And a camera with video capability. You want me to post this entire altercation on YouTube, with a label mentioning the TV show you write for?"

Charming suppressed a grin. He had no idea why Bourke took on the woman. Bourke was clearly outclassed.

"You wouldn't," Bourke said, sounding desperate.

"Why not?" the barista asked. "After all, *hon*, I am the maker of the crap coffee, and I really don't feel like serving you any longer. So if I put this on YouTube, my boss will see what an asswipe you are, and he'll back me up."

"Just because I'm not pretty like Encanto here," Bourke said, "you think you can push me around."

"As pretty as your friend is," the barista said, "I would throw him out too if he were as rude as you."

Charming stood very still. He could feel everyone looking at him. He'd never been described as "pretty" before. What ever happened to "the handsome prince"? It probably went the way of Prince Charming. Or of the hair at the top of his head.

"I think you should go, dude," said the kibitzer to Bourke, and this time, no one told the kibitzer to shut up.

Bourke gave him a sour look, then grabbed his laptop bag. "This isn't the end of this," he said to Charming. "You have no right to her."

"Of course I have no right to her," Charming said. "Women stopped being property a century ago."

Mellie gave him an odd look. Was that the wrong defense?

Probably.

But he felt a little outgunned here. He hadn't expected to be in a fight, even if it was a verbal one, with a real Dave.

"I don't ever want to hear from you again," Mellie said to Bourke.

"I got that, sweetheart," he said snidely. "You're no prize either. I just felt sorry for you, that's all. That's the only reason I spent time with you."

Mellie drew herself up to her full height.

"Don't," Charming said softly. "He's not worth it."

Bourke finished packing up his laptop. "I never liked this place anyway," he said as he grabbed his coat and headed out the front door. It banged closed behind him.

Only after he vanished from the windows, did Charming move. His hand was still on Mellie's shoulder.

"You okay?" he asked softly.

"I didn't date him," she said. "*I* felt sorry for *him*."

"Okay," Charming said, and then winced. He sounded like he didn't believe her—probably because he really didn't believe her.

"Seriously," she said. "I talked to him because he was explaining screenplays. I figured if I couldn't handle a book, maybe I could handle a screenplay because I like movies."

Charming smiled and eased her toward her chair. "It's okay, Mellie," he said, not certain if he was comforting her or just trying to change the subject.

"I didn't realize he was such an—what did you call him?" She looked at the barista.

"An asswipe," the barista said as she set her phone down. "He was too piddly to be an asshole."

Mellie barked out a laugh. "Piddly," she said. "That's perfect. You're good with words."

"Yeah, well, I've written a screenplay too," the barista said.

"Haven't we all?" said the kibitzer.

Charming shook his head. He pulled out Mellie's chair. She sat down. "I didn't mean for that to escalate," he said.

"That's okay," she said. "I didn't mean to get so mad."

He pushed the chair in, like a perfect gentleman. Then he went to his chair. He pushed the books aside so that he could see Mellie.

He waited until conversation started around them, and then he said, "What would have happened? You know, if you had gotten all the way mad?"

She looked at him, startled. "What do you think? Poison apples raining from the ceiling?"

He tried not to smile. He knew she was sensitive. "No. I was just wondering. The way that felt—" he lowered his voice so that he was nearly whispering. "—it seems like you have real magic."

"As opposed to what?" she asked.

"Charm," he said sheepishly.

To his surprise, she grinned.

"I used to have real magic," she said. "It's gone now."

"I thought I could feel it," he said.

"Oh, there's remnants," she said. "But it's never come back."

He studied her for a moment. She didn't seem upset about her lost magic. Which meant she sacrificed it for a good cause.

He had a hunch he knew what that cause was.

"You used up your magic saving Snow's life, didn't you?" he asked quietly.

"What?" She looked stunned.

"You're the one who prevented her from dying when she ate that poisoned apple." He knew he was right, just from her expression.

"Who told you that?" she asked.

"No one," he said. "It's just logical. She was in a stasis because you weren't anywhere near her. So you couldn't keep her alive and get the poisoned apple out of her throat at the same time."

She blinked hard and looked away. "I never told anyone that," she said.

"I know," he said softly.

"No one's ever figured it out," she said.

"No wonder you've been so upset," he said. "Everyone in the Kingdoms and in the Greater World believes the worst of you, when you actually saved her."

Mellie shrugged. "No good deed goes unpunished."

"Why didn't you just tell Snow?" he asked.

"She wouldn't have believed me." Mellie grabbed her plate and pulled it close. "Besides, she thought her charming prince saved her. I would have ruined that."

"I thought it didn't work out."

"I didn't know that then, did I?" Mellie said.

He stared at her for a moment. She had done a brave and courageous thing, had saved a life at great cost to herself, and had never taken credit for it.

For the first time, the one thing he had disliked about her—that bitterness he had seen at the book fair—finally made sense.

"You could tell her now," he said.

"No," she said. She looked at him. "It doesn't matter anymore. Besides, she would think I was lying."

Her eyes were clear now, although her nose was still a bit red from the near-tears.

"My relationship with Snow is what it is," Mellie said. "But she's alive, and she's doing well, and she has lovely children, even if I've never gotten to meet them. At least they exist."

"That doesn't break your heart?" he asked.

"No," she said. "It's a victory. I cherish my victories."

"Well, you're certainly not a damsel in distress," he said, thinking of Ella, thinking how romantic he had found that damsel, that distress.

He thought Mellie would smile, but instead she looked rueful.

"You don't want to be a damsel in distress, do you?" he asked, feeling a bit incredulous.

"Oh, heavens no," she said, but she sounded funny. Then she cut into her cinnamon roll. "We're so sensitive about the strangest things, you and I. You can't handle someone criticizing books, and I can't handle anything to do with fairy tales."

He nodded. She clearly wanted to change the subject.

He had gotten too close to something painful. He would give her a minute to catch her breath.

He followed her lead and stopped discussing Snow.

"Were you really talking to Bourke about screenplays?" Charming asked.

"Yes," she said.

"You really want to do this, right? To make a difference."

"Yes." She sounded impatient.

"You do know how many screenplays there are in this town and how few get made, right?" Charming asked.

Mellie looked at him sideways. "Noooo."

She sounded wary, as if she expected him to hurt her somehow.

"I counted at least three in this shop alone," Charming said. "Four if we count yours."

"I only have a few pages," Mellie said. "And Dave has written several."

"We're not counting his TV show," Charming said.

"That's right," Mellie said. "I'm not counting his TV show."

"And he actually knows people who might be able to get production money," Charming said. "It's easier to publish a book than it is to get a screenplay produced."

"Not if you can't write the damn book." Mellie stabbed her fork into her cinnamon roll and peeled off half of it. "I doubt reading all of these books will make me a better writer."

"I doubt it too," Charming said, and immediately wished he could take the words back. He didn't mean it the way it sounded.

The hunk of cinnamon roll hovered near her mouth. She raised her eyebrows. Fortunately, she looked amused.

"I mean," he said, "it would take a lot of practice as well—"

"That's not what you meant," she said. "I really don't care about characters and stories and made-up stuff. I was thinking of writing a blog."

He frowned. "A blog."

"About wicked stepmothers and how that's a lie," she said.

He nodded and thought about it. People got a lot of traction from blogs. But the blogs had to be consistently interesting. He wasn't sure Mellie could do that. He was already getting to the point where he wanted to interrupt her when she started into her evil stepmother rants.

And he liked her. He liked her a lot.

He decided to approach the blog suggestion cautiously. "Have you thought about how you would structure it?"

"The blog?" Mellie shook her head. "I don't even know how to design a website. And I don't know if it would be worthwhile. I mean, how many people get more than their family reading their blogs?"

"I don't know," he said.

"Of course, there's no guarantee a book would sell very well," she said more to herself than to him. "Just like there's no guarantee that a screenplay would become a film."

"If you sell your book to a major publisher," Charming said, "people will read it."

"And then what?" she asked.

"Then you write another book," he said. "Keep the idea in the public eye."

She made a snorty sound. "I can't even write one book. How could I write two?"

"The idea was to start a trend, remember?" he asked. "Follow the vampire model and remake your image."

She shook her head. "I can't do that. It's ingrained. This whole culture hates older women."

"That's not true," he said, then stopped when she glared at him. She wanted to believe it was true, so he was going to let her believe it was true.

At least for the moment.

"I can't even hire one of those ghosts you talked about," she said. "They're all part of the Greater World. No one from the Kingdoms knows how to write. Even those horrible Grimm brothers were from the Greater World."

"I know how to write," Charming said softly.

"Well, of course you do," Mellie said. "We all know how to write. Literacy became a requirement, what, two hundred years ago?"

He picked up his own fork and picked at the cinnamon roll. His heart was pounding. He wasn't quite sure why. What was he risking here?

He wasn't sure he wanted to answer that question, even to himself.

"I mean," he said softly. "I know how to write fiction."

She dropped her bit of cinnamon roll. "How come you didn't tell me this before?"

He shrugged. He was about to make a blithe comment, then he stopped himself. Honesty. He needed to be honest with this woman.

"I figured you'd want to do it," he said.

"I don't even like to read," she said. "Why would I want to write?"

Good point. He hadn't thought about that part until just now. "I just figured, it's your story."

"Like that has stopped people before," she said.

His gaze met hers. She was so beautiful. He wasn't being entirely honest. He didn't want to write her story because he didn't want to do anything that would drive her away. And writing—that really was about honesty. The good and the bad.

"I probably couldn't write this book," he said.

Her eyebrows curved into matching perfect Ns. "Why not?"

"Um, because I'm male?" he said.

"What?" she asked as if he were making a comment as offensive as Bourke's. "What does *that* mean?"

"Um," Charming said, unable to find his verbal footing. "It means that this is a woman's book, for women, about women's issues. It's not really… cool… to have a man write it… um… because the woman… can't."

He winced, and she glared at him. He'd really blown it now. He'd insulted her as badly as Bourke had.

Charming wanted to pick up his briefcase and leave. But he didn't dare. Not when she was staring at him so intently.

"I can't believe you just said that," she said.

He held his breath, bracing for the worst.

Chapter 21

CHARMING HAD A HORRIBLE LOOK ON HIS FACE, AS IF HE expected her to slap him.

What kind of person did he think she was? If she were easily offended, she'd be hiding in a room in the Kingdoms, rather than making her way through the Greater World.

"Good heavens," she said. "How ridiculous can you get?"

His beautiful blue eyes opened and he leaned away from the table, as if he expected a slap. He wasn't timid—if he were timid, he wouldn't have stood up to Bourke—but he was emotionally fragile.

Mellie didn't know if that was Ella's fault or the fault of Charming's father, and at the moment, she didn't care. She was more intrigued by Charming's reaction and his idea.

"You're being politically correct, aren't you?" Mellie asked.

"Um," he said, gulping air as he spoke.

"That's a Greater World thing, isn't it?" she said.

"Um—"

"I mean, really, what am I supposed to do if I want to change the world and I need help doing it? Enlist only women because it's a women's cause?"

"It's been done before," he said, then bit his lower lip. He looked very uncomfortable. And vulnerable.

And cute. She had never thought of him as cute before, but he was when he lost that cool façade, a façade that seemed more about hiding shyness than actually being cool.

She tried not to smile. She had riled him. She liked that. Beneath the cool exterior of this man was tamped down passion, passion he seemed afraid of.

"So who would I enlist?" Mellie asked. "Selda? She's already told me she hates writing. Lavinia? She knows nothing about the Greater World. Snow? She hates my guts. Ella? She—"

Mellie stopped herself before she said something she regretted. She always did that. She let down her guard and she said something stupid.

"It's okay," Charming said in a flat tone. "She's not much of a mother, so how would she be a stepmother?"

His tone was so sad, so wistful, that Mellie reached across the table and caught his hand. She didn't say anything. After all, he had finished the very sentence that she had been about to say. He often said what was on her mind. He had with Bourke. And even if he didn't, she liked the way that Charming thought.

She liked him. She liked him so much.

"You said you can write fiction," she said. "How do you know that?"

He shrugged one shoulder again.

"Charming," she said. "You can't make a statement like that without backing it up."

"I've… written a few things," he said. But that sounded like a lie. Only "lie" was too harsh. It sounded more like a humble misdirection.

"How few?" she asked.

That shoulder went up and down again.

"Charming…"

He sighed. "I don't know. I wrote a lot when I first came to the Greater World."

"And put it all in a drawer?" she asked.

"Noooo," he said.

"What did you do with it?" she asked.

"Sold it," he whispered.

"To…?"

"Magazines," he said. "They're called little magazines. And literary magazines. And some digests."

"Under what name?" she asked.

"Names," he whispered.

She rolled her eyes. "Is any of your writing here?" she asked, putting her hand on one of the pile of books.

"No," he said. Then he leaned forward. "I can understand why you'd want to see my writing first—"

"Hell, no," she said. "I'm just relieved you've done a lot of it. If you were to ghost my novel, how would it work?"

He looked at her as if she had grown another head. She almost touched her neck to make sure she hadn't.

"I don't know," he said. "I mean, you'd have to tell me what you want."

"You're the guy with the vision," she said.

"But it would be your book," he said.

"If I could write the damn book, I would," she said. "So how would this work?"

"We'd come up with a story together," he said, "and then I'd write it. And we'd put your name on it."

"Which name?" she asked. "The Evil Stepmother?"

"Um, no. We'd use your Greater World name."

He was being serious and she had been snide. He had caught her off guard again, and when she was off guard, she was snide. It was a defense, and not an attractive one.

She didn't know how to be attractive to this man, a man every woman watched: from the business women in the coffee shop to the Goth barista behind the counter.

Her hand still held his, and he hadn't tried to move away. But maybe that wasn't because he liked touching her. Maybe that was because he was still talking.

She had to focus on what he was saying.

"...and we should probably have another story lined up, because it might take a book or two before we get it right."

"By right, you mean without rants," she said.

"Oh, no," he said. "We'll put your rants in. If we do it right, they'll be one of the most memorable parts of the story."

Then he blinked at her, his eyes widening. She was beginning to realize that was his look of dismay.

"I mean, you know, your opinions. It's not fair to call them rants."

"It is too," she said. "I like to rant. I'm good at it."

He nodded, then winced again. Poor man. How many people had yelled at him for his opinion?

"Do I pay you?" she asked. "Is that how this works?"

He opened his mouth, then closed it. Then frowned. Then opened his mouth again and closed it again.

"I don't need money," he said after a moment.

"You told me at that book fair that ghosts got paid," she said.

"I did," he said.

"So if you do this as a favor, neither of us will be happy," she said. "We need to keep it strictly business."

He looked down. She had a sense that he was disappointed, but at what, she wasn't sure.

"Yeah, you're right," he said after a moment.

"So how do I pay you?"

"If it sells," he said, "fifty-fifty split?"

"When you're doing all the work?"

"You'll do all the publicity," he said.

She caught her breath. Then she shook her head. "No," she said. "You're the charming one."

"You're the one with opinions," he said.

"You're the one who can sway people to your point of view," she said.

"You're the person with the agenda," he said.

"I'm the person people don't like," she said.

"But you're *interesting*," he said.

"And you're not?" she asked.

"No," he said softly. "Not really."

She stared at him for a long moment, this handsome, charming man with two daughters and a long life, a man who liked to read and knew about all kinds of things, a man who cared deeply about things. This man thought himself uninteresting.

In fact, he didn't think himself uninteresting. He seemed convinced of it.

She knew from long experience that telling him he was interesting wouldn't help him. She would have to show him.

"Fifty-fifty," she said.

He nodded.

"You write, I promote," she said.

He nodded again.

"Not every book gets promoted, though," she said. "I mean I've never heard of half these books."

She waved her hands at the books on the table.

"If your book is one of those that gets no promotion," he said, "you can do it yourself. It'll be your excuse to call radio stations and do online chats."

"It didn't work for PETA," she said.

He blinked at her. Apparently he'd forgotten the acronym.

"People—"

"I know," he said, and she realized then that he wasn't blinking oddly because he had forgotten the acronym, but because he was being polite. "It's not the same."

"I can rant when I have a book, but not when I have a cause?" she asked, feeling confused.

"Do you watch television?" he asked. "Listen to talk radio?"

"Not really," she said. "I mean, I watch TV shows. With plots. But not that talky stuff. It has nothing to do with me."

He nodded. "It will now."

She picked up her fork and finally ate that bite of cinnamon roll. It tasted good. Her coffee was cold, but she didn't care. She was using the time to think as much as to refresh herself.

"You really don't mind writing this?" she asked.

"It will be fun," he said.

"But you have your daughters, your bookstore—"

"My bookstore is in the Kingdoms," he said. "I'm not going there for a while."

"You said you were going to open one here," she said.

"The last thing LA needs is another bookstore," he said.

She frowned. She wasn't sure she agreed with that.

"Besides," he said. "I can look for suitable property while I'm writing the book."

"Will you have time?" she asked.

"Writing would keep me at home with the girls," he said. "And they need me right now."

Writing would keep him home. He wouldn't have time to see Mellie. But they could stay in contact. And that would be good, right? And when the book was done, maybe he would think favorably of her. Maybe he would be comfortable enough to introduce her to his girls.

Maybe they could spend some real time together, not talking about books or fairy tales or evil stepmothers.

She took a deep breath. "What about me?" she asked. "How would I be involved?"

"After we do the planning?" he asked.

"Yes," she said.

"I'd write it, and then you'd read it."

"But the rants," she said. "Would I get to write those?"

"When we get to rant time," he said, "I'll call you and ask for one."

Not visit her, not meet her in the coffee shop. Call her. She took a deep breath. "So," she said, "a collaboration wouldn't mean working together every day?"

"No," he said.

"But Dave said that he has to write in this room with other writers—"

"That's television," Charming said. "We're doing a novel. Novels are solitary activities."

"Even with two authors?"

He looked at her. Her cheeks heated. "I mean one author and one… ranter?"

He smiled. It was a warm smile. She really liked all his smile variations. "Even with two authors," he said. "One cover name and one ghost."

She took another bite of the cinnamon roll, trying to figure out how to ask the next question. "What if I don't like what you've done?"

"Then we don't submit it to publishers," he said.

"You wouldn't mind?" she asked.

"I'd mind," he said. "Didn't you mind when I was less than enthusiastic about your pages?"

"Less than enthusiastic," she said. He *was* good with words. Because that was an understatement.

"We'll need something in writing," he said. "Some kind of agreement. Something simple. And we can meet to talk about this, and plan it, but not here."

"Why not here?" she asked.

He looked pointedly at the guy in the baseball cap who had interrupted their fight with Bourke. Then Charming looked at the barista.

"You want to talk about the Kingdoms here?" he asked softly.

"Point taken," Mellie said.

"Besides," the baseball cap guy said, "someone might steal your ideas."

"And write an unproducible screenplay," Mellie snapped.

Charming chuckled. To her surprise, so did the baseball cap guy. He got up, grabbed his laptop and his briefcase, and came over to their table.

"You two are entertaining," he said. "You finish your

little project, whatever it is, and call me. I'll help you promote it."

He dropped a business card on the table and then, without a word, left the shop. Mellie picked up the card. The man's name was emblazoned across it, with a company logo below, and the word Publicist in big letters.

She handed it to Charming. "Do you know what that is?" she asked.

"Twenty thousand dollars a month that we don't need to spend," Charming said.

She looked at the door. "He makes twenty thousand a month?"

"If he works in this town, he does," Charming said. "But he is spending his afternoons here, so he's probably just getting started."

Mellie took the card back. "So are we," she said.

"It's a deal, then?" Charming asked.

"Oh, yeah," she said. "It's a deal."

The Final Manuscript

Chapter 22

CHARMING FINISHED THE BOOK ONE SUNDAY AFTERNOON in early April. The ending surprised him—not because he wrote something he hadn't planned (hell, he hadn't planned the whole book; nothing went according to his initial vision), but because he wrote "the end" pages (no, chapters) ahead of where he thought it would actually end.

He got out of his chair, wandered around his study, and felt like he had screwed up somehow. He had no sense of whether or not the book was any good. Nor did he trust Mellie to make that judgment. She had made it clear in their many phone calls that she was slogging through his favorite books, pretending to like them, when it was clear she didn't like them at all.

He stood with his hands clasped behind his back, looking out the window at his garden. The flowers were in full bloom, something he and the girls enjoyed. In the Kingdoms, spring would have just arrived. Here, it felt like summer—without the actual killer heat of a real LA summer. Pleasant.

What he needed was a first reader, someone who could be totally honest with him about the quality of the book, someone who would understand the risk Charming was taking just in writing it. Someone who would respect the secrecy that Charming had to maintain as a ghost writer.

Charming only knew one person like that, someone whom he could trust, not just with his book, but with his writerly ego: Sheldon McArthur.

Sheldon (Shelly to his friends) used to own the Mystery Bookshop in Los Angeles. In fact, Shelly started the business, selling it only when he decided to retire to a small town on the Oregon Coast. But Shelly couldn't really retire any more than Charming could stop reading. So Shelly opened another bookstore up north, called North by Northwest Books.

Charming had stayed in touch with Shelly after the move. Shelly sent books that he felt Charming should read, and Charming did the same for Shelly (not that there were many books that Shelly missed).

Charming went to his desk, and called Shelly. Shelly cheerfully told him to email the entire manuscript. Then Shelly added, "It's about time you wrote a novel."

Charming hung up, feeling relieved. The book was in the hands of someone who knew good literature, someone who would be completely honest if the book failed.

But there was one other person who had to read the book in this draft. By that agreement Charming had signed with Mellie, she had to read the book too.

On good days, he had no idea what she would think of it.

On bad days, he worried that she would hate the book.

On terrible days, he worried that she would hate him because of the book.

This was a terrible day. But he screwed up his courage (more than he even knew he needed), picked up the phone, and called Mellie to set up an appointment.

He was going to hand her the manuscript in hard copy, just like she had asked.

Then he was going to leave, and fret about whether she would ever talk to him again.

Chapter 23

THEY MET IN THEIR FAVORITE COFFEE SHOP. WELL, MELLIE'S favorite coffee shop. She had never asked Charming if he had liked it or not.

But he was the one to suggest it, rather than his house or her Malibu beach house.

She understood. He probably figured they needed to see each other in a public place to keep the discussion to a minimum. He had said on the phone half a dozen times that he wanted her to read it before she made any judgments about it.

She understood that too. She had felt that way when he had looked at her manuscript, all those weeks ago.

She arrived early. She ordered the cinnamon rolls and the coffees, asking the barista—the same one who had threatened Dave Bourke with a call to the police—to hold the second cinnamon roll and coffee for Charming's arrival.

Only Mellie had enough presence of mind not to call him Charming to the barista, who had smiled at her and asked how the relationship was going.

"Oh, it's not a relationship," Mellie said with airy good cheer (or so she hoped). "It's just business."

"Hmm," the barista said. "It never looked like business to me."

Mellie frowned. How could it not look like business? They had books, they had briefcases, they had laptops.

"What did it look like?" Mellie asked.

"Like a major flirtation," the barista said. Then she smiled. She looked a lot younger and more vulnerable when she smiled. "I mean, how can you not be attracted to that guy? He's so handsome. And nice."

"A regular prince charming," Mellie said dryly.

"Oh, hell, I don't think so," the barista said. "He's a bit too battered to be Prince Charming. I mean, Prince Charming has to be, like, you know, Zac Efron with shoulders or like, I don't know, George Clooney but younger. You know."

George Clooney but younger? Mellie already thought George Clooney was young enough. And handsome. Although not as handsome as Charming.

"I mean, Prince Charming," the barista was saying. "He's like twenty-five, right? Not married? Square jaw, perfect features, black hair—"

"Like the cartoon," Mellie said dryly.

"What cartoon?" the barista said.

"I don't know," Mellie said. "Take your pick. *Cinderella*? *Snow White and the Seven Dwarfs*?"

"Maybe *Cinderella*," the barista said. "There's something off about that prince in *Snow White*. I mean, what guy wants to kiss a woman in a coffin?"

In spite of herself, Mellie grinned. "I've often wondered the same thing."

She took her coffee and her cinnamon roll to her regular table. The coffee shop looked no different, except that Dave Bourke didn't sit at the next table. The kibitzer guy sat in the corner, engrossed in his computer, his baseball cap on backwards. He didn't even see her.

All the other regulars were there too—a couple of men with laptops sitting at one of the bigger tables, chugging their way through half a dozen lattes in the space of a morning; a woman with a pen in her hair, writing on something that looked like a cross between a laptop and a smart phone; and five other people reading, although only three were reading physical books. The other two had some kind of e-reader, something Mellie wouldn't have even known about if it weren't for Charming, and his various reading assignments.

And her afternoon in that book fair.

If she was honest, she had to admit that day changed her. She was reading more, although she wasn't really reading fiction per se. Nonfiction and how-to books, mostly. But still, that counted. Or so she hoped.

She'd brought back six of Charming's books—nowhere near all the ones he had given her, but still a lot, for her anyway.

He entered the coffee shop exactly on time. So on time, in fact, that she actually wondered if he had been sitting outside in his car, waiting for the clock to inch up to the appointed hour. Then she reminded herself that that was something she would do. It didn't mean it was something someone else would do.

He looked fantastic. He was wearing perfectly creased pants and a white shirt that set off his skin and dark hair. That barista was wrong; he didn't look battered. And he looked *better* than Clooney.

Before she'd gone to the book fair, Mellie wouldn't even have thought that possible.

Charming came over, set his briefcase down like he had the last time, smiled at her (what a great smile. What a delicious smile. Oh, how she had missed that smile), and headed to the counter.

The barista was the one who told him that Mellie had already ordered his food. Then the barista handed him a tray with the warmed up cinnamon roll and freshly poured coffee.

Mellie smiled, happy that it had worked out as planned.

She closed her laptop, set it on the chair next to her, and waited for him to return to the table.

——⁓——

She looked good.

No, she looked better than good. Her features seemed softer, and her eyes sparkled.

Or maybe she had always looked like that and he had just forgotten. Although he didn't know how he could forget anything about her.

Especially considering he spent each and every day since he took on this project thinking about her.

He took the tray back to the table, saw that she had already nibbled on her cinnamon roll, and almost offered to get her another.

But, he realized, he was stalling. He resisted the urge to kiss her hello. He didn't want to startle her.

He didn't want to startle himself.

"Hey," he said as he sat down.

"Hey yourself," she said.

He was shaking. He had never shown his work to anyone in person. He'd always mailed it out, and if someone didn't like it, they just had to slap a form on it and send it back. No in-person critiques, no need to look someone in the eye.

It was what made writing different from the performing arts, something he had always appreciated. He had no idea how those people on *American Idol* (which his girls had discovered and adored) withstood the judges' comments at all, let along getting them in front of a national audience.

He would have withered and died of embarrassment.

Right there, in front of the studio audience, and all of those cameras, beaming everything to television screens all over the nation.

He was so happy the Kingdoms didn't allow television. He had no idea how it would have gone if his meeting with Ella—his dance with her on that one truly magical night of his life (a magical night that had led to years of misery [and two marvelous daughters])—had been filmed for the enjoyment of all the Kingdom's subjects.

He would have hated it.

His father would have hated it.

Although Ella would have loved it. She liked being famous, something Charming abhorred.

Good thing Mellie was the one who was supposed to do the promotion of their novel.

If, of course, she liked it.

"You seem nervous," she said. She sounded surprised.

He was surprised. He hadn't expected to be read as easily. He made himself smile. The smile even felt nervous.

"I'm not used to showing people my work," he said. "It's not—"

He stopped himself before he could continue. He wasn't going to apologize for the book. He wasn't going to say anything that prejudiced her against it.

"Well," he said, "you'll see."

Without looking at her face, he opened the briefcase

and removed the manuscript. He had put it in a box and then put rubber bands around the box. It felt weighty, and important.

A tome.

It hadn't felt that weighty and important when he emailed it to Shelly.

"It didn't take you very long," Mellie said.

Charming flushed. She clearly thought he had written the book too fast. Maybe he had. He wanted to finish it. He wanted to see her again. He wanted...

Well, what he wanted really didn't matter now, did it?

"I mean," she said. "I was surprised when you called and said it was done."

"It surprised me when I finished," he said. "The book really didn't turn out—"

He stopped himself again.

"I mean," he said, sounding like her, parroting her, "writing a book is different than talking about it."

"Don't I know that," she said, sounding wistful.

He made himself look at her. He had forgotten how green her eyes were, how the fringe of lashes around them made them stand out. A man could get lost in those eyes, forget that he ever worried about anything. A man could fall in love with those eyes...

He closed his own. He didn't want to fall for her. He didn't want to fall for anyone. It hadn't worked the first time.

It wasn't going to work this time either.

He opened his eyes. Mellie was watching him. He couldn't read her expression.

"Sorry," he said. "I'm just, you know—"

"Nervous," she said.

He nodded.

She took the box, and removed all the rubber bands, wrapping them around her wrist. Then she opened the lid and stared at the cover page.

"That's my name," she said.

"Yes, of course," he said, frowning. Had she forgotten that part?

"Where's yours?" She asked, looking up.

"We said it would be your book," he said. "I'm a ghost. I was just writing it."

"Don't you get credit for that?"

"No," he said. "I get money for that, not credit. It's your story. Your book. A lot of your words are in it, from those phone calls—"

"Is that why you called it *Evil*?"

His breath caught. He had known the title would be a problem. But he couldn't come up with anything else.

"No, no, it's not that I think you're evil," he said.

Her face was blank, as if she had wiped all emotion off of it. He had seen that expression only a few times before, and it worried him.

He had planned to explain the title before she saw it, but in his nervousness, he had forgotten.

"It's that, oh, crap." He ran a hand through his thinning hair. He was making a mess of this, right from the first word. "It's a take-off of *Wicked*. You know, that book was about the Wicked Witch of the West. At least that was what everyone called her, even though her name was Elphaba. And everyone calls you—well, not you, but the character, you know—the Evil Stepmother."

"Or the Wicked Stepmother," she said, with a bite to her voice.

"Or that," he said, "but I couldn't use *Wicked*, it had already been taken."

"So you opted for *Evil*," she said.

"It's not a good title. I was hoping we could come up with something better. It's a first draft, Mellie." God, he was begging. He heard that sound in his own voice. Begging.

He hadn't ever begged before.

He blurted, "Just read it before you make up your mind. We don't have to do anything with it, you know."

There, he had said it. The words that completely negated all of his work from the past few months.

"I know," Mellie said, looking down at the manuscript, at that horrible word. What had he been thinking? *Evil*. Evil indeed. Jeez. "We had talked about that when we finalized the agreement."

"Yes, we did. Right," he said.

She took the lid and put it over the box, hiding the manuscript. "I don't like seeing my name under the word *Evil*," she said.

"I know, I'm sorry," he said.

She studied him. His heart was pounding. Why was he so nervous? How did he get so nervous? He had no idea he had had so much at stake in this manuscript.

In this project.

With this woman.

And now she was angry at him. He could feel it. He had ruined everything.

"I'll read it," she said.

"If you don't like it," he said, almost before she finished talking, "you can just chuck it. We don't have to do anything with it."

"I know," she said. "You just said that."

Had he? He didn't remember. He was a complete and utter mess. He hated the feeling.

He hated the whole idea.

What had he been thinking when he offered to ghost this book?

Obviously, he hadn't been thinking.

"You know," he said, reaching for the box, "this was probably a bad idea. I'll just take it back. We can forget the whole thing."

"No," she said, putting her hand over the box. "I want to read it."

"I'll make it better," he said. "I'll change the title."

"Charming," she said, "let me at least look at it before you offer to change anything."

He made himself take a deep breath. Then another. And another.

"Okay," he said. "But if you don't like it—"

"We don't have to do anything with it," she said. "I know."

"I know you know," he said, "but that isn't what I was going to say."

She looked at him. "What were you going to say?"

"Just that you don't have to tell me," he said.

"I don't have to tell you what?"

"That you don't like it," he said.

"How is that practical?" she asked.

"What do you mean?" he asked.

"Well, if I like it, I tell you and if I say nothing, you'll know I don't like it," she said. "So you'll know no matter what."

"Oh," he said. He hadn't thought that through. "You're right. Never mind."

WICKEDLY CHARMING 229

"I'll like it, Charming," she said and smiled. But her smile was wobbly and she didn't sound convincing. Or convinced. "Really, I will."

He smiled back, then closed his briefcase. "Good," he said, feeling a little light-headed and a lotta stupid. "I'll just be going then."

"There's no need," she said. "I thought maybe we could talk."

She moved her hand over some books.

"No time," he lied. "I have to meet the girls."

He was halfway out the door when he remembered it was a school day and it wasn't even lunchtime yet.

Mellie would know that he lied. But he couldn't change that now.

He had to leave.

He was too nervous to stay.

And they both knew it.

Chapter 24

MELLIE HAD NEVER SEEN CHARMING SO FLUSTERED. SHE HAD thought of him as unflappable. A man who got angry, yes, but a man who could remain in control of that anger.

But he had been nervous with her. Nervous and worried and uncharacteristically insecure. No wonder he wanted her to do the publicity on the novel: If anyone criticized his writing in public, he would probably faint dead away. And she thought he got too upset when someone criticized the books he *read*. How would he be on the books he'd written?

She already knew the answer to that. He would be a disaster.

She took the manuscript back to the Malibu beach house, made herself some iced tea, and went onto the balcony overlooking the ocean. The day was warm, the breeze light, the sun sparkling on the water. The beach was empty. Since it was the middle of the week, most people were either working or hadn't come to their vacation homes. Kids were in school.

She felt like she had the beach to herself.

She needed the privacy because, if she was honest, this novel scared her.

She was glad Charming had given her an out. Now that she held the manuscript in her hand, she no longer wanted to do this project. She didn't even want to look at it.

Evil, indeed.

Just like *Wicked*, which had been a novel she hadn't even enjoyed. (Although she did like the music from the Broadway show. In fact, the Broadway show made her cry.)

But a Broadway show, a movie, a series of books like Gregory Maguire had done with *Wicked*, that would change her image. That would change the image of step-mothers forever.

She spread out on a lounge chair, put on sunglasses, and opened the box, picking up the offending cover page and turning it quickly so that she wouldn't see her name with that offending word.

From the beginning of the book, she felt discombobu-lated. She and Charming had plotted a basic romance. In fact, they had stolen the plot from some successful novel—something she hadn't read and could now no longer remember.

But she remembered the plot: a beautiful but misun-derstood woman marries a man whom she thinks loves her, raises his children, and gets accused of magically hurting them. She hasn't, of course, and must defend her misunderstood self. He leaves her (or dies—she couldn't remember that part either) and she falls in love with the perfect man who helps her and the children and the world understand what a wonderful and misunderstood person she really is.

But this book didn't go that way at all. It actually started in the Kingdoms, told by another stepmother—Lavinia, with a made-up name (Laverne, of all things. Who did he think he was fooling?)—who talks about what fairy tales really are: Tales of Misunderstood (or Twisted) Love.

That very idea caught Mellie's attention. The Laverne

character explained it—everyone in fairy tales is searching for something spectacular, something important,
often finding love and forsaking it.

*But no one notes the love of a mother for her chil-
dren*, says Laverne. That's missing in the fairy tale.

And the love of a stepmother for her children is, of
course, never mentioned at all.

As Mellie read, she felt more and more uneasy.
Charming was writing her story. Her life story, narrated
by Laverne, the surviving member of the friendship.

And the novel wasn't a romance at all. There wasn't
even a sympathetic male character until her first husband appeared a third of the way into the novel. Her
father was horrible (and he was; she made no bones
about that), and her brothers disowned her, forcing her
into her first marriage.

Charming got all of that right. He got her emotions
right too. It was as if he had crawled inside her mind
and plucked out her memories, writing them onto the
page—more beautifully than she ever could, of course.

Because that was the other thing: The language here
was utterly lovely. Rich and full, the descriptive pas-
sages so vivid that she could smell the flowers and see
the cracks in the palace walls.

She almost stopped after the first section to call
Charming and find out if he really and truly could read
minds.

But then he would know how uncomfortable he made
her, and they would have another of those awkward
conversations.

Instead, she kept reading, engrossed in her own life as
told by a man she had met just a year before.

He caught it: the sense of loss when her first husband died, the need for security, the way that she couldn't rely on her now-grown children (because that wasn't fair to them or to her). He showed how her second marriage had been a partnership—she was in charge of the children, he in charge of their well-being, something he had provided for, even after his death.

And Charming showed spectacularly the prejudice against second wives, against women in general in the Kingdom, how they were mocked and hated and considered inferior.

She wondered if some of this hadn't come from his sympathy for Ella—after all, she had been mocked and hated and considered inferior—but that didn't explain all of it.

Ella, after all, angered him, and bewildered him.

And there was none of that in this novel. No bewilderment at a woman's behavior, and no anger at her behavior either.

Although there was anger—a lot of it.

Many of Mellie's rants made it to the page, word for word.

And they fit.

They actually fit.

The attempted murder of Snow, the false accusation, the defense that Mellie had gotten from her own children and her stepson Raymond, all made it into the book.

And so was Mellie's rescue of Snow. Hidden, difficult, the way she had to use her magic for weeks, just to keep Snow alive. And how it felt to have that magic slowly burn out, to have it fade, and the fear she felt that she might not be able to keep Snow alive after all.

The relief when Snow's handsome prince showed up, and then the worry when Mellie realized what kind of man he really was.

Charming managed to follow Mellie's life *and* the fairy tale, forcing the stepmother to leave when Snow's Prince Charming took over the castle and became King. Snow's Prince Charming, who didn't play real well in this book— a dark, evil, necrophiliac buffoon, whom the "evil" stepmother (whose name was Malinda—*that* wouldn't fool anyone) had repeatedly warned Snow about, only to get told by her rather naïve, pigheaded stepdaughter that she didn't know anything about men and she was just jealous.

Anyone reading the novel knew that Snow was heading for disaster with that man, and knew that the stepmother was right trying to stop it.

At the end, the stepmother gets banished from the Kingdoms, and leaves, misunderstood, saddened, unhappy, a symbol of all that has gone wrong in a world once lovely and magical.

The novel made Mellie cry.

She wasn't sure if it made her cry because it was about her life, because it was somewhat accurate, or if it actually had power all its own.

One thing she did know: No one would want to read the damn thing. No one would want to cry at the end of a novel.

It was a beautifully written embarrassment, one she certainly couldn't have out there under her own name. What would people think of her? They would know everything about her, from her young and somewhat unrequited love for her first husband to her businesslike relationship with her second.

They would also know how much she loved Snow and Raymond, and how sad she became when the relationship with Snow fell apart.

The accusations, the lies—all of it on the page, for everyone to see.

It didn't matter that the stepmother character in the book was, as Laverne said, the only one whose love was truly pure. No one would see that.

They would see what an idiot she was, how dumb she had been, how much she had believed in the true fairy tale—that love could conquer all.

It was dark when Mellie finally put the lid back on the box. Lights from the houses nearby fell on the beach. The ocean shushed beneath her, a soothing sound.

But it didn't really soothe her. It just made her uncomfortable.

Charming made her uncomfortable.

He had seen all of that, everything about her, all of her secrets, her deepest fears, and her greatest needs.

Then he had titled the book *Evil*.

He had defeated her, just like Prince Charmings always did to evil stepmothers, in a way that she couldn't really admit to him, in a way that she had never once thought possible.

He had completely and utterly, absolutely and thoroughly, broken what some had called her nonexistent heart.

Chapter 25

WHEN CHARMING GOT HOME FROM THE COFFEE SHOP, HE found an email from Sheldon McArthur—lower case, in a hurry, cryptic: *you might need an agent*.

Charming sat in the sunlight pouring in from the windows in his lovely home office and stared at the computer screen. No matter how hard he studied the email, it did not change.

It said that he might need an agent, and that was all, except for Shelly's virtual signature and his store's address and phone number. By the time Charming got to the email, the store was closed. He got the voice mail. He could have called Shelly at home, but he didn't want to disturb his old friend.

Although he should have.

He had no idea what was behind Shelly's email, although he found out the next day, as the offers for *Evil* started pouring in.

Apparently, Shelly had shared the manuscript with a few editor friends, all of whom wanted the book *now*.

Which made Charming nervous. He hadn't heard from Mellie. He had no idea what she thought of the book. He didn't know if her silence meant she hadn't gotten around to reading it yet or if she completely absolutely and utterly hated it.

He suspected the latter, but he knew he was already nervous about the project, and no real judge of his own work.

All he knew was that he had tried to write a *Twilight* kind of novel, and it had seemed silly to him. So he tossed out that draft and started again. And this time he wrote a story about life in the Kingdoms, and he used Mellie's life to build a kind of truth.

She had to have hated it.

But they were going to have to discuss it.

He printed out all the emails marked "Offer" from the various editors, rerecorded the voice mails onto his cell phone, and then he called Mellie.

"We need to talk," he said when he got her voice mail for the fifteenth time.

Yep, she hated the book.

No doubt about it.

⁓

Mellie got Charming's voice mail. She also saw all the missed calls.

She just couldn't bring herself to return them.

Nor could she bring herself to leave him a message at all.

Still, that didn't explain how she found herself in his neighborhood early the next afternoon. She had lunch at a restaurant she'd always wanted to go to—one he had mentioned on the phone in fact during their calls about the book, a restaurant very close to his house.

And after she finished a delicious lunch—at least, she hoped it was delicious; she hardly tasted it—she found herself driving down the street that he lived on.

"On the Street Where You Live"—one of those Broadway musical songs. Of course, sung by the guy in *My Fair Lady* who *didn't* get the girl. That was probably

a sign. Because Charming was the pretty one in this relationship, and Mellie wasn't ever going to "get" him.
Especially since he was clearly so ambivalent about her.

Mellie sighed. And looked, following the addresses.
The neighborhood was—oh, she hated to think it—charming. And Charming's house, appropriate, a two-story
mock Tudor with faux rock and mullioned windows.

Lovely, lovely house, with a handsome, handsome man
standing on the stoop, looking stunned to see her vehicle.

Of course, she couldn't just drive by now. She had
to stop.

So she did.

She wanted to stay in the car and have him come
to her, but that wasn't right. Instead, she forced herself
out. The sidewalk leading to the house wasn't really a
sidewalk at all. It was a cobblestone path, beautifully
designed to fit into the lovely garden that was blooming
with seasonal flowers.

The air smelled sweet—some kind of flowering
California plant that she couldn't recognize. There were
no tulips here, no daisies, no plants that needed cold to
go dormant in the winter. Just plants that could handle
the warm winters and the even hotter summers.

She ran a hand through her hair. She was focusing
on flowers because she couldn't bear to think about
anything else.

"Mellie?" Charming said as if he couldn't believe she
was actually there.

She swallowed hard and hoped her voice would
sound calm when she spoke.

"I got your messages," she said. "What could be so
urgent?"

He hadn't moved from the stoop. He looked a bit mussed—his at-home clothes, instead of his in-public clothes—khaki pants that looked well worn, a polo shirt with a rip along the sleeve. Even his hair was tussled, as if he hadn't combed it yet that day.

The look made him seem less formidable, more boyish.

"Um," he said, sounding as nervous as he had at their last meeting. "I—um—well, once you might have thought it was good news."

"What?" she asked.

"Come on inside," he said. "Have you had lunch?"

"Yes," she said.

He nodded, as if he had expected it. He opened the door, and waited for her, like a perfect gentleman.

She tottered along the walk, her heels catching in the uneven stone. She had hated cobblestone in the Kingdoms and she hated it here. It was an affectation, even if it did look good with the garden and the mock Tudor house.

He smiled at her as she stepped past him into the darkened interior. She tried to ignore that smile. It was one from his arsenal of lethal smiles—warm and welcoming and insecure all at the same time.

As she walked past him, she realized he wasn't wearing shoes, that he was completely barefoot. With her wearing heels and him barefoot, he wasn't that much taller than she was. The look suited him more than she wanted it to.

He put his hand on her back as he guided her through the door. His palm was warm through her shirt, making her breathless.

He was so casual in his touching, so comfortable with the motions of politeness. Like that kiss on the hand, the one she had found so very erotic.

And she didn't want to think erotic thoughts about Charming because she might turn around and kiss him. Really kiss him, not like she had at the book fair, but full on, shove the man against the wall kissing, the kind that might lead to clothes getting ripped, and parts getting caressed and—

She made herself stop. She couldn't think of that.

She didn't dare.

"Nice house," she said, and meant it.

The interior smelled faintly of a young girl's perfume mixed with a stronger scent of garlic. The entry was neat, but not too neat. Shoes were pushed haphazardly against the wall, the front closet door was slightly open, and someone had left a stack of books on the stairs leading up to the second floor.

Charming led Mellie into the kitchen. A woman she didn't recognize was browning some meat. That was where the smell of garlic came from. Some chopped onions sat on the sideboard along with some glistening tomatoes.

The woman was heavyset, with soft, careworn features. She wore a blue T-shirt and faded blue jeans. She was barefoot too.

Charming introduced her, but Mellie missed her name. His housekeeper, and the person who kept him honest, he said. Mellie wasn't sure what that meant.

He got a lime cooler from the fridge and offered her one. She shook her head. She wasn't going to stay very long.

Then he led her to the back patio. The patio was also made up of cobblestone. A glass table with matching chairs stood in the center. The glass was perfect because it showcased the riot of flowers back here. Even underneath the table itself, flowers bloomed in a circular planter around the base.

Mellie sat, but he didn't. He walked to the edge of the cobblestone patio and looked out over his backyard, showing off that perfect back again. How could she be so attracted to a man's back?

She made herself look away.

"I know you don't like the book," he said. "You don't have to tell me about it. Your silence says it all."

"Charming," she said, then let her voice trail off. She really had nothing to say about the book. She couldn't tell him how disconcerted she felt that he had seen her clearly. And she couldn't tell him how much it had hurt her because then she would have to explain why, and she didn't want to.

She no longer wanted to be vulnerable in front of this man.

"But we have a problem," he said. "When I gave the book to you, I also gave it to my friend Sheldon McArthur, who is a book dealer and knows a lot about literature."

Her cheeks heated. She bit her lower lip. She wanted to excoriate him for letting someone else read the book, but she didn't want to start yelling now.

If she started yelling now, she might never ever stop.

"I thought, you know, that if you liked it, we had to make sure that it was an okay novel before we marketed it, and since neither of us were experts…" Charming shrugged. He was still facing the garden.

She was glad for a moment that she couldn't see his face. Or, rather, that he couldn't see hers.

"Anyway," he said, "Shelly liked the book, and he gave it to a few people—"

"He what?" she asked.

"He does that," Charming said. "I didn't know that he did that, but he's done it with some now-famous mystery writers. He uses his connections to make sure the book has a hearing."

Mellie's heart pounded. Other people had read this book? She was going to die of embarrassment.

She closed her eyes. And part of her heard her own thoughts: she sounded like a teenager. Worse, she sounded like an inconsistent teenager, one who could protest a book fair but not let people see her life story.

As written by Prince Charming.

"So far," Charming said softly, "I've gotten six offers on the book."

"What? You have?" She opened her eyes.

He had turned around slightly, so that he could see her face. She could see his. It was filled with trepidation and regret.

"They seem to think I'm your agent," he said. "Shelly sent the manuscript, and put them in touch with me, but my name isn't on the document. Just yours."

"Offers?" she asked.

He nodded. "Better than anything I could have hoped for. The kind of offers you wanted. The kind you needed to get the attention we initially talked about."

"But the book is *sad*," she said. "It doesn't have a happy ending."

His smile was rueful. "I know. They're calling it women's fiction. One editor said it might start a trend of stepmother lit. They say the market is huge, given all the second marriages and blended families in this country. Everyone has a stepmother or knows someone who does."

Mellie's heart was pounding. "What does this mean?"

"It means we could have an auction," he said. "It means that whoever buys the book will want to send you on tour and have you do publicity, and will promote the book as the definitive stepmother story. And—I hate to tell you this—they all seem to love the title."

"The title is horrible," she said, then stopped herself. She almost told him the whole book was horrible.

"I know," he said and made his way over to the table. "I was going to turn it all down, but it didn't seem right without consulting you. So I've told you. Now all I have to do is email them with a thanks but no-thanks."

She swallowed hard. She hadn't expected this. She hadn't expected any of this. Initially she had thought about the talks and the tours, the publicity and the promotion, just as a way to get her message across. But even all that got lost in her efforts to write the book.

And she had been so relieved when Charming took that over.

Until she saw the book of course.

Then again, she'd been trying for years to get a hearing on the mistreatment of stepmothers in fairy tales. Not just years. Decades.

He was right: she would have been happy about this a month ago. Hell, a week ago, before she had read the book.

But now the book was a reality, and it wasn't quite her reality (but it was close—too close for comfort, in fact. But who would know that, outside of the Kingdoms? And how would it get to the Kingdoms, except for Charming?)

"Let me see the offers," she said.

He grabbed a folder off a nearby chair. Inside were printed out emails—six of them—with the word "Offer" emblazoned across the top.

"I have voice mails too," he said. "Some people left messages."

She glanced at him. "They did?"

He nodded. "A lot of messages. These editors are afraid they'll miss out. They really think you have the next best thing here."

"You have the next best thing," Mellie said. "You wrote the book."

"Using your words," he said softly.

Her cheeks heated. She spread the papers on the glass table top. Offer after offer after offer. He had arranged them from the smallest—if you wanted to call six figures small—to the largest, which made her gasp.

Not that she needed the money. But she had no idea there was so much money in publishing, particularly for a book like this.

"The money is just representative," he said. "I've been talking to some writer friends. They tell me that these are advances, and they indicate how much push a publisher is willing to put behind a book. These advances mean that a publisher would try to make this book a national—maybe even an international—bestseller."

Mellie looked up at him. He had wiped his face of all expression—probably deliberately—and he was just watching her.

Then he leaned forward, and moved some pages.

"Here's what I think is interesting," he said and tapped the middle of one of the sheets. "It's an advertising and promotion plan, something they tell me is really, really unusual at this stage. But the publisher's really afraid that they'll lose out to someone else, so they're letting us know everything they plan for the book. See? You'd go all over the country on a whirlwind tour. There'd be appearances on *The Today Show*, on *Regis and Kelly*, and they'd even try for a special *Oprah* segment, although they are really clear they can't guarantee that."

"Oprah?" Mellie asked. Oprah was the holy grail. Oprah promoted books, but more importantly, Oprah promoted causes.

"And *The View*," he said. "If you're a really good interview, they'd want you to spend a lot of time on *The View*. And none of that counts all the radio interviews. They also think the book would do well on the book club circuit, so they'd publish an edition with questions in the back specifically designed for book clubs."

She scanned the document. All kinds of plans were laid out here, from the advertising budget (which was eye-popping) to the various promotion types, down to viral videos on YouTube.

"I showed this to Shelly," Charming said, "and he warned me that you'd lose a month, maybe more, of your time, as you promoted this thing. But he said that he thought it would work, and it would make news. It would be something everyone would talk about for a nanosecond anyway, which is about all you can expect in this culture these days."

"But would it change perceptions?" she asked, almost to herself as an aside. She was still staring at the numbers and the plans, and the exclamation points. All of the editors had used exclamation points to show their enthusiasm for this book. (*Tremendous! Fantastic! I'm so glad that someone realized that stepmothers could be heroines!*)

"It certainly did for the vampire," he said. "They're sexy romance heroes now."

"You've said that before, but what about other archetypes? Has anyone rebuilt, say, ghosts?"

"I don't know," Charming said, "but werewolves are showing promise."

Then he smiled. This smile was tentative, almost as if he was wondering if he dared hope that she might go for this project.

"What would you do?" she asked. "If this was your book."

Then she took a sharp breath, realizing what she had said.

"I mean, it is your book, you wrote it, and—"

"It's not my book," he said. "It's yours."

She shook her head. "I can't write."

"But you have a way with words," he said. "That's what makes this live. Those speeches. See?"

He tapped another part of a different email:

What's most astonishing about this book are the diatribes. They shouldn't work. Instead they flow and convince and make us sad all over again for the life that this poor woman has led.

"This poor woman," Mellie said. "Is that what people are going to think of me?"

"They'll think you're a survivor," he said. "And remember, if you do go out and do all those tours, it won't be about you. It'll be about a character in a book that you wrote."

She took a deep breath. She'd have to work on keeping that separate.

"So," she said again, "what would you do if it was just you?"

He sank into the chair across from her. "This is every writer's dream."

"Touring?"

"Recognition," he said. "Readership. You'll get people reading your book, discussing it, *thinking* about it. They might not agree with it, but they'll be talking about it, and what more could you want?"

It was what she had wanted all along. She wanted people talking about how unfair fairy tales were, how no one should believe in them, how harmful they could be.

And she would finally have a platform.

If she could stay calm—and remember that the book wasn't about her, it was fiction. If she could try not to rant. If she could present herself well.

She gathered up the papers. Of course she could do that. She had done it, with several local television stations in interviews that got cut to pieces or didn't air. But she hadn't talked about herself as a fairy-tale stepmother. She had talked about herself as a stepmother— which she was, in the Greater World as well as in the Kingdoms—and how hurtful it was to see stepmothers portrayed as something less than human.

"Could we change the name?" she asked.

"They like it," he said. "They even have a marketing concept—a black cover with a beautiful apple in the center of it, and a bite taken out of it. One editor even suggested a subtitle. *Evil: The True Story of the Woman Who Raised Snow White*."

"I didn't raise her," Mellie said.

"I know," he said, "but you see what they're trying to do."

She nodded. She did see. She could imagine that cover everywhere. It was lovely, even in her imagination.

"We'd have to tell them you wrote it," she said.

"Why?" he asked. "You hired me to ghost. That's between us. Just thank me in the acknowledgements for help with the manuscript, and never say that you wrote every sentence while you're on television. That'll work."

"But I don't know the novel as well as you do," she said. "Shouldn't you do the interviews?"

"I wouldn't be as passionate as you," he said. Then he sighed and rubbed his nose. "Hell, Mellie, honestly, the idea of doing all that publicity—it scares me to death."

She studied him. He did seem nervous all over again.

"And you," he said. "It's got you interested in the project, doesn't it?"

"I'm not vain," she snapped. She hated that accusation. It came from the Disney film too. *Mirror, mirror, on the wall. Who is the fairest one of all?* Like someone would actually care about that.

He held out his hands in a placating gesture. "I didn't say you were. But you're a lot more extroverted than me. You like the idea of this publicity. Me, I just want to go into my office and hide."

He said it with such sincerity, such force, that she actually laughed. He probably did want to go hide.

"You'd want to come with me on this, though, right?" she asked, and tried to keep the wistfulness out of her voice.

He shook his head. "I can't," he said quickly, as if he had already thought about it. "I have my girls."

"The girls could come," she said, and realized she sounded just a bit desperate.

He smiled—the third smile of the afternoon, this one altogether different from the others. This one had no finesse, no regret, just a bit of amusement, as if he understood how uncertain she was.

"No," he said. "They're just getting used to being here. And they're finally enjoying school. I can't uproot them."

She nodded. She understood. She really did. She just didn't want to.

"Of course," she said.

She stood up and looked out over the garden, just like he had. It was a lovely view, with that soft, flowery perfume in the air, the green, the reds and yellows and pinks, the overgrown vegetation. A person could get used to this place.

She could get used to this place.

But she wasn't going to.

She was going to accept one of those offers.

"You'll take half the money, right?" she asked.

"That's in our agreement," he said.

"Good," she said. "Then let's figure out which of these offers we want to accept."

The Book

Chapter 26

MELLIE HAD NO IDEA HOW LONG IT TOOK TO PUBLISH A BOOK. Nor had she any idea how many steps were involved. She had expected to go out on tour within a month of signing the contract—only it took three months just to get the contract, and that was after two weeks of intensive negotiation, with the help of an agent that Charming's friend Sheldon McArthur helped them hire.

But even then, the book wasn't tour-ready. Charming had to explain to Mellie that there were other steps involved. He knew some of them, but not all of them.

There were revisions—which scared her, since the editor called and wanted to discuss them before sending them and the very idea just confused Mellie, who finally decided to be agreeable, take copious notes, and let Charming handle them. Then there were things called copyedits, where someone wrote all over the manuscript and sent it to her for approval—("What am I supposed to do?" she asked Charming. "Tell them that the words look better with little pencil marks?" "I'll handle it," he said.)

Then they got "proofs" of the cover—several iterations of the cover. Someone decided that the black and red apple cover was too *Twilight*. So then there was an evil stepmother cover that was too Disney ("I think the suits are afraid of a lawsuit," the editor, whose name was Mary Linda McIntosh said, as if that explained everything). The final cover was simple—just the title and the subtitle, and Mellie's name, embossed over a tasteful and shiny emerald green background.

If anyone had told her before she saw that cover that she would be able to use the words "tasteful" and "emerald green" in the same sentence without sarcasm, she would have been shocked.

But she liked it, and Charming liked it, and Mary Linda the editor liked it, and more importantly, according to Mary Linda, the sales force liked it, and the buyers for the superstores liked it. Everyone thought the book had possibilities, and everyone in the publishing house was reading it and passing it around.

("It's our word-of-mouth book this year," Mary Linda said, "and I can't tell you how good that is.")

Mellie gave a lot of things to him—and those were the only times she dealt with him. She would show up at his house with the latest thing from the publisher, and he'd invite her into the garden, and they'd talk about the publishing process, and he would stay distant, and she would think about kissing him or telling him how gorgeous he was or how much she liked him, and then she would remember that he was *Prince Charming*.

Every woman he ever met told him how spectacular he was. How nice, how charming, how handsome. His other name, of course, was the Handsome Prince and he lived up to that as well.

She wanted to kiss him, to caress him, to touch him, but she didn't. Because they were in his home, and his girls might come home. He'd been very clear about his girls. He wanted them to adapt to life in the Greater World.

More than that, he wanted them to adapt to a life without their mother.

Mellie understood that. She *respected* that. And sometimes (most of the time), she wished she wasn't so damn sympathetic.

Ironically, she never saw his girls, always showing up during the middle of the school day, although one afternoon she noticed photographs on the wall, school photographs of stunning young beauties with the kind of golden hair that usually didn't make it outside of the Kingdoms. His daughters, clearly. Beautiful, intelligent, and of course, the center of his attention.

The last few meetings hadn't even take place at the house. They took place at his brand new bookstore in Westwood. He spent a lot of his portion of their advance buying a building there, renovating it, and making it the premiere bookstore in the entire area. Coffee bar, yes, and back stock, and an area for children, another for teenagers, and a place where adults could sit and talk and read, even if they didn't want to buy.

Mellie wasn't a book person, and she liked the store. From everything she heard, so did real book people.

Charming had a hit on his hands.

Not counting the book itself.

Which showed up in the form of an Advanced Reading Copy or ARC. It still wasn't done. It had all kinds of disclaimers on it—saying there were grammatical errors, and any final quotes should be compared to the final. It had publishing information along the back, release dates and ship dates, and the highlights of her proposed tour.

Which she had been discussing with the publicity department. They started her in the Midwest—three days of practice from Minneapolis to Fargo to Des Moines. Then the real tour began in Chicago, with two days there, two days to blitz Chicago media. From there she went east, D.C. to Philadelphia to Boston to New York, which was a three-day stint filled with media.

She would then fly to Denver, Seattle, San Francisco, and she would end in Los Angeles more than a month after she started, with no days off (except fly days). She would be working from seven or eight in the morning ("Morning talk shows," the publicist said. "Big business") to nine or ten in the evening ("Night time signings are best," the publicist said. "You get people after their workday is done.")

Mellie would do blitz radio interviews from her hotel room, all on her cell phone "visiting" a dozen radio stations all over the country in a single morning. She would do some bookstore talks courtesy of Skype. She was supposed to blog about her travels—although she begged out of that, pleading possible exhaustion (not the real reason, which was an inability to write). Instead, the publicist offered to do it, because the publicist was coming along, to hustle Mellie from one location to the next.

Mellie was scared, she was excited, and she was thrilled.

Finally, she would get her message out.

Finally, people were going to listen to her.

Finally, she had a chance to change the world.

Charming thought it ironic that he actually had to beg Mellie's publicist to give him one of her final signings in Los Angeles. He wanted to do a big show at the store. He had to promise extra media coverage, and for that he had to call in yet another favor from Shelly, who knew how to promote bookstore events in Los Angeles, even though he hadn't owned a store there in more than five years.

Charming's store was wonderful, his dream business. It had a welcoming first floor filled with a coffee shop and areas for kids, a place for signings, and a small stage for bigger events. There was a great area for new arrivals and for titles he felt needed highlighting.

But that wasn't his favorite part of the store. His favorite part was the second and third floors. He built a windy, showcase staircase, one his architect argued against because it would take away shelf space. But Charming didn't care about shelf space. Instead, people would go up the grand staircase and see the entire first floor. They'd see the books on the upper shelves of the first floor, and then gradually, the books on the lowest shelves of the second floor.

This was the kind of bookstore he'd always wanted.

And if his girls hadn't been with him, he would have considered adding an apartment onto the fourth floor (which was now storage space), and living right here, in the most perfect place on Earth.

All of Earth. Including the Kingdoms.

This was Charming heaven.

He was happy about it all, except for Mellie. He didn't know how to bring Mellie deeper into his life. She came to see him whenever she had a publishing question, and then she fled as if he frightened her.

Maybe he did. She was the one person he knew outside of his family whom he didn't try to charm. Maybe his baseline personality—the one not masked by charm magic—was frightening. Ella certainly hadn't enjoyed it.

But the girls weren't frightened of him, although they did (to his surprise) respect his fatherly authority. He was finding his rhythm with them too.

And they liked to come to the store in the evenings to see what new books arrived.

They couldn't take inventory out of the store, but they could read it here, and they both did.

To his eternal gratification, his daughters loved books as much as he did, and in the case of Grace, maybe even more.

He knew things were going well. In fact, he knew they were going too well, and he knew at some point, they would change.

So he wasn't surprised when Ella showed up at the bookstore one day. Although he was surprised by the feeling of foreboding that he got when he saw her.

He realized, at that very moment, that he saw Ella as a harbinger of bad things to come.

He just had no idea how bad those things could get.

Chapter 27

IT HAPPENED A WEEK INTO MELLIE'S TOUR. CHARMING WAS manning the main desk in the bookstore, the one closest to the main entrance. It was Monday morning, one of the slowest times of the week.

He had a high speed computer running beside his work station. He was at work, but for once, he wasn't thinking about the store. He was thinking about Mellie. He'd seen the numbers—*Evil* was selling out. The distributors were reordering so fast that they couldn't keep up with demand.

Mellie's appearances hyped interest in the book. And she was starting to get coverage on the "stepmother" issue.

Everything she had wanted, and more. He was so thrilled for her.

And he missed her. He missed her a lot. When she got back, he would start to court her.

He'd already read a few books on how to do it.

He was multi-tasking, trying to watch a series of interviews Mellie had done over the weekend on the computer, and keeping an eye on the entrance. He had three employees scattered around the place, moving books, changing displays, and manning the upstairs information/check-out counter.

Charming had designed the front of the store so that lots of sunlight poured into the entryway. Most bookstores didn't let in much light, afraid it would damage the books. But he had his staff rotate the books daily, so no book got too much sun exposure.

He loved the way the sun fell on the carpet, the warmth it added to the cavernous room, the way it glinted off the book covers. In addition to listening to Mellie—she had done a series of radio interviews that morning, and he was listening to each one, in order—he was also going through book catalogs, placing his orders for the following week.

He often forgot what he was trying to do, because his eye kept wandering to Mellie's face, animated on the blog that the publishing company had started for her. She talked, without sound, in the small upper right hand corner of the screen. If he clicked on her image, he got a choice of videos from the tour so far, some from interviews she had done for television, some from readings she had done at various bookstores (she was good—quite professional and theatrical, making the book sound better than he thought it was).

Her initial interviews were shaky, but that's why the publicist started her in the Midwest (which New York considered flyover country—even though it was really fly-to country, considering how many hubs were there [not to mention how many people]), but she had been getting progressively better, and her appearances in Philadelphia this past weekend looked stunning.

The publicist was doing a great job running the blog. Charming was trying to keep up with all that Mellie was doing, not because he cared so much about the book (although he did, he really did, he just tried to pretend that he didn't) but because he cared about her.

She looked lovely at all the appearances and not a

bit tired, and she rarely repeated herself. She had even had the grace to look surprised and grateful when one of the morning show people mentioned that they'd read the book "cover to cover" and "enjoyed every bit of it."

He'd been surprised too. So many interviewers never read the books, only the promotional material.

He was about to click to a new interview when the entrance pinged.

From the second floor, one of his employees looked over the rail, clearly making sure Charming was still at the front desk.

He smiled an I-got-it smile at the employee, then looked for the customer. It took him a moment to see her, bathed as she was in that bright sunlight. When he did see her, his heart stopped for a brief, horrifying instance.

Ella.

He hit pause on the interview with Mellie, then slept that computer screen. He would need all of his abilities to talk with his ex-wife.

She didn't look out of place in this part of the Greater World, even though he had never seen her in the Greater World before.

She had once professed a hatred of it.

Apparently that went away.

She was too thin, much too thin, like so many rich, middle-aged women in Hollywood. She was almost skeletal. She wore black Capri pants, black flats with no socks, and a black mesh top over a rose-colored T-shirt. Her blond hair was pulled back away from her face, which seemed as skeletal as the rest of her, or maybe more skeletal. And shiny, the way that a person's face got when they'd had too much plastic surgery.

She hadn't had any—he could see some frown lines near her still-beautiful blue eyes—but she was wearing too much make-up, which was probably why her skin had that shiny look.

"Ella," he said, trying to keep his tone neutral. But all he succeeded in doing was sounding flat. His heart was pounding. What was she doing here, in the Greater World? Why hadn't she contacted him? Had she already tried to see the girls?

"So this is your castle," she said as she walked to the front desk. "How... pedestrian of you."

He smiled reflexively, not willing to let her know how much her very presence had upset him. "To what do I owe this pleasure? It can't be because you want a book."

The dig slipped out before he could stop it, but she didn't even seem to notice.

"I do want a book," she said. "And I even decided to buy it from you."

She paused while he took in that information. Ella wanted a book? Something really *had* shifted.

"I figured I'd get the book here because I did want to see what's been taking all of your time," Ella said. "The girls told me this is your pride and joy."

He jolted at the mention of the girls, until he remembered that they called her every Sunday, whether she wanted them to or not.

"They like it here too," he said.

"They've told me." She rolled her eyes. "You're turning them into creatures I don't even recognize."

He didn't say *good*, although he wanted to.

"Your father certainly wouldn't approve," she added.

"And that would be unusual how?" he asked.

She smiled. Her smile was still lovely, giving an echo of the beauty she had once been. He realized suddenly, with great surprise, that Ella was younger than Mellie and looked much older. He wasn't quite sure what had caused that—except that his ex-wife was clearly an unhappy woman.

"Your father does care about what you do," she said.

"I know," Charming said dryly. "He's terrified I'll continue to embarrass him."

Ella walked up to the desk, and rested her arms on it. They were sun-browned, and too-thin. She held some parchment in her right hand.

"What are you doing here, really, Ella?" he asked.

She slid the parchment at him, but kept one hand over it, so that he couldn't read it. "Tell me, Charming," she said in her softest voice. "Are the rumors true? Are you dating one of the stepmothers?"

He could answer that honestly. "I'm not dating anyone."

"Yet the girls say you've been seeing a lot of—what's her name? Mellie? Snow's stepmother."

"We're friends," he said, wishing he could tell the girls not to talk about his personal life. But he didn't want to get between them and their mother. The phone calls were all they had now. "Why?"

Ella shrugged. "Just curious. I'd been hearing the strangest rumors."

"From the girls?" he asked.

Ella didn't answer directly, which was another of her maddening habits. "She's written a book, hasn't she? This stepmother of yours."

"She's not my stepmother," he said, disliking the

implication. Ella made it sound like Mellie was older than he was. She wasn't.

"There's a copy of Mellie's book right near the desk," Charming said. "You can buy it if you like."

"You're not going to comp me a copy?" she asked.

"Ella, you aren't going to read it. We both know that."

"It's a gift," she said. "For a friend."

He almost said, *You have friends*? but thought the better of that too. "Just put it on the desk and I'll ring it up. You want anything else?"

"From here? Are you kidding?" Ella asked. "I don't see why anyone would waste their time or their money in this place."

The words were designed to make him angry, and they worked. But he wasn't going to let that anger out. He told her the price of the book, and she paid him with cash, which surprised him.

Then she took her hand off the parchment. "I want you to sign this."

His breath caught. Now what was she trying to do? Steal the girls back? They had just calmed down and settled in. He wasn't about to give this woman his daughters again.

He took the document. It was one page, handwritten in the lovely calligraphic style of the courts in his Kingdom, and as he read, his heart sank.

"You're giving up all rights to the girls?" he asked, looking at her. It would break their hearts. "Why?"

But he knew why. There had to be a man involved. A man and money and prestige.

"You're doing such a fine job with them," Ella said. "You're a much better parent than I could ever be."

"But you're disowning them, Ella," he said. "That's just wrong. That'll destroy them."

She frowned at him. "It will not. Children are resilient. Tell them what you want. It really doesn't matter to me."

"All you're doing is talking to them on the phone once a week," he said. "That can hardly be a strain."

"It promotes a tie that we don't have," she said. "I think it's better to have a clean break, don't you?"

"No," he said. His heart ached. How did he fall for this woman? She was everything the fairy tale said she wasn't—self-involved, self-centered, self-important. And she couldn't feel love. That had surprised him when he married her, although the court wisewoman had an explanation.

A child raised without love, she said, *often cannot learn how to give it*.

"They're your daughters," Charming said. And then his trump card: "They love you."

Ella nodded. "I know," she said, as if love were an expected thing, even after the way she had treated them. "But this is better."

"For whom, Ella?" he asked.

"For all of us," she said.

He shoved the parchment back to her. "I'm not signing this thing."

"You don't want them to be yours one hundred percent?" she asked.

"They *are* mine one hundred percent," he said. "I have sole custody. You have the right to talk to them once a week. That's good enough."

"I don't want to be tied down," she said, her voice rising in a whine. "Don't you understand?"

"And a single call to the phone you carry with you is tied down?" he asked.

"Yes," she said.

He shook his head. "Who is he?" he asked.

"Who is who?" she asked.

"It's a man, right?" he asked. "You're giving up your daughters for a man."

"No," she said in that tone she used when she was lying. "I am not giving up my daughters at anyone's request except yours."

"I never asked you to give them up," Charming said. "I just wanted to raise them."

Then he looked at the document again, and read it very carefully. She wasn't disowning the girls. She was annulling them. It negated not just Ella's custodial rights and her parental rights, but the motherhood itself. As if it had never happened.

He felt chilled. Kingdom court documents could be very dangerous. They actually had a bit of magic. If he signed this, there was a good possibility his daughters would cease to exist, because Ella would no longer be a mother.

He took the document back. He wanted to tear it up, but he couldn't even do that, not without taking a large risk. He had to consult someone magical, someone who knew what kind of magic this document held.

"What happens if I don't sign this?" he asked.

"You have to," she said and sounded a bit desperate.

"Or…?"

She shook her head.

He ran a finger along the document, then touched the edges of the letters. Secondary writing appeared—the spell itself—and an expiration date. If the magic was not used within twenty-four hours of the creation of the document, the words would vanish.

He gave her a measured look.

"I'll read this over, let my lawyer look at it, and talk to you about it next week," he said.

"No," she said. "Now."

"I don't make any decisions about our girls rashly," he said. "I'll call you when I've made my decision."

"I'm leaving the Greater World in an hour," she said. "I'll need it then."

"No," he said.

"Then give it back." She reached for it.

"No," he said.

She stamped her small foot. His daughters hadn't done that since they were little, but his ex-wife seemed to do it all the time.

"You're going to ruin everything," she snapped.

"I just want time to consider this," he said in his most reasonable tone.

"You know that it won't work if you wait. You know it. I want you to sign it now."

"And I want you to be a better person," he said softly. "Neither of us will ever get what we want."

"I hate you, you know that?" she asked.

"Yeah," he said softly. Those words no longer had the power to hurt him. "I do know that."

"I'm not calling those girls ever again," she said. "I am disowning them, with or without that document."

"Fine," he said.

"You're a cold-hearted bastard," she said.

"I'm not the one abandoning my children," he said.

She glared at him. Then she started to stomp out of the store.

"You forgot your book," he said as a parting shot.

To his surprise, she stomped back in and grabbed it. "It's not my book," she said as if that made it better.

And then she did stomp out.

He watched her shadow make its way across the store's carpet, until she rounded the corner and disappeared.

His heart was pounding. He put his head in his hands for just a brief moment. His wife had just tried to wish his girls out of existence. He would need to contact his attorney, and Lavinia, and anyone else he could think of.

Ella had just gotten dangerous. Or even more dangerous. She had clearly gone off some kind of deep end.

And it wasn't his to wonder why (although he did). It was now his duty to protect his daughters.

Somehow.

Chapter 28

MELLIE WOULD HAVE TOLD ANYONE WHO ASKED THAT THE entire tour experience blurred into one long mess, filled with signings and interviews and impersonal hotel rooms. But she would've been lying. Because she thrived on this—the lack of sleep, the horrible food, the hurry-hurry-hurry to the next stop, the next town, the next airport.

The only thing that bothered Mellie was Charming. She missed him. She missed seeing him, consulting with him. She even missed wishing she could flirt with him.

When this tour was over, she'd get off the plane, run to his beautiful bookstore, wrap her arms around him, and give him the biggest, best kiss of her life. She would literally throw herself at him, and if he balked, she would step back and say it was all a thank-you for saving her.

Because that was what he had done.

The wonderful man.

Mellie was hearing daily how the numbers on the books were trending upwards. After her Minneapolis appearances, the book started selling well in the Midwest. After she did some syndicated radio interviews, people showed up early at the stores to make sure they got copies of the books.

And by the time she reached Philadelphia, the stores had sold out of their copies of *Evil* before she arrived.

The people who showed up at the signing had bought the book a few days before.

Things started to go sideways in Philadelphia, though. Until that point, she thought she could predict the questions in the interview:

1. What caused you to write the book?
2. Did the idea come out of your own life?
3. Do you really believe stepmothers are misunderstood?
4. What made you choose fairy tales as your vehicle of self-expression?
5. What was it about the Snow White story that spoke to you?

Those questions usually comprised the entire interview, and after the third day of the tour, she could answer them by rote.

She tried not to, though, because then the interviews would start to sound canned, and what people liked—according to LaTisha the publicist who, in addition to traveling with Mellie, monitored blogs, and reactions to the signings—was Mellie's passion for her topic.

Her readers surprised her too—or her potential readers, anyway, at the first part of her tour. The people who bought the book weren't all stepmothers. Some were stepchildren who loved their stepmothers ("My mom abandoned me," she heard more than once, "but my stepmom was there, and she raised me. She's my real mom."). Others were husbands who had second wives ("Finally, someone who has told the world what we're going through."). And the most surprising group—at least to her—stepfathers ("I know women get the bad rap in fairy tales," they'd said, "but all stepparents get a bad rap in real life.").

By the time Mellie reached D.C. half of the people who came to the signing had already read the book, and wanted to engage her on its contents. Most of the comments were positive, although a few—mostly from young girls—complained about the portrayal of Snow White as selfish.

Mellie wished she could answer that truthfully. It was the only part of the book she didn't like. Yes, Snow had been self-involved, but she had also been eighteen years old. She hadn't really understood all the things she was feeling. If the blood weren't so bad between them (Mellie would say), she would be able to tell Snow her side of the story, and Snow would finally understand.

But Mellie hadn't told Snow her side of the story. She couldn't change that.

But it looked like she might be able to change the perception of it.

Until that last round of interviews in Philadelphia. Mellie hadn't realized it at the time, but a day later— after things changed in Boston—she thought back, and saw the seeds in Philadelphia.

She had been in a television studio in Philadelphia at W-something-something-something. She had just come from a marvelous hour-long radio interview at WHYY with Terry Gross of *Fresh Air*, discussing books and women's issues. LaTisha thought that was Mellie's best interview yet, and she did as well. It would air later in the week, and it would, Mellie thought, bring a whole new class of reader to the book.

Now, television studios, like hotel rooms, tended to

look alike. Lots of cables, lots of teleprompters, lots of segmented areas with "permanent" sets that looked like they'd been designed fifteen years before.

Mellie got to sit in front of a desk, as if she were an anchor, while someone pinned a mike to her lapel. She was told to answer questions "naturally," and she had to watch the screen in front of her, for the different interviewers, from different stations across the Northeast, who were going to ask her a few questions and then use them in their noon (or morning) "entertainment" segments.

She wasn't sure where the first question came from— Delaware? Vermont? Connecticut?—but it was one of the few she had never heard before: "Tell me about your writing day."

Fortunately, LaTisha had prepared Mellie for that. *Sometimes*, LaTisha said, *someone who really loves reading asks what your writing day is like, expecting it to be glamorous. The key is to answer the question politely without being insulting.*

Mellie gave the answer she'd been trained to give, how in the confines of her own home, she could go on adventures without ever changing out of her pajamas.

She got the question twice more in that round of interviews, and even LaTisha had commented on it, saying how rare it was to get that question more than once a tour.

But Mellie didn't mind. Nor did she think much about it when the host of one of Philadelphia's morning shows—a man who, all things considered, would rather *not* be in Philadelphia—commented that she looked too glamorous to be a writer.

"And not an ounce of fat," said the weather guy, who (LaTisha told her later) had been hired as comic relief.

"How do you stay so thin when you spend all your time reading and writing?" the host asked as if her slender form was some kind of conspiracy.

"I believe in exercise," Mellie said truthfully. "It's the one thing I miss when I'm on tour like this."

She had effectively changed the subject, and then she deftly brought it back to parenthood ("Of course," she said, "I've been through that before. As the mother of young children, I didn't get much exercise either.") and LaTisha had complimented her on her smoothness.

Those incidents seemed like comfortable (and much needed) blips in an otherwise routine group of questions.

And then she was in Boston, Boston with its major media, Boston with its famously aggressive press corps, Boston which had its own mini-publishing industry (some of whose members had bid upon and lost the opportunity to publish *Evil*).

On the cab ride in from Logan International Airport, LaTisha (who had been hugging her BlackBerry as if it were an old boyfriend) told Mellie that the publicity department had heard from Oprah's people.

"A tentative gesture," LaTisha said. "They want to know how the sales are going, what kind of person you are, and if you're going to be all interviewed out before Oprah even gets to you. I told them that you have hidden depths, and that they might want to consider a topical interview instead of one focused on the book."

"Topical?" Mellie asked.

"One about fairy tales and how they discriminate against women," LaTisha said, "*and* how that has led to the stereotyping of stepmothers as evil."

Mellie's heart leapt. Her dream interview. From the

best interviewer in the world. Oprah, with all of her followers, all of the people who loved her, all of the people who thought about the topics Oprah asked them to think about.

Mellie had always hoped she would get that kind of platform. She just never permitted herself to dream it would be possible—not so soon in this media blitz as Charming had called it.

Charming. She contacted him as often as possible. She wanted to hear his voice. (Honestly, she *needed* to hear his voice.) And he seemed interested.

He listened with enthusiasm to her strange, tired phone calls, and told her he had watched each and every interview (and from some of the details he mentioned, he clearly had). He bucked her up after her first disastrous Minneapolis interview, although LaTisha and the segment producer hadn't thought it disastrous and neither had Charming after he saw it.

But he raised her spirits before he saw it by saying, "You're practicing, Mellie. You'll get better with each and every interview. You don't want to start at the top of your game."

Of course, she did want to start at the top of her game, but she knew that wasn't possible. And she *had* gotten better, with each and every interview. LaTisha told her that she was unlike most writers who got worse as time went on.

And then Boston happened.

Chapter 29

After Ella left, Charming moved like a man possessed. He put one of his employees in charge of the store, called his manager and told her that he needed to her to find a way to cover his shifts this week, since he might be gone, and then he left the store, so fast he wouldn't have been surprised to see a dust cloud in his wake.

He had to fight to control his car's speed as he headed to his daughters' school. He wouldn't put anything past Ella, not even kidnapping the girls and taking them to someone who could achieve the destruction of Charming's family without the paperwork.

He had called ahead, and the girls were waiting for him in the principal's office. Imperia had her arms crossed and she was tapping her foot, her blue eyes flashing. Charming had always thought Imperia, in her pissed-off mode, looked like her mother, but actually she looked like a beautiful female version of Charming's father—strong, demanding, and brooking no disagreement.

Grace sat on a nearby chair, her feet crossed at the ankles and swinging back and forth as she waited. She was reading a book when he arrived and finished her page before looking up at him.

"I have a test," Imperia said. "I can't go anywhere."

"You'll have to make it up later," Charming said. Then he thanked the principal's secretary, put his hands on the back of both girls and propelled them to the parking lot.

He felt particularly vulnerable. The document, folded and inside his breast pocket, hummed with power. He had nothing, no real magic at all. The power to charm had its uses, but it also had its drawbacks, particularly when faced with magic so real that it could destroy his entire family with the stroke of a pen.

He put the girls in the car, locked the doors, and drove to the nearest portal. It was in Sherman Oaks, on a road made famous by countless movies and television shows. On one side, a dirt cliff face (with tons of homes built on the rambling roads above). On the other, a hillside with steep drop-offs, so wild you could still hear coyotes at night.

He parked in a small gravel-covered turnout.

"Daddy?" Imperia asked, her voice trembling, "What are we doing?"

She knew where they were because she had gone through this portal countless times. Grace, on the other hand, hadn't used this portal in nearly five years and, if Charming remembered correctly, she had been asleep the last time they had gone through.

"We have to go home for a bit, baby," he said.

Normally, she would have protested it. This time she just looked scared.

"What happened?" she asked.

"Nothing, I hope," he said. "But we're going back just in case."

And he wasn't going to let the girls out of his sight.

He unlocked the doors and slid out, then glanced at the dirt wall on the side of the road. The portal still gleamed, as if someone had pasted a thin sheet of water over the sandy dirt.

His heart was pounding. He figured this portal was far enough away from his store that Ella wouldn't know about it. He had rejected portals in the Beverly Hilton, another in a major store on Rodeo Drive, and his favorite one, in Grauman's Chinese Theatre.

The portals all led into the Kingdoms. In fact, by thinking about where he needed to go, he could pick where he came out in the Kingdoms. He was pretty sure it worked that way for all Kingdom members heading home. But it didn't happen that way in reverse. He couldn't enter a portal in the Kingdoms and pick where he was going to come out in the Greater World. He had to find the portal most directly linked to his exit.

Fortunately, a lot of Greater World portals were linked to Los Angeles, although most of them dumped him in Anaheim, much too close to Disneyland for his own comfort.

"Take my hands, girls," he said, extending them. Both girls grabbed on without protest. Grace used her other hand to clutch her book.

"Something bad happened, didn't it, Daddy?" Grace asked quietly. She seemed certain, and he hoped it was her natural intuitiveness and not the beginning of some magical ability he couldn't quite understand.

"Not yet, hon," he said. "Maybe not ever."

He led the girls to the portal, and as they stepped through, he realized he hadn't let Mellie know he was leaving the Greater World.

Well, he thought as he sank into the transition between worlds, he could only hope that she would be too busy to notice that he was gone.

Chapter 30

It was Mellie's first experience with a Gotcha! interview, and it left her speechless. And terrified. But she couldn't confess terrified to LaTisha. She couldn't confess anything at all because she was afraid of making things worse.

Everything started out well. LaTisha had booked them in the nicest hotel yet, with a stunning lobby that paled in comparison to the expansive room. For the first time, Mellie wished she had more time to just luxuriate in the oversized tub or sprawl on the bed covered with linen so soft that it made her want to cry from pleasure.

But she only had a half an hour to freshen up from the trip, so she took a quick shower (and steamed out her blouse), dressed for television—no stripes, no plaids, no small repeating patterns, and no white—and headed back to the lobby with five minutes to spare.

The Oprah rumors had started a cascade of media "gets." The *New York Times* wanted to interview Mellie when she came to New York. One of *Nightline*'s producers had called, as had one of the booking agents for the *David Letterman Show*. Some of the scheduled appearances—like *Live with Regis and Kelly*—wanted more time, and she was even going to get a better segment on *The Today Show* (whatever that meant).

The cab ride was filled with much texting (LaTisha) and Tweeting (LaTisha) and telephone calls (LaTisha) and blogging (LaTisha). Mellie pulled out her phone just so that she could look busy, and because she wanted to let Charming know what was going on.

Only she didn't dare talk to him, not with LaTisha there. So she sent him a text message, telling him she'd call later with very good news. *Things going well*, she wrote.

She had no idea that "things going well" would only last another thirty minutes or so.

The segment, for a major Boston public affairs and entertainment program, was a prelude to a WGBH interview that would be compiled into a series on writers and writing later in the year. Mellie had those two interviews, and one major bookstore appearance later in the evening.

After a quick round make-up session (and arguments about how red her lipstick should be ["Not red," Mellie said. "Soft." Again, a prelude of things to come]), she settled into a round, uncomfortable blue chair in a very blue studio with huge windows behind her. The set-up was supposed to look personal and comfy, but only ended up looking like a cross between an anchor's chair and a bad 1960s home design.

The interviewer was not the person that LaTisha had spoken to the day before. That person had been a young-ish woman who was trying to make her bones with a "soft" interview about a trendy book on women's issues.

This interviewer was not young. She was a hard-edged woman who had clearly graduated from the ingé-nue's chair to an anchor position at a C market, and was now trying to make her way into the top tier of television news programming. LaTisha had stopped cold when she saw the woman and had pulled the segment producer aside, quietly begging for someone else.

That, more than anything, panicked Mellie.

When the segment producer said the original inter-viewer was unavailable, LaTisha asked to see a list of interview questions and was denied. She then tried to pull Mellie out of the interview, but Mellie, in her naïveté, refused.

Later, she would wonder how different her life would be if she had actually listened to the woman whom the publisher had sent along to protect her from herself.

Instead, Mellie settled into that uncomfortable chair, smiled at the overly made-up woman across from her, a woman whose unnaturally brown hair (with very blond highlights) looked like it had been lacquered into place, much like the skin around her eyes, that had already been tucked one time too often.

The woman held an iPad with a series of notes on it. She didn't speak until the red light above the camera came on, then she smiled at Mellie. The smile seemed feral, and for the first time, Mellie had a sense of foreboding.

The woman didn't introduce herself, although the voice-over announcer identified her as news anchor Cindy Jordan.

"Mellie," Cindy Jordan said warmly and then paused, looking at Mellie theatrically. "May I call you Mellie?"

What was Mellie going to say? No? Although she was tempted to bolt. However, she'd been in the Greater World long enough to see what happened to television interview subjects who got cold feet while on camera—the footage got replayed and replayed and replayed, making the interviewee look like an idiot.

"Of course you can," Mellie said, smiling her warmest smile. It was the last time she'd smile during that interview.

"I understand that you had help writing your book," Cindy said.

Mellie wasn't sure if she heard the question right. After all, she was tired, and things seemed strange. "Excuse me?"

She knew that was a lame response, but it was better than trying to answer a question she hadn't properly heard. LaTisha had told her that as well.

"I've been told you didn't write a word of *Evil*," Cindy said. "Is that true?"

Mellie didn't like lying. She never wanted to lie, not about something important. She'd even discussed this line of questioning with Charming, who had said it would never happen (dammit). When she convinced him she needed a way to answer the question, he said to say...

"*Evil* is my story," Mellie said as calmly as she could. "It's filled with my life and my opinions, my experiences and my thoughts."

"But did you write it?" Cindy leaned too close, and Mellie could smell the minted Listerine on her breath.

Minted Listerine covering just a bit of alcohol. A train wreck, just like this interview was going to be. Now Mellie understood why LaTisha was panicked, why Mellie shouldn't have sat in this chair.

But she was here, and either she could stammer her way through the interview or she could take control.

She opted for control.

"Did you hear the question?" Cindy asked. "Did you write this novel?"

"Did you read it?" Mellie asked in the exact same tone. Behind the camera, LaTisha covered her mouth with her hand. Apparently Mellie had not given the right answer.

"That's not relevant," Cindy said, as if brushing off a comment about the weather. "What's relevant are all the rumors flying around that you have not written a word of this novel, that you're passing yourself off as the author when in fact a bookstore owner in Southern California wrote this book. A *male* bookstore owner."

Mellie's mouth had gone dry. She understood all the implications. She even understood how it sounded. Hell, she and Charming had even discussed it—the political correctness of a man writing a woman's novel. Of Prince Charming writing an understanding book about an evil stepmother.

"Is that true?" Cindy asked.

Mellie had no answer. She didn't even open her mouth.

And Cindy Jordan, consummate professional that she was, knew that silence on television was called "dead air" for a reason, and that reason meant the end to an interesting segment, so the woman became judge, jury, and prosecutor all on her own.

"Because," she said, "in this era of James Frey and all those lying memoirs, all the misinformation and un-substantiated facts, all the people who plagiarized other people's works and passed them off as their own—"

"I didn't plagiarize anything," Mellie said, and winced, knowing how awful she sounded.

"Well, yes, how could you when you haven't written a word?" Cindy said, looking at the camera. She wasn't talking to Mellie. She was playing to her audience.

But in doing so, she had given Mellie an out.

"I've written a word," Mellie said. "I wrote and wrote

and wrote on this novel. It seemed like I wrote the book forever. It takes a lot to learn how to write, you know, especially when you're a woman like me who has had no formal education. I spent more time on this book than you can imagine."

"Are you saying you had no help writing it?" Cindy asked.

"All writers have help," Mellie said. "My editor, my friends—"

"But you wrote every word?" Cindy leaned even closer, as if she could intimidate Mellie into an answer.

She certainly was making Mellie uncomfortable.

"What exactly are you accusing me of?" Mellie asked.

LaTisha's hand moved from her mouth to her eyes. She peaked through her fingers as if she were afraid to watch. Maybe she was.

"I'm accusing you of perpetrating a fraud on your readers." Cindy had a triumphant tone, as if she were the defender of innocent readers everywhere.

Even though she had probably never voluntarily opened a book in her entire life.

Mellie squared her shoulders. "I'm no fraud," she said softly. "I'm the prototypical evil stepmother. I haven't lied."

The segment producer made a motion with his hand.

"We'll get to the bottom of that after this," Cindy said, and the red light on top of the camera went off.

"What the hell was that?" LaTisha stayed behind the camera. Obviously she didn't want this part filmed. But she was glaring at Cindy Jordan.

Cindy smiled. She had clearly been waiting for this moment. She waved her iPad at LaTisha, pointing to something on the shiny smooth screen, something Mellie couldn't see.

"I have documentation showing that your client didn't write a single word of her novel," Cindy said. "Someone named Dave Encanto who has a bookstore in Los Angeles, wrote every word. I have a letter here from a screenwriter named David Bourke, who says that he knows for a fact that your so-called writer here can't write. And I'm scheduled to interview a woman named Essy White-Levanger, who claims that Mellie is her stepmother and can't even read—"

"I can too," Mellie said.

"—and certainly wouldn't be able to write anything."

"What is all of this?" LaTisha asked Mellie.

"I don't know about these charges," Mellie said as she took the microphone off her lapel. "I don't know where they came from or why they're happening now. But I do know that I'm done here."

She stood up and set the mike on the chair. Then she glanced at the camera. The red light was still off.

Thankfully.

"I'm sorry," she said as she took LaTisha's arm. "I should have listened to you."

"Yeah," LaTisha said dryly. "You're going to have to listen a moment longer because I need to talk to these kind folks. And you're not going to say another word."

Mellie nodded. She wasn't about to say another word.

"I need your so-called evidence," LaTisha said. She hadn't moved, even though someone turned a camera toward her. She glared at the operator. "And if you film this, I'll sue your ass every which way from Sunday."

The camera operator turned the lens away from her.

Mellie stood behind her, heart pounding.

Cindy still sat in her interview chair, as if expecting both LaTisha and Mellie to join her at any moment.

"You have no right to our information," Cindy said.

"I have every right," LaTisha said. "You either deal with me or our lawyers."

"Lawyers don't scare me," Cindy said. "Why don't you both stick around? Then you'll see my evidence. Otherwise, wait until the six o'clock news."

LaTisha made a face, then grabbed Mellie's arm and propelled her forward. They headed down the hallway.

"Why didn't you stay?" Mellie asked, tripping on her heels as she tried to keep up.

"Because we are on the cusp of a PR disaster," LaTisha said, "and I could spend my time fruitlessly arguing with a woman whose career was going nowhere until this afternoon or I could find a way to protect us. I opt for protection."

"Thanks," Mellie said.

LaTisha frowned at her, and then pushed open the double doors leading outside. "I'm not going to ask you about this Encanto or this Bourke guy until we get somewhere private, but really, is your stepdaughter named White-Levanger?"

Mellie looked at LaTisha. "White's her maiden name," Mellie said.

"You've got to be kidding me," LaTisha said and hustled her to the nearest cab.

Chapter 31

THE PORTAL DUMPED CHARMING, IMPERIA, AND GRACE IN the reception room of Charming's attorney's office.

The building was squat and made of stone. It had stood in this site for more than a thousand years and had once been a wine cellar and a dungeon. It had windows, but only because someone—about five hundred years ago—had pushed out a few of the giant round stones that made up the wall and had glassed in the front. To see out, you'd have to crawl into the circular opening, something Charming couldn't do (his shoulders were too wide) but Grace or Imperia could if they were so inclined.

He had no idea why they would be so inclined. Despite the fact that the janitorial staff scrubbed the walls nightly, they still had a coating of moss. Water dripped through them, making the entire place smell slightly damp.

It was also chilly—the kind of chilly that caves deep underground got. Some trees grew in the interior—the reception desk was made out of one of the larger fallen branches—and they used that water to thrive. Their trunks went through the roof in several places and their canopies hid the building from any inquisitive visitors.

To come to this office, you had to know it was here.

Attorneys in the Kingdoms were great scholars and even greater magicians, able to use words and spells to sway judges and peers, which was what the juries were called here. Often cases got adjudicated in front of the greatest local authority—the King, in the case of the Third Kingdom, where Charming lived.

The last thing Charming wanted to do was go in front of his father.

Charming's attorney had the largest client list in the Third Kingdom. She often didn't have time for someone who dropped in unannounced.

Charming hoped today would be different.

He led the girls up to the reception desk. Grace was clinging to his hand so tightly that she cut off the circulation. He wanted to comfort her, but he couldn't let go of Imperia's hand. It was trembling ever so slightly, but he knew if he mentioned that to Imperia, she would pretend everything was just fine.

Fortunately, the receptionist was someone Charming knew. William the Younger, he was called, even though he was an only child. But he had gotten the name as the apprentice to Charming's valet, also named William, back when everyone thought William the Younger had no magic. Turned out he had an organizational magic, one that was more geared to legal niceties than to the proper way to thread a needle.

He smiled at the girls. They smiled back.

It bothered Charming that he had come to this office so often that his girls liked the receptionist.

"Is Gustava in?" he asked.

"You caught her between cases," William said. "I trust this is important?"

"Urgent," Charming said.

"Then go in."

"I need to leave the girls out here," he said. No way

was he going to let them overhear what their mother had done this time. "But they need to be watched at all times."

"Da-a-ad!" Somehow Imperia had made that word three syllables. Three upset syllables.

"Not because of you, baby," Charming said. "It's just a bad day, and I want to make sure you girls are being taken care of."

Grace hadn't let go of his hand. "Can I come with you?" she asked quietly.

Usually that tone, so serious and so needy, had a lot of sway with him, maybe too much. But not today.

"William will keep an eye on you," Charming said gently. "Fortunately, you brought your book."

"I didn't," Imperia said.

"We have plenty to read," William said. "I even have a rather fascinating history of the Third Kingdom somewhere around here...."

Charming left him searching for the book—which Imperia would not like—and made his way down the snaky arched corridor to Gustava's office.

The damp smell faded here because Gustava kept a fire burning in the corridor's fireplace. The air smelled of wood smoke. She liked her office warm, and she hated the dampness so common to this part of the Kingdom, so she burned excess fuel just to keep herself comfortable.

And, unlike most people, she loathed the outdoors—and with good reason. It terrified her, and nothing she or anyone else did made that terror go away.

Charming knocked on the solid oak door, then pushed it open. It groaned as it moved, which he thought appropriate for a door that weighed more than Grace did.

Gustava's office was beautifully appointed, with another fireplace—this one better vented than the one in the corridor. A patchwork fur rug, made from the pelts of half a dozen animals, covered the area in front of the fireplace, and another decorated the area in front of the desk.

The office had no windows, but made up for the lack with grand paintings of other buildings, indoor scenes, and one rather gruesome oil of a raven being strangled by a beautiful woman.

On closer inspection, anyone would realize that the woman was a young version of Gustava herself, a gift from a grateful client years ago who wanted to free Gussie from the terrors that held her so deeply hostage.

She loved the painting, but it hadn't freed her. Charming doubted anything would.

When Gussie saw him, she got up from behind her desk and came around to give him a hug. She was almost as tall as he was, thin in an ascetic way, wearing scholar's robes. Her chin was long and pointed—a witch's chin, like those out of the wood etchings that used to accompany the early volumes of Grimms' fairy tales. Her nose was pointed as well. Even with those flaws, she had been a beauty when she was young, although never the beauty her stepsister had been.

It was Charming's fault that Gussie hid herself in these offices, Charming's fault that she was terrified to step outdoors. He hadn't realized the power of magic when he was young, and he told the wrong person—whom, he would never know—that Ella's stepsisters had treated her cruelly because they were jealous of her looks.

Her stepsisters had treated Ella badly, in the way of

teenage girls, but not because they hated her looks, but because she made them feel intellectually inferior. She could read; they couldn't. She had an education; they didn't. She had known and loved her father; they had never known theirs.

Charming hadn't known that his careless comment to a handful of unknown people would result in an event that marred his wedding and (he privately thought) tainted his marriage forever.

Songbirds—dozens of them—carried Ella's veil, lifted her train, and sang as she walked down the aisle. But the crows and ravens, jealous of the songbirds' special place in the ceremony, had attacked Ella's stepsisters, plucking out their eyes.

He could still hear the screams. Initially he thought it all caused by some kind of bird magic. Only later did he learn that birds had to be spelled by a human to behave in that way—from the songbirds to the ravens—and he never found out who.

But he did discover that the stepsisters were falsely accused. He had hired a wise woman to reverse the spell. When she couldn't, she did her best, along with a healer, to give the sisters back their sight.

Gussie's sister had refused the gift, saying she found comfort in darkness. But Gussie took it, and then used that sight to study law, so that the perpetrator of that crime against her—whoever it might be—would eventually be punished in a proper and fair way, not in a magical violent way.

Charming had supported her in her studies, although Ella never approved. Gussie and Charming started up a true friendship, and when his old lawyer retired shortly after Charming's divorce, Gussie had taken him on as a client. She had helped him establish his Kingdom bookstore in a way that would prevent his father from having control, and she enabled Charming to emancipate himself from his family in other ways, mostly protecting his girls from his father's all-powerful touch.

Gussie felt fragile in his arms, her bones brittle. And as she stepped back, he could see the scars around her eyes, scars she never had covered over with any sort of magic, although she did wear stylish glasses that made the scars seem more like a fashion choice than a horrible, disfiguring accident.

"I take it this isn't a social visit," she said.

"That's right." He reached into his pocket and pulled out the parchment. He started to hand it to her, but she put her hands up.

"Put it on the desk," she said.

He did, in between leather-bound books so old that they were written in the Kingdom's first language. Gussie went behind the desk and took out tweezers, pulling the document toward her without touching it.

"Did I do something wrong in handling it?" he asked, not quite able to keep the fright from his voice.

She stared at it. "You're part of the document. It needs you."

She spoke almost absently, as if she wasn't really paying a lot of attention to him.

"Where did you get this?" she asked after a moment.

"Ella brought it to my store in the Greater World," he said.

She raised her head, her mouth a thin line. "No."

He nodded.

She bit her lower lip, looking younger than she was. "And the girls?"

"In with William," he said.

"Good." She looked down and studied the document for a long time.

He made himself stand still, his worry growing the longer she stared at that bit of parchment.

Finally, he couldn't take the silence any longer. "It'll negate itself, right? It's got a time limit."

"It should," she said. "But I think we need to neutralize it."

"Because it tries to undo my girls, doesn't it?"

She looked up, her expression so sad that his heart twisted. "I was trying to figure out how to tell you that. I forgot how smart you are on legal matters."

He grimaced. "I'm just a worst-case scenario kinda guy."

"Thank everything magical that you are," she said. "Your caution stopped this entire part of our world from unraveling."

She moved the parchment aside with the tweezers, then set those in a lead-lined box as if touching the document had contaminated them.

"I'm going to have to unspell this line by line," she said, "and search for more hidden meanings. It'll take time to undo."

"And my girls?" he asked.

"Should be fine, so long as you never sign this document."

"I wouldn't," he said.

"But I can't guarantee what else she'll try." Gussie

pushed up her glasses with the knuckle of her index finger. "I knew Ella was unhappy, but this—this is serious stuff. This is nasty magic, the kind that I thought she had forsworn."

"Forsworn?" he asked.

Gussie sighed. "I thought, maybe, she was behind the attack at the wedding. I made her swear she would never use magic to harm again."

Charming's breath caught. "Was she behind it?"

"She said no. I wasn't in the mood to trust her. But she did seem happy with you then, and that kind of magic isn't the act of a happy person."

Charming nodded. "I never thought she was vindictive. Just self-centered. This could be interpreted as self-centered."

"Or," Gussie said softly, "it could be something else."

He looked at her.

"She would have had to pay someone to do this spell. And maybe that someone took advantage of her, thinking it might harm the entire royal family to lose the girls."

"I hadn't thought of that," Charming said.

"Whoever did this spell," Gussie said, "had powers well beyond the average magic user here in the Kingdoms. This is one powerful person, and one twisted person. The best thing you can do is find out who Ella got to create the document."

"I doubt I'll ever talk to her again," he said. "She really wants nothing to do with the three of us. Ever. She wishes we did not exist."

Gussie blinked as if the thought hurt her. "Then the document would do that job, but in a way that might have even harmed Ella. Undoing the fabric of the world around us is a dangerous spell, one that can have side effects none of us understand."

"So someone is using Ella to get to my family," he said.

"Ella is part of your family," Gussie said, "whether you like it or not."

"And yours," he said.

"Yes," Gussie said dryly. "Only I'm not required to interact with her. You are."

"Not anymore," he said. "We agreed that I'd raise the girls and she wouldn't have to see them again if she didn't want to."

"You agreed to that?"

"My choice was between that or this damn document," he said. "Which do you think I'd chose?"

Gussie leaned back. He realized just how much vehemently he had spoken.

"Is there any way to protect my girls? I'm terrified to let them leave my sight."

"That seems practical at the moment," Gussie said.

"It's not," he said. "We're building a life in the Greater World. They have school and friends on their own. They can't be with me all the time."

"For the next few days or so, keep them at your side," Gussie said. "By then, I'll know how dangerous Ella's friends are."

"I think we can handle a week," he said. "But I have no way to fight serious magic. What if someone comes after us?"

"I can give you a protection spell," Gussie said. "I'll recite it over the three of you. But it'll only protect you against Ella and anyone sent by her. Do you understand?"

"If someone comes after us with a Greater World weapon, the protection spell won't work," he said.

"Unless Ella asked them to come after you," Gussie said.

"So if I know who is threatening my family, I can have you whip up another protection spell?" he asked.

"Yes," she said. "But it's best if you don't investigate. Let me. You keep an eye on your girls. Get them out of the Kingdoms, because magic is stronger here. And I'll contact you as soon as I've neutralized the document."

"Gussie," he said, "you're a lifesaver."

"No," she said. "You are."

They'd had this bit of banter before, and it always made Charming uncomfortable. "Come see my daughters," he said, deliberately changing the subject. "You'll be surprised at how much they've grown."

"And I can do the protection spell without them even realizing it," Gussie said.

"That too," Charming said. "That too."

Chapter 32

MELLIE TRIED TO EXPLAIN WHERE CINDY JORDAN HAD gotten those interview questions as LaTisha opened the door to the cab. LaTisha shook her head, and slid into the cab. Mellie followed.

She tried to explain again, but LaTisha held up a very imperious finger. She then bent over her BlackBerry and texted for the entire ride.

"Can't we talk about this?" Mellie asked.

"When we get to the hotel," LaTisha said as she nodded toward the front of the cab. "When we're by ourselves."

Mellie glanced at the cab driver. He was a big, hulking man whose shaved head was covered with tattoos. He had gold posts running down the outside of both ears.

Somehow she doubted he was part of the target demographic for her novel. She had a hunch he wouldn't care if she wrote the book or if she had stolen it from someone who was less media savvy but a better writer.

She pulled out her cell, hoping for a message from Charming. But nothing appeared on the screen. She had no messages at all.

As distressed as she felt, she should have had a few messages. Somehow she felt like the entire world had just seen her humiliation.

But she knew that wasn't the case. No one would see the interview for hours.

The cab finally stopped outside the hotel. Mellie wanted to flee to her ostentatious room and never, ever leave it.

But she waited as LaTisha paid the driver, then they walked inside together.

"Act normal," LaTisha said, as they walked toward the elevator bank.

Mellie had no idea what normal was. Would she have been giddy after a good interview or just plain tired? Did she ever act normal? She wasn't sure.

Still, she managed to keep pace with LaTisha as they walked across the lobby. No one looked at them; no one even seemed to notice them. Mellie hoped that was what LaTisha wanted.

An elevator stood open and as they got inside, Mellie turned to LaTisha.

"What the hell happened there?" Mellie asked.

"Something we'll discuss away from cameras," LaTisha said, staring at the little red numbers going steadily upward beside the sliding doors.

Mellie didn't see any cameras, but she decided to trust LaTisha. When the elevator stopped, LaTisha got off first, and headed toward her room.

"What cameras?" Mellie asked, as LaTisha unlocked the door to her room.

"Security cameras," LaTisha said. "All the public areas have them."

Both women stepped inside.

"So?" Mellie asked.

"If any of that crap Cindy Jordan said back there is true, you're about to become the flavor of the week. Every newscast, every entertainment program, every magazine, and every newspaper will cover your story."

"That's good, right?" Mellie asked.

"Are you kidding me? They're going to lump you with all of the horrible publishing scandals of the past decade. You're going to be the new poster child for an out-of-control industry."

"Is the industry out of control?" Mellie asked.

"*No*!" LaTisha tossed her purse on a nearby chair. The room wasn't nearly as fancy as Mellie's but it was still lovely. A sofa and chair filled the main area, along with a round dining table, and a huge television set. A door opened to the small bedroom. The entire place smelled of lemons.

"Well, if the industry's not out of control," Mellie said, "why would they claim it is?"

"Oh, Christ." LaTisha collapsed on the couch. "Look, do you know how many books get published every year?"

"No." Mellie cautiously made her way to one of the dining chairs.

"Hundreds of thousands," LaTisha said. "No one knows exactly for sure. Maybe a million. And there are always big books, splashy books, bestselling books, game-changing books."

"You said *Evil* is one of those."

"Yes." LaTisha looked annoyed. "I said that because it was a game-changer, just this morning. But now it's a crisis book."

"Crisis?" Mellie asked.

"We get one of those every two or three years—statistically insignificant, really," LaTisha said. "But you'd think from the press attention that it's every book at every publishing house, and everyone fails to do their due diligence, although for the life of me, I can't figure out why we would have had to do due diligence on a book that's just a simple retelling of a fairy tale."

"I don't understand," Mellie said.

"Neither do I," LaTisha said. "I have no idea why Cindy Jordan decided she could resurrect her dying career by attacking you, but the one thing I know about that woman is that she checks her sources before she uses them. So she has something on you from this Dave guy—there were two Dave guys, right?"

"Um—yeah." Mellie had trouble thinking of Charming as Dave.

"She said she had a letter from a Dave…" And here LaTisha checked her BlackBerry, because she'd clearly been taking notes. "David Bourke. Who is that?"

"A guy I met in a coffee shop," Mellie said.

"And?"

Mellie's cheeks warmed. "He's a screen writer for some TV show, something I don't watch—about some macho guy who goes after terrorists?"

LaTisha rolled her eyes. "That could be half a dozen shows. I'll look him up. Tell me more."

"I was trying to write the book, and it wasn't working. He was a writer. I thought I could pick his brain. But he turned out to be a horrible jerk who—he said—just wanted to get into my pants. We had a fight in the coffee shop, and he got thrown out. For good."

"So he hates you," LaTisha said. "And you can prove that?"

"I suppose," Mellie said. "The barista was the one who was going to call the police on him."

"Crap," LaTisha said. "This just gets worse and worse. So who is the Encanto guy?"

"He's a friend," Mellie said. "He helped me with the book. He's the one who sent the book to Sheldon McArthur who gave the book to Mary Linda."

"So he's got ties to the book," LaTisha said.

"And he was there, fighting with Dave Bourke, when Dave Bourke got kicked out of the coffee shop."

"I suppose your stepdaughter, Miss White, was there too?"

"I haven't seen her in a long time," Mellie said.

LaTisha frowned at her. "There's more to all of this, isn't there?"

"Everybody's life is complicated," Mellie said, not sure what she could say and what she couldn't say. She wanted to talk to Charming. She needed to talk to Charming.

"Yes, I know," LaTisha said. "But now I have to figure out if your life is good-complicated, and the press we get is going to be favorable or if your life is bad-complicated, and we're going to have to duck every single interview from here on out."

LaTisha checked her watch, then reached for the remote.

"The six o'clock news is five minutes away," she said. "You want me to order room service?"

"We're still doing the signing tonight, right?" Mellie asked.

LaTisha nodded.

"Then I'd like to rest for the next hour or so," Mellie said. "Just come get me when it's time to leave."

"I think we should watch this together," LaTisha said.

"I'm sure I'll hear about it," Mellie said. She got up and headed to the door. She needed the time alone. She needed to reach Charming.

She needed to think about everything that happened.

And she didn't dare watch that television show beside LaTisha. Mellie fully expected to get angry, and she was apt to blurt something she would regret.

She had been so close to a success. In fact, she had been having a great success. And then someone had to spoil it.

Dave Bourke. Who knew?

And Snow. How had she even heard about the book? And why did she care?

Mellie stepped into the hallway. It was cooler than LaTisha's room had been.

Snow cared because the book revealed what Mellie had done, how Mellie had saved her life. At this late date, Snow wouldn't believe it. Mellie knew that. And she knew it would make Snow angry, make Snow believe that Mellie was just making herself look good at Snow's expense.

Mellie was shaking as she used the key card to unlock her own door. She got inside the big, fabulous room, and realized her original instincts were correct. She did want to stay here forever. She never ever wanted to go outside again.

She had a hunch everything that waited for her outside this room was going to be bad. She'd been in this position before. She had entered both of her marriages with great hope, only to experience great disappointment. The death of her first husband had hurt. The death of her second had hurt as well, but it was what came after—that horribleness with Snow and Mellie's loss of reputation, loss of friends, loss of almost everything she believed in—that hurt worse.

She had just started to recover. This book was helping her recover.

And now she was going to lose it too.

In a very public way.

Chapter 33

THE MOMENT CHARMING STEPPED INTO THE RECEPTION AREA of Gussie's office, his phone started vibrating. He kept it in his breast pocket, and the vibration was startling. He had forgotten that Gussie's office was a magic-free zone.

Still, he didn't look at the screen right away. Instead, he scanned for his daughters.

Grace sat on the sofa against the wall, legs curled under her, reading her book. She didn't look up as he came in, so she really was reading.

Imperia, on the other hand, glanced at him immediately. She was surrounded by books, most of which looked older than he was. On her regal face, he saw a mixture of expressions—impatient teenager and terrified little girl.

He gave her a reassuring smile.

William the Younger was digging through a box in the back of the room. He held up a few more books. "How about *History of the Fates and the Magical World*," he said. "Or *The Law, the Fates, and Magic*?"

"It's okay," Imperia said. "My dad is here."

Grace still didn't look up, but she turned the page. She was lost in the story. His girl.

Charming glanced at his phone and was startled to see that he had missed fifteen text messages and twenty phone calls.

His heart twisted.

"Just give me a minute," he said, and stepped outside.

Outside was a dense forest, dark and gloomy. The tree canopies, which mostly hid Gussie's office, touched the ground here, giving everything the scent of green leaves. That was the plus side. The downside was the preponderance of moss, which made his Greater World dress shoes slip with each step.

He stood just outside the door, and listened to the drip, drip, drip of rain through the leaves. He didn't mind getting wet. The leaves protected him from the worst of it.

He looked at the texts first, mostly because he knew that people who couldn't reach him by phone often sent their messages by text.

All of the messages were from Mellie. The first was upbeat—she had great news. But the rest got increasingly desperate:

Need to talk

Where are you? Call me right away.

Call me.

CALL ME.

She took to leaving her phone number, as if he didn't already know it. The missed calls were from her as well—all of them, even though she only left two voice mails. He listened to the first:

Terrible interview today, she said. *My publicist thinks this is the beginning of the end. Maybe it'll destroy the book. Please call.*

He frowned, then listened to the second.

I sent you a link in your email, she said. *Please watch it, then call.*

He opened his email program, not sure it would work in the Kingdoms. He didn't get any mail except Mellie's.

Briefly he wondered how the program could know who was a Kingdom native and who wasn't.

Then he remembered it was magic, which was answer enough.

He clicked on the link, which took him to a video on a Boston TV station's website.

Two generic anchors sat side by side—the square-jawed middle-aged male anchor, and a perky young female anchor. Off to the side, sat a middle-aged woman with helmet hair, who looked like she had once been a perky young female anchor.

"I hear you had a surprising interaction today, Cindy," the male anchor said.

"I did," said Miss Helmet Hair, sounding as scripted as she probably was. "You've all heard of the step-mother blockbuster, *Evil*, by now. If you haven't, then you've been living under a rock. Its so-called author has been touting it on various shows and appearances all over the country."

Charming's breath caught at "so-called author."

He listened to the rest of the report in disbelief. It was a long segment, maybe eight minutes. Helmet Hair had an interview with the odious Dave Bourke, done "with thanks to our Los Angeles affiliate," where Bourke sat like a victorious toad, telling the world that Mellie didn't write the book.

"She can't write," Bourke said. "I read what she put on the page. She doesn't know grammar or how to spell. Worst of all, she has no sense of story. When I saw her last, she was searching for a ghost writer, and she clearly found one. There's no way this woman could have written her way out of a paper bag."

"Neither can you," Charming whispered to the image on his phone.

"I understand she asked you to write the book," Helmet Hair said.

"Actually, she wanted me to write a screenplay. But when I told her that most screenplays don't get produced, and showed her the excellent screenplays I'd already written that hadn't yet been made into films, she got discouraged. She asked me if I could write a book, and I told her that I was a macho guy who couldn't get the female perspective right—no real man could—"

Charming rolled his eyes at the dig.

"—and gave her information on classes to take to learn how to write. But no one learns that fast, especially when they're not a reader. And she made no bones about the fact that she didn't read books."

"Not only that," Helmet Hair said in her voice over, "but she also doesn't write them. Her stepdaughter, the much maligned Essy White-Levanger, says her stepmother hired a man known for shady dealings, a shadowy man known as David Encanto, to write the book for her and to keep that work a secret."

The film cut to a sad-eyed woman with hair so raven-black that the streak of white along one side looked like an affectation. Worse, it made her look like the prototype for Cruella de Vil.

"Dave Encanto is a well-known ghost," she said. "He had the ability to write that novel, not my stepmother. She's a hideous woman who'll stop at nothing to obtain fame and fortune."

The report went on from there, with Helmet Hair saying that the publisher had been duped, that no one had heard of this Encanto, and that there was a possibility that Mellie had actually stolen the book from him.

Charges, unsubstantiated and salacious, filled the rest of the report.

And then they got to Mellie. Who, when she was asked if she wrote the book, vacillated between belligerent and dumbstruck.

It didn't play well. All of her media skills had failed her there.

And some of that was his fault. She quoted the words he had given her when she asked what she should say if someone asked if she had written the book.

It's my story.

Yeah, it was. But he wrote it.

And unless they figured out how to deal with the public relations nightmare, that one little fact might destroy everything they had worked toward.

Worse, it might make Mellie hate him. Forever.

Chapter 34

THE SIGNING WENT BETTER THAN MELLIE EXPECTED. MOST people hadn't even seen the news report. Only one person asked about it, and he had said, bravely, that he thought it was a hatchet job.

Nice man.

The line snaked around the new arrivals section, went into the bargain books section, and then disappeared out the side door. Most of the people who wanted her to sign had already read the book.

"You spoke directly to me," said one tired-looking woman. "I'd love it if we could change every single fairy tale to be more female-friendly. Women are either witches or evil or helpless in them."

"I don't know why we still read fairy tales to our children," said another woman.

And a third added, "No matter how hard I tried, I couldn't stop my own little girl from wanting to be a princess."

Mellie had smiled at her. "I think secretly we all want to be princesses," she said, and a lot of people laughed.

Mellie stayed until each person made it through the line, which took an extra hour. LaTisha tried to hustle her out, but Mellie wouldn't be hustled. This was probably the last time she would enjoy one of her signings, and she was going to stay until the bitter end.

Which she did. As she left, rubbing her sore right arm, and swaying with exhaustion, her phone rang.

She looked at it. The call was from Charming.

"I'm going to take this," she said to LaTisha. "I'll meet you back at the hotel."

"I'll wait in there," LaTisha said, and pointed at a bar across the street. Mellie didn't blame her for going to a bar. If Mellie were the drinking type, she'd be in a bar right now.

She walked past the bookstore windows, filled with *Evil*, as she answered the phone.

"Where have you been?" she asked, knowing she sounded desperate and not really caring.

"Something came up," Charming said. "I had my phone off."

"Did you look at my email?" she asked.

"Did that news thing really air?" he asked. "It was awful."

His voice sounded thin and tinny. She could hear rain in the background. She knew it wasn't raining in LA. It hadn't rained in LA in weeks.

"You sound funny," she asked.

"I'm in the Kingdoms," he said.

"Oh, no." Her knees buckled. It took all of her strength to remain upright. He was gone. She was going to have to do this on her own after all.

She allowed herself one second of panic, and then reminded herself that she had always done things on her own. She had survived.

Still, it would have been nice—it would have been great!—to have help. Sometimes help kept you out of trouble; at least, that was what she used to tell her kids.

She had never experienced that.

"It's okay," Charming said. "My business here is done. I'm coming to see you. We'll figure out how to handle this."

She put a hand on the bookstore's outer wall. It was brick and warm against her palm. "You're coming here?" she asked, not sure if she believed him.

"I'm in the Kingdoms," he said. "If I take the right portal, I can be there in an hour. Where are you?"

"Boston still," she said, and gave him the name of her hotel.

"Make me a reservation," he said. "I'll be there soon. And make sure the room is a suite. I have the girls."

Then he hung up.

She stared at the phone for the longest time. He would come here? He wanted to help? Really?

Had anyone ever offered to help her when she was in trouble before?

She couldn't think of a time that had happened. She'd had help before, but never when she really, really needed it.

Like now.

She stuck the phone back inside her purse. Then she squared her shoulders and headed across the street.

As she walked, she realized her mood had lightened just a little bit.

Charming would come here. He would help her figure out how to handle this crisis.

Just being able to share it took some of the pressure off. For the first time since the middle of the afternoon she felt a little bit of hope.

And a little bit of hope was all that she needed.

Chapter 35

THE NEAREST PORTAL TO MELLIE'S HOTEL WAS IN BEACON Hill, in the yard of an ancient house that was once rumored to house a witch. Charming had been there before, and had actually looked up the house's history. It had housed a witch—if anyone with magic from the Kingdoms could be considered a witch. In fact, that woman was the first recorded Kingdoms member on American soil.

He would've told the girls that, but he didn't have time for the history lesson. Instead, he had to walk them quietly off the hill to a business district where they hailed a cab.

Boston was warmer than the Third Kingdom, even though it was clearly much later at night. The streets were empty and the cab drove in and out of streetlight puddles, making the interior of the cab light, then dark, then light again.

Grace clutched her book like it could save her. Imperia sat upright, back straight, her entire body rigid. They knew they were coming to Boston because he had to be in Boston. They knew that their mother had done something dangerous, which was why they couldn't go home just yet.

But he hadn't told them about the threat to their lives—and he wasn't ever going to, not if he had a choice. (He hoped that Ella would give him that choice.) His right fist clenched, then he forced himself to unclench it. He had no time to deal with his own anger at his ex-wife, although he wanted to.

She upset him so much that he found he really wanted magic—the fire-and-brimstone magic that only a few people ever had. He'd even burn it all out in one gigantic spell that would keep Ella and her minions away from his girls forever.

But he didn't have that choice.

Probably just as well.

"I don't like it here," Imperia said as the cab wound its way through the deserted streets.

"We won't stay long," Charming said.

"When are we going home?" She wouldn't look at him. She was clearly very upset.

Still he found a small measure of hope in her words. By home, she meant Los Angeles. The mock Tudor house, her school, her routine. Slowly his girls were becoming creatures of the Greater World, which was what he wanted for them.

Grace had her thumb on the middle of the page on her book. Her head was tilted slightly upward. To the casual person, it would still look like she was reading, but Charming knew better.

She was listening.

"We'll be home within the week," he said in his warmest, most reassuring voice. "Maybe even sooner."

"I'd like to be home now," Imperia said.

"Me, too," he said, and as he did, he realized that unprepossessing house, with its beautiful garden and its somewhat messy interior had become home for him as well. He was beginning to love it there.

Damn Ella for messing that up.

The cab stopped in front of a spectacular hotel. It looked expensive, even from the exterior. Charming was glad he always traveled with his wallet, even to the Kingdoms, because there was no way he was going to be able to walk into this place and charm his way past the front desk.

Not to mention that the price of the suite Mellie had reserved for him had to be as much as one of his house payments.

But he wasn't going to think about that. He could afford it, even if it was wasteful.

He paid the cab driver, hustled the girls out, and realized, at that moment, they had no luggage. It took him the entire trip across the sidewalk to realize he had a lie for that too.

He and the girls walked into the lobby. Fortunately his daughters were used to fancy places. Neither girl felt uncomfortable among the gold fixtures, the overstuffed furniture and the high-end plants. Even the rug looked expensive—too expensive for a public place. The hotel probably had to replace it every single year.

One pinch-faced young woman stood behind the black reception desk. She had pulled her long red hair back severely, making her pale skin look ghostly against her high cheekbones.

"May I help you?" she asked in one of those tones that meant *What the hell do you want?*

That was when Charming realized he had to look a mess. He'd been in the same clothes since that morning. He'd worn them around Los Angeles, and in the rainy Kingdom forest, not to mention the smoke-filled corridor at Gussie's. The girls looked all right, but none of them were carrying luggage.

He let his shoulders wilt, allowing himself to look as tired as he felt.

"My name is Dave Encanto. You should have a reservation for me and my girls."

The woman clicked the computer, and perked up. "Ah, yes, Mr. Encanto," she said in a decidedly friendlier tone. That suite had to be worth a fortune.

Charming braced himself for the price.

"Everything's in order," the woman said. "Just let me see some identification…."

He held out his driver's license. She took the number, then slid a piece of paper at him, along with a key.

"Would you like a key for your girls?" she asked.

"Um…" he said, "don't you at least need my credit card?"

"All expenses, including incidentals, were paid when your friend made the reservation," the woman said.

Charming was tired, but not that tired. Mellie paid? Why? He would have to talk with her about that.

The woman was still looking at him expectantly.

"Yes," he said. "Two extra keys for my daughters."

"Would you like help with your luggage?" the woman asked.

He had a lie prepared for this one. He hadn't briefed his daughters on it, but they would understand. They knew that no one in the Greater World should know about portals or magical travel.

"I'd love some help with my luggage," he said, "if only I had some. The airline lost it all."

"Oh, dear," the woman said. "Do you need personal items?"

"Yes," he said, "toothbrushes and combs at least,

and maybe some large T-shirts for my girls to use as nightshirts."

"Certainly, sir. We'll have it all delivered to your room." She handed him the extra keys. "Enjoy your stay."

He smiled at her, a warmer smile this time, then gathered his daughters. Grace was nearly asleep on her feet, but Imperia was watching the entire lobby as if she expected someone to attack her. She knew he hadn't told her everything. And, honestly, he wasn't sure how much to tell her.

He steered his girls to the elevators, glanced at the paper the woman had handed him with the room number, and pressed the right button. The elevator was as gaudy as the lobby, with mirrored walls. As the door slid closed, he saw that he didn't have to force himself to look tired; he clearly was tired.

Grace leaned against him, wrapping one arm around his leg. Imperia stood straight, still on alert. He didn't know how to relax his oldest daughter.

When the elevator doors eased open, he followed the signs, leading the girls to the end of a long hallway. He used the keycard to open the door, and stepped into luxury. A bank of windows opened onto a long balcony. Behind it, the Boston skyline winked in the night.

The main room had two couches, a dinner table for six, a big screen television set, and a baby grand piano. Still the room looked just a bit empty.

To the left, an opulent room done in white and gold. Two beds and another television, which he promptly unplugged. The private bath had a third television, which he also unplugged.

Neither of his girls protested. Either they were too tired or they really didn't care.

Housekeeping had been here ahead of him and left two large T-shirts with Boston written in flowing script on each bed. Both beds were turned down, and a small mint graced the pillow. Toothbrushes, combs, and other toiletries sat on marble counter in the bathroom.

"Let's get you guys ready for bed," he said.

"Where will you sleep?" Imperia asked with some concern. His eldest was needy but trying to hide it.

"Let's go see," he said.

They trekked across the oversize living room to the master bedroom. The king-sized bed looked small, but it was covered in pillows. The curtains were drawn, but clearly they overlooked that balcony as well. Another couch and two chairs sat on one side. This was a hotel room all by itself—and the bathroom was large enough to hold a family of four.

"Wow," Imperia said. "It's big."

"Scary," Grace said. "You wanna sleep in our room?"

He smiled—a real smile for the first time in a while. "I think I'll be fine here. But now you know where I am."

"Seems far away," Grace said.

"That's just because it's a new place," he said. "We'll be fine here for the night."

"Are we leaving tomorrow?" Imperia asked.

"I don't know the answer to that yet," he said.

"What about clothes?" she asked.

"We'll find some in the morning," he said. "We have to get you girls to sleep."

And then he did just that, helping them with their routine as much as he could. Teeth got brushed, hair untangled, faces washed. The girls opted to sleep in the same bed. Grace put her book on the bedside table, but asked for a story anyway.

Charming had barely gotten out the "Once Upon a Time," when he realized his youngest was sound asleep.

"You want me to finish?" he asked Imperia.

She shook her head and curled against her sister. "'Night, Dad," she said.

"'Night, Imp," he said, and smoothed a hand over her forehead. She smiled just a little, her eyes closing. Within a few minutes, she was asleep as well.

His girls.

Damn Ella for threatening them. Thank all that was magical that Gussie could clean up the mess. Now if she could only discover what had inspired Ella to go after the wrong kind of magic.

He sighed and headed out of the bedroom, shutting out the light as he went. He left the door cracked open. Then he went into the master bedroom and picked up the phone, letting the automated phone system put him through to Mellie.

Chapter 36

SHE WAS WAITING FOR HIM. SHE, MELLIE, A WOMAN WHO prided herself on her independence. Waiting for a man. Because she needed his help.

She sat on the uncomfortable couch in the giant living room, with the television on behind her. She had it turned to a movie channel, so she wouldn't see news headlines, afraid she might see herself or her book.

She had on all of the lights, including the weird lights that shone down on the art. The curtains were closed, though. She had made herself a cup of chamomile tea—this room had everything—but that hadn't really calmed her down.

She was afraid he wasn't going to show up. Why would he, really? It wasn't his problem. He had written the book, yes, but his name wasn't on it. Besides, the book was acclaimed. The writing was not just good, it was spectacular—everyone said so. The book was passionate and heartwarming, it was well-paced, and it made its point.

Mellie had done none of that. She had provided the raw materials, and Charming had created a masterpiece.

She leaned on a pile of overstuffed pillows. Her problem really wasn't the *Gotcha!* interview. It was the way the *Gotcha!* interview made her feel.

It made her feel as if someone had pulled back a curtain and revealed her for the fraud she was.

Charming couldn't make that feeling go away, no matter what he came up with. Even if he showed up.

Besides, something was happening to him. He had called from the Kingdoms and he had his daughters with him. Which meant that his ex-wife had done something screwy again.

The last time he had gone to the Kingdoms, he'd had to rescue his abandoned daughters.

Mellie wondered what had happened this time.

She wondered if he would tell her when he showed up.

If he showed up.

Mellie ran a hand over her face. She had no idea what the next day would bring. She and LaTisha were leaving, and they would have a meeting with the publisher. Things Would Get Decided, whatever that meant.

Mellie had even used her laptop to refer to all those cases that the reporter and LaTisha had mentioned. James Frey, whose book started as a novel, but whose agent sold it as memoir, which meant it was "truthful," when it was not. The scandal when people discovered he'd made up parts of the book must have been unbearable.

After Frey, there were a handful of others, leading to the charge the publishing world didn't know how to handle dicey legal aspects. And she was in that category now, lying about writing a book, promoting it as if it were her own.

The phone rang, startling her. She grabbed the receiver.

"Yes?" she asked, expecting LaTisha.

"Hi, Mellie. It's Charming."

Like he had to introduce himself. Like she wouldn't recognize that voice. Like it didn't make her feel warm and tingly all at the same time.

"This is some room you reserved for me," he said. "You didn't have to pay for it."

"You're doing me a favor," she said.

"The girls are asleep," he said. "You want to come down here and talk? I really shouldn't leave them alone."

"Sure," she said. "I'll be down there in a minute."

He gave her the room number, and hung up.

She clutched the receiver for a moment. He had come. Even though he was having some troubles of his own, he had come.

In spite of her best intentions—she didn't want to have expectations, she didn't want to think of him as anything other than a friend and business associate—in spite of all that, her heart beat just a little faster.

She combed her hair, freshened her make-up, slipped on a new dress, because she couldn't go see him looking sloppy and terrified.

Then she grabbed her key, let herself out of her room, and headed down the hall.

Chapter 37

CHARMING SHOULD HAVE ASKED FOR ONE MORE T-SHIRT, BUT he hadn't thought of it when he was at the desk. He had been thinking of his daughters only, thinking of night-shirts, thinking of the evening ahead. And while a large T-shirt would double as a nightgown for his daughters, it wouldn't cover anything except his chest.

He hadn't realized he would need something to change into before he saw Mellie.

After he hung up the phone, he opened the closet door in the master bedroom. There he found freshly laundered robes with the hotel's monogram on the right breast pocket. As if he wanted to show up at the door like some low-rent Lothario in an ill-fitting bathrobe and nothing else.

He settled for washing his face, wetting back his hair, and using the mouthwash the hotel had so thoughtfully provided. But he couldn't do anything about the smoky smell on his clothes or the mud on his shoes. He finally just took his shoes and socks off. The carpet was soft and plush, and he felt better, just doing that little bit.

At that moment, Mellie knocked softly on the door.

He hadn't told her to be quiet, but she had figured that out. He liked that about her. She knew what other people thought, and adjusted her behavior accordingly.

Unlike Ella.

He sighed, wishing he could get thoughts of his ex-wife out of his brain.

Then he pulled open the door, and all thoughts of Ella fled. Mellie stood in front of him, looking more vibrant than she had on television, as if seeing her in person added a whole new dimension. He had forgotten just how beautiful she really was.

She looked exhausted. And defeated, even though he could see that she was trying to hide it. Her eyes were red, and he wondered if she'd been crying.

Before he even had a moment to think about it, he extended his left arm and pulled her close.

She felt good leaning against him, soft and round and warm. He buried his face in her black hair, enjoying the scent of her mixed with the rose of her perfume. He had wanted to do this from the moment he met her.

This woman didn't need a man like him groping her.

But right now, she looked like she needed a hug, and he was more than willing to provide it.

The problem was, he was more than willing to provide a lot more.

He eased her inside and closed the door. Then he leaned back just enough to see her face.

She tilted her head up to his. He looked in those emerald eyes, so sad and tired, and got lost all over again.

The next thing he knew, he was kissing her—his mouth over hers, his hands on her cheeks (how had that happened?), his body pressed against hers.

She wrapped her arms around him and pulled him closer, kissing him back, making soft sounds in her throat.

He had a moment of clarity—just barely—remembering his daughters, and somehow he maneuvered Mellie into the master bedroom. He wondered—briefly—if she minded the scent of smoke, then realized that if she did, she would have pulled away from him by now. And then he had another moment of clarity as he debated whether or not to close the door.

If he closed the door, he was breaking a promise to his daughters that he would be accessible this night.

If he left it open, he was violating his own standards of decency.

Of course, if he let go of Mellie, he wouldn't have this dilemma, but he wasn't willing to do that.

All of this ran through his mind as he continued to kiss her, enjoying the taste of her, the feel of her pushing against him, the smoothness of her skin beneath his hands.

He almost forgot his door dilemma when Mellie solved it for him, by pushing the door shut with one stockinged foot. Had she been wearing shoes when she arrived?

He didn't know, and he really didn't care.

Her hands slipped down the back of his pants, and his hands slid away from her face, unbuttoning her blouse.

She stepped away for a half-second—he felt an actual physical sense of loss—and then she smiled at him, doing the unbuttoning herself.

Before she took the blouse off, she unbuttoned the top button of his shirt—a silent command to join her—so he did, fingers fumbling with his own buttons as he watched her shirt slide off.

She was wearing a white lace bra that revealed as much as it concealed. With a practiced movement, she unhooked it, and it fell away, revealing still-perfect breasts.

He couldn't breathe.

She had to help him with his shirt, with his pants, and then he helped himself, kicking off the rest of his clothes, as she wriggled out of her skirt. She playfully pushed him backwards on the bed, and then tumbled on top of him, her body over his.

She kissed him and wrapped her arms, her legs, her entire self around him, stealing his breath, stealing his mind, stealing everything except this moment, this woman, these sensations.

He lost himself in them, and loved her like he had never loved anyone before.

Chapter 38

THEY ENDED UP LYING KITTY-CORNER ON CHARMING'S gigantic bed, their heads almost sliding off the side. Mellie propped herself up on one elbow. Somewhere along the way, Charming had lost his glasses. His face had a naked look, a private look, as if she were seeing him like no one else saw him.

His cheeks were flushed, his blue eyes so bright that they looked alive, his mouth bruised. She nuzzled his neck, and he wrapped his arms around her.

He felt good. He felt better than good.

He felt marvelous.

She straddled one leg across his hips. She had never ever made love like that before. She had never felt such urgency before, which, she supposed, reflected badly on both husbands. Although she doubted it was the fault of her first. She was so young and inexperienced. Her second tried, but he hadn't really cared for her.

Not like this.

And she hadn't cared for him.

Not like this.

She wrapped her arm around Charming's chest, putting her ear against his rib cage. She could hear his heart beating.

She had fallen in love with him, against all her best efforts. Deeply, irrevocably in love.

He was going to break her heart, and at this moment, she really didn't care.

"Wow," he said, his hand twined in her hair.

"Yeah," she breathed.

They lay in silence for several minutes, listening to each other breathe. She wanted to say so much— *I missed you. I can't believe you got here.*

I love you.

But instead, she said, "Thank you for coming here."

"My pleasure," he said, laughter in his voice.

She flushed, not realizing until just now that she had unintentionally spoken a double entendre.

"I meant—"

"I know what you meant," he said, easing himself back just a little. He put a finger under her chin, and raised her head so that she was looking directly at him. "This really upset you."

"No." She shook her head without moving away from his gentle touch against her skin. "I'm not upset at all."

"I meant," he said with a smile, "the interview."

"Oh." Her bad mood suddenly hovered. She sighed. "Yeah. That upset me. LaTisha thinks I committed fraud."

"And LaTisha is?"

"My publicist."

"Well," he said, "publicists are such legal experts."

She smiled in spite of herself.

"What did you tell her?" he asked.

"Nothing," she said. "Except what we agreed on."

"And right now, that's not enough," he said.

She nodded, and put her head back on his shoulder. She didn't want to look at him. She felt tears threaten— and she never cried.

Why did this make her tear up?

It only took a moment for the answer to come. He had broken through her defenses. She was more emotional than usual—and so she actually felt how deep her disappointment went.

For decades, she had worked to repair the image of stepmothers. She had fought the fairy tale, and just as it looked like she was going to win, someone pulled the rug out from underneath her.

"You didn't commit fraud," he said. "We have an agreement between the two of us. If we did anything wrong, it was not informing your publisher."

"But it seems like we did something wrong," she said.

He sighed. "We probably did. But it's not something that'll tank the book or your wonderful publicity work. You have to remember the publisher wants the book to do well as much as we do."

"I doubt that," she muttered into his neck.

His fingers played with the skin along her rib cage, moving but not quite reaching her breast.

"We can resolve this, Mellie," he said. "I promise."

Then he kissed her again. She kissed him back. And as he rolled them away from the edge of the bed, as his clever hands found parts of her he had neglected before, she forgot her worries, she forgot her fears.

She forgot everything but him.

Chapter 39

He didn't know how long he had lost himself in her.

But when he finally surfaced, sated and pleasantly exhausted, he remembered: The girls.

It had been so long since he made love with his daughters in the next room that he couldn't remember the last time.

Then his stomach growled, and Mellie laughed.

"Sounds like you need sustenance," she said.

"Only if you intend to ravish me again," he said.

She smiled. "Of course I do," she said. "But I think I can wait until you've had something to eat."

He laughed. It shook his entire body. "I'll call room service," he said.

"Will that wake the girls?" she asked, and he loved her for asking that question.

"Not if we do it right." He got out of bed, went to the closet, and pulled out one of the robes. He slipped it on, then grabbed the other and tossed it to her.

She caught it and rubbed her face against it before slipping it on. That moment of unconscious sensuality caught his eye. She had so many facets—he was only just beginning to see them.

He belted his robe, then grabbed the phone and pressed the number for room service. He ordered an assortment of pastries, fruits, and cereals as well as some eggs.

"You were hungry," she said as he hung up.

He smiled at her. "The girls will want something to eat when they wake up. I figured we won't eat all of this, so there will be something left over for them."

Mellie tied her robe and slipped off the bed, her expression serious again. "Why are the girls traveling with you? I thought they were in school."

He sighed. He didn't want to discuss this, but it was a perfectly normal question. In fact, it was a sensible, concerned question.

But Mellie had enough on her plate. She didn't need his burdens too.

She walked over to him and, from the back, slipped her arms around his waist.

"I won't break," she said as if she could read his thoughts. "And I'm smart enough to figure out that you wouldn't pull the girls from school unless something went seriously wrong. Did the bullying come back?"

"No," he said. "You solved that."

"I had nothing to do with it," she said.

"I wouldn't have been able to tell the girls what to do without you," he said. "You helped more than you could know."

He couldn't see her face. She pressed it against his back for a brief moment, then let her arms drop. She walked around in front of him, and pulled open the bedroom door.

"We'll need to be able to hear room service," she said.

"I told them to knock softly," he said before remembering she had overheard his side of the conversation.

He glanced at the clock. They told him to expect them in twenty minutes. He figured five had gone by already.

"If you don't want to tell me, that's okay," she said, in a tone that sounded almost convincing.

He sighed, then closed the bedroom door. He didn't want any chance of the girls overhearing this.

He lowered his voice, and told Mellie about his encounter with Ella. When he got to the parchment and what it did, Mellie's face paled.

"Ella wanted to annul her relationship with her children?" Mellie whispered, as if she understood his unwillingness to speak that too loudly.

He nodded.

"Did she know what a dangerous spell that is?"

He swallowed hard. "I'd like to believe she had no idea."

Mellie bit her lower lip. Clearly she disagreed with him. "That's why you went to the Kingdoms. To get rid of the document."

"And to get a protection spell on us. No one connected to Ella can get near us."

"Good," Mellie said.

He opened the door. The girls' room was still dark. He wanted to go check, to make sure they were both sound asleep.

"Go," Mellie said. "I'll wait."

He glanced at her. "How do you know what I'm thinking?"

"If I were you, I'd want to check on them right now," she said.

He smiled, then headed across the living room. He stopped at the girls' room and peered inside, waiting until his eyes adjusted to the dark.

Both girls slept, curled against each other. He could hear their soft rhythmic breathing.

But he couldn't help himself. He went inside the

room, and adjusted the covers, not because they needed adjusting, but because he wanted to make absolutely certain the girls were all right.

When he had reassured himself, he stepped quietly out of the room, then made a detour to the main door. He braced it open slightly. That might discourage the room service attendant from knocking.

But he couldn't leave the now open door. He was too nervous.

He hovered there until the service elevator dinged. He peered out the door and watched as a room service waiter wheeled the heavily laden cart toward the room.

Charming held the door open. As the waiter came close, Charming put a finger to his lips.

The waiter nodded. Charming helped him inside, then added an elaborate tip, and signed the ticket.

The waiter left without saying a word.

Charming locked the door after him.

Mellie stood in the doorway of the master bedroom. Charming beckoned her. She walked over as he took the lids off the two plates of scrambled eggs. He added silverware, then nodded toward the bedroom. She smiled, got a glass of water, and took the plate into the room as he grabbed some napkins.

Then he went in, not closing the door entirely.

Mellie sat on the sofa near the windows. She looked fetching and vulnerable in that bathrobe. It was much too big for her. She curled her legs on the sofa, and leaned against the arm rest.

"What happened to you today was really serious," she said so quietly he had to strain to hear her. "I'm sorry I bothered you with my very small problem."

"It's not small," he said. "It's important."

"Not as important as your daughters," she said.

Her words warmed him. He sat down in the armchair so that he could see out the open door. He wanted to know if his daughters got up.

"I needed to keep them out of LA for a while," he said. "This worked perfectly."

Suddenly it felt as if there was an awkwardness between them. He balanced his plate on his knees and took her hand.

"I'm happy to be here," he said. "What happened to you is our problem, not yours."

She shrugged a shoulder. "It's mine, Charming."

"No," he said. "It's ours. We'll solve it. And here's how I think we can do it."

Chapter 40

CHARMING'S PLAN WAS DECEPTIVELY SIMPLE, SO SIMPLE that Mellie didn't think it would work. But she didn't have a better one, not even after the few short hours of sleep she got after leaving Charming.

She had fallen in love with him. And, it seemed, he cared for her. Otherwise, he wouldn't have come to Boston in the middle of one of the greatest crises of his own life.

If she still had magic, she would have added her own protective spell to the one he had gotten in the Kingdoms. But she had used up her magic long ago, and she wasn't sure it would ever return.

For the first time in a long time, the lack of magic bothered her. She wanted to protect him and his daughters. She wanted to make sure no one harmed them again.

Not that she could understand how a woman would want to deny her own children. She knew other women who had wanted to do the same thing, women who hadn't understood what motherhood entailed, didn't plan for the work and the difficulties along with the great love.

Or the handful of women who, for whatever reason, never really felt love for their children. Mellie always wondered if those women could feel any love at all for anyone other than themselves.

Sadly, she had a hunch Ella belonged in that category.

And it was clear how much Ella's actions had hurt Charming. He was worried for his girls and heartbroken that someone wanted to wish them away.

Sometimes—often—magic was more of a curse than a blessing.

Mellie knew that, which was why she usually didn't miss hers. She hadn't even missed it after the *Gotcha*! interview. But this, this made her want something she hadn't had in a long, long time.

She got up feeling more refreshed than she should have, given how little sleep she had gotten. She felt like a beautiful woman again for the first time in years, and she felt cherished.

She also felt just a little tender, which made her smile. It had been a long time since she had cared about someone enough to make love—and that was some lovemaking.

The best of her life.

Mellie packed her carry-on and brought it to the lobby. Then she took her laptop to the business center and printed out the agreement she had with Charming, folding it, and putting it in her purse.

She met LaTisha in the lobby, and together, they left for an early morning flight to New York.

LaTisha was quiet and sullen. She looked a little hung over.

Mellie didn't say anything to her about the publicity or the turn the tour had taken. The only thing they discussed was the timing of the meeting at the publishing house. When Mellie had the exact hour, she texted Charming.

Then she settled in for the short trip to a city where she had expected to be welcomed as a successful author.

Her expectations had now been shattered, the interviews with all the big-name hosts about to be canceled.

And she found that she cared a lot less than she thought she would. Her reputation didn't matter nearly as much as it had even a few days before.

Charming had made her feel good about herself. He had made her feel important.

He had made her feel loved.

And that made more of a difference than she had ever imagined it would.

Chapter 41

CHARMING HAD FORGOTTEN THE BENEFITS OF STAYING AT an upscale hotel. The concierge knew someone who could open a nearby department store early, so that Charming and the girls could get some clothes for this trip.

In these days of megamalls, Charming hadn't realized there were still department stores. Then he took the girls into this one and realized it wasn't what he remembered department stores to be.

This was an upscale name-brand store, something the average shopper couldn't easily afford.

He could afford it, but he didn't like shopping at these places, even when the clerks fawned all over him, as they were doing here. They expected to make some money—since they worked on commission—and they would, but not as much as they had hoped.

The store had clearly been in its location for a long time. It was made of brick, the kind he never saw on the West Coast. The interior smelled like cologne, disinfectant, and plastic. The men's department covered half of an entire floor.

The girls sighed when he went to the men's department first, but there was method to his madness. He knew his suit would need a bit of tailoring, and he knew a store like this could do it on the spot.

As he looked at the suits, his phone rang. He looked

at the display and saw that the caller was Gussie. His stomach clenched. News, then, of some kind or another.

He held up a finger, like the mogul he was pretending to be, and walked out of menswear into men's shoes. The area smelled like leather. The shoes on display glinted in the fluorescent lighting.

The girls followed him, but he shook his head.

"I need a minute alone," he said to them.

Imperia frowned. Grace bit her upper lip.

"Find me something to wear," he said. "I trust you."

At least, he hoped he did. When the girls were out of earshot, he answered the phone.

"Hey, Gus," he said.

"My," she said, her voice sounding so close it seemed like she was sitting next to him. "You're even starting to talk like you're from the Greater World."

He almost said, *I am*, but decided that would derail the conversation.

"You have news?" he asked.

"Tracked down Ella," Gussie said. "Which wasn't easy. You know she's made friends with Snow White, right?"

"I hadn't realized," he said.

"Yeah, Ella's the one who gave Snow your book, and Ella's the one who told everyone that you wrote it. Your father's not happy, by the way. He says writing is for monks and eunuchs and is worse than being a merchant."

Charming looked at his girls. He hoped he would never be the kind of father to them that his father was to him.

"Clearly, my father and I disagree," Charming said. "How did Ella hook up with Snow?"

"We're still trying to figure that out. Something to do with fairy godmothers, we think."

"We?" he asked.

"That investigator I told you about," Gussie said. "We have some theories, but no proof."

"Okay," Charming said. "So what's the headline?"

"You do talk like them," Gussie said.

Across the aisle Grace held up a grape-colored suit, and pointed at it, meeting his gaze. Charming did everything he could not to wince. Instead he shook his head with a rueful smile.

"The 'headline,' as you so quaintly put it," Gussie said, "is that Ella is not your problem any longer."

He sat up straight, his heart pounding. "How can that be?" he asked, afraid she had died or something.

"She's moved out of the Third Kingdom," Gussie said. "She's starting over in the Sixth Kingdom, and not calling herself Ella anymore. In fact, she tells people she never married and is childless."

He sighed. He wasn't going to tell his girls that either. "That's fast. She just left the Greater World yesterday."

Although it felt like a week ago to him.

"She was going back to the Sixth Kingdom. She'd been staying there since she abandoned the girls. You, by the way, didn't tell me she had abandoned the girls. I had to find that out on my own."

"Sorry," he said.

"Eh." Gussie made a dismissive noise, more interested in her news. "Apparently someone told Ella she could make her lies about being single and childless come true. But you thwarted that. She's not going to try anything, Charming. She wants nothing to do with any of us."

He hunched over and said as softly as he could, "Would you bet the lives of my girls on that?"

"Yes, as a matter of fact," Gussie said. "You have my protective spell, and I had a few other spells placed around the three of you for good measure. You'll be fine. All of you. Of course, the upshot of the spells is that Ella can't contact any of you, ever, but I figure if she wants to, she'll talk to Mother."

Mother, in Gussie's case, being Lavinia. And the chances of Ella talking to Lavinia were pretty slim.

Ella was out of his girls' lives, and by definition, out of his.

He waited, expecting to feel something—a wave of loss, and grief. Instead, he just felt sadness that his girls lost their mother.

Or rather, lost the idea of their mother. They had never had the kind of mother they deserved.

"I'll let you know if there are any updates," Gussie said. "I don't expect any. But then, I've never been one for keeping an eye on Ella."

"But your investigator will?"

"Oh, yeah," Gussie said. "We have alerts set all over the Kingdoms. We'll hear if she goes off the deep end again."

"Thanks, Gus," he said.

"Don't thank me until you see the bill," she said, laughed, and hung up.

He sat for a moment on the chair, one foot resting on the stool the salesman usually sat on. Charming clutched the phone in his left hand, and bowed his head.

His marriage was officially over, his wife gone. The fear he'd had, just hours ago, dissipated.

He looked at his girls, so lovely as they thumbed through the racks of men's suits. Those girls were one hundred percent his now. His responsibility. If they turned out badly, it would be on him. If they turned out well, it would be on him too.

And now he'd have to deal with the loss of their mother, which would be tough, because she hadn't died. But the net effect was the same. She was gone from their lives forever.

He wished he could speak to Mellie. Mellie understood children. He didn't. Mellie would know how to raise them, how to soften the blow.

Mellie would know what to tell the girls and what to leave out.

Imperia held up a dove-gray suit. It wasn't a color he would normally wear, but even from here, the suit looked regal. Leave it to Imp to find something offbeat but beautiful.

He smiled at her, a real smile, and stood. Then he tucked the phone in his pocket and made his way to the girls.

"Who was that?" Imperia asked, clutching the suit to her chest.

"Gussie," he said.

"Is it about yesterday?" Imperia asked.

Charming nodded. He waited for her to ask about her mother, but she didn't.

"Everything's okay now," he said.

"Except the stuff with your friend here in Boston," Imperia said with a bite to her voice.

"I hope we'll solve that this afternoon," he said. "In New York."

He looked at the salesman, who held up a pale silver-blue shirt, a black silk tie and a matching pocket handkerchief. It all went with the suit, and none of it was something Charming would have picked out for himself.

But he had said he trusted his daughters, so he tried the outfit on. The suit made him look slimmer. The shirt and tie, with the matching pocket handkerchief, made him look stylish.

He touched his hair, feeling good for the first time in months. He would like to have blamed that on the suit, but he had a hunch it had more to do with Mellie and the night they spent together.

Or the time they spent together. She had left long before the night was over.

He smiled to himself, thinking of her. She would never leave children, like Ella did. In fact, Mellie had suffered a lot for her children and her stepchildren, including the damaged reputation.

It took a lot of strength not to defend herself against all the charges that people in the Second Kingdom had leveled against her. She had never told anyone that she had burned up her magic saving Snow's life.

Which was probably the best decision, given what people thought of her. So many people wouldn't have believed her, even though the magic proved that she hadn't lied.

Only powerful good magic drained like that. Evil magic fed on itself, twisting and perverting the user. But Mellie had sent her magic away, using it to prop up Snow, until someone could find a way to give her back her life.

But that wouldn't give Mellie her magic back. She had to wait for that well to refill, and it might take another hundred years.

He closed his eyes for just a moment, as he realized what was going on. He was falling in love with Mellie.

Or maybe he had already fallen.

He just wasn't sure when.

He came out of the changing room. His girls *oo*ed and *ahh*ed. The suit needed hemming. The salesman measured, and promised to have the light tailoring done within the hour.

Once the measuring was finished and he had changed back into his own clothes, he took his daughters to the girls' department. He bought (exceedingly expensive) underwear and (slightly less expensive) socks. Then let the girls each pick out two outfits. Grace wanted a nightshirt as well, but he told her that she was going to sleep in her T-shirt for this trip.

He had them change into the dressier of their new outfits in the changing room. Even though the girls hadn't wanted dressy outfits ("Dad, we're *traveling*," Imperia said), he insisted, since they had to accompany him to Mellie's publishing company in the afternoon.

Fortunately for all of them that meeting was after lunch, which gave him time to finish up here and catch a train to New York. He was pushing the timing, but he hoped it would all work out.

Grace came out first, wearing a short-sleeved pink tunic over a matching pair of pants. The entire outfit made her look older than she was, which tore at Charming's heart.

He almost told her to put the clothes back, but the clerk beside him gasped.

"What a beautiful little girl you have, sir," she said softly.

Grace smiled, her entire face lighting up. "Me?" she asked.

"Of course, you," the clerk said. "You're stunning."

Grace loved the compliment. Usually people called Imperia beautiful and Grace sweet. He'd never be able to get her to buy something else now.

"C'mere, beautiful," he said.

Grace came up beside him and slipped her hand in his.

"Where's your book?" he asked.

"Imp has it," she said.

"Okay."

While they waited for Imperia, he paid for the clothes. He spent more than he had planned to.

As the clerk bagged the last item, Imperia came out of the dressing room. She wore a pale blue short-sleeved jacket over a pair of blue pants. Her shirt was black with a slogan written across it.

That's Imperial Princess to you, Buddy.

She had found the shirt and loved it. He loved it too. It looked like it had been made for her. But he had warned her it was too casual for the afternoon. Only she had found a way to dress it up.

His Imperia was going to be a fashion maven as she got older.

"Wow," he said.

"That's striking," the clerk said, and Charming was absurdly grateful she hadn't told Imperia she was beautiful too. He didn't want Grace to lose the joy she had in that compliment.

"Thanks," Imperia said, nodding and heading toward her father.

She carried a shopping bag filled with their clothes. Grace opened it, and made certain her book was inside.

"I *told* you I'd bring it," Imperia snapped.

"Imp," Charming said, a warning in his voice.

"I *did*," she said.

"I know," he said. "She was just making sure. I told her to."

Imperia glared at him, but she didn't flounce off. She waited as he thanked the children's wear clerk for coming in early.

Then he took the girls back down to menswear. As they rode the escalator, he turned to Imperia.

"What's bothering you this morning?" he asked, expecting a litany about showers, breakfast, and being away from home.

"That woman," Imperia said.

He wondered what the clerk had done, and he hoped it wasn't calling Grace beautiful.

"Which one?" he said, hoping to steer the conversation away from clothes.

"The one who came to our room last night."

Charming stiffened. He had thought the girls were asleep.

"She's the woman you wrote the book for, right?" Imperia asked.

"Yes," he said.

"I didn't know she was pretty," Imperia said.

Charming smiled. "She is, isn't she?"

They reached the bottom of the escalator.

"She's just using magic to make herself look pretty," Imperia said. "She's really an ugly old hag underneath."

Then she flounced away, heading toward menswear.

"Is that true?" Grace asked.

"No, honey," Charming said. "Mellie doesn't have magic anymore."

"How come?" Grace asked.

WICKEDLY CHARMING   345

"I think she used it all up." He took her hand and followed Imperia to the menswear section. "I thought you guys slept through the whole night."

"*I* did," Grace said. "Imp spied on you guys."

Great, Charming thought. *Just great.*

"Did she tell you what she saw?"

"She said you had breakfast in the middle of the night."

"We did," Charming said, worrying that Imperia had seen the prelude to breakfast.

"The smell woke her up," Grace said. "It didn't wake me up. I was tired."

Charming nodded. If breakfast woke up Imperia, then she saw nothing untoward. And more importantly, she didn't hear what her mother had done.

Grace frowned. "Imp said that woman is an evil stepmother. Is that true?"

He sighed. "That's what I wrote the book about. Mellie's not really evil."

"Like Gramma Lavinia?" Grace asked.

"Like Gramma Lavinia," Charming said, silently thanking the gods for his understanding youngest daughter.

They reached the menswear section. Imperia was waiting for them near the ties, pretending interest in the gaudiest of them.

He wanted to ask her right then and there what she saw, but he didn't dare. The other clerk came over with Charming's newly adjusted suit.

"I'll be right back," he told his girls. "You wait just outside this door."

He went into the changing area. He could see their feet through the opening at the bottom of the booth.

He changed in a hurry, his mind working overtime,

worrying about what Imperia overheard. Clearly it all upset her.

He just wasn't sure what he could do about any of it.

He came out, feeling like a certified grown-up in expensive grown-up clothes. He had grown-up problems too.

He bought one more item—a small rolling suitcase—and packed their other clothes inside.

Then he led the girls to the train station, so that they could catch the express to New York.

Chapter 42

THE FIRST THING MELLIE NOTICED WAS THAT PUBLISHING offices looked nothing like she expected. Oh, they started out exactly like her imagination told her they would. They were in big New York buildings, many floors, banks and banks and banks of elevators, and name after name after name listed on sign boards against the wall.

Mellie didn't have time to look for her editor's name. LaTisha led her to an elevator marked *15 to 34*, and got inside. The elevator made the elevators at the Boston hotel look like they needed an upgrade. This one was roomy and big enough for a dozen people. The only floors it stopped at were the floors between 15 and 34.

The doors opened on a stunning reception area. Wide, filled with plants and books, the reception area looked incredibly inviting. The latest *New York Times* bestsellers published by the company sat on a display, as well as on some of the nearby tables. Mellie was surprised to see *Evil* there. She would have thought they had taken the book down already.

The receptionist nodded at LaTisha. "The meeting is in Conference A."

LaTisha headed toward steel doors at the back of the room. Mellie was supposed to follow, but she didn't. Instead, she stopped at the reception desk.

"A friend is supposed to join us," Mellie said. "His name is Dave Encanto. He'll be here shortly."

At least, she hoped he would. She hadn't heard from him all morning and that made her nervous. But this was his idea, so she was going along with it.

"Should I send him back?" the receptionist asked.

"Better bring him back," LaTisha said. "He'd get lost otherwise."

She waited for Mellie with the door half-open. Mellie smiled at the receptionist, then headed to LaTisha.

As LaTisha opened the door the rest of the way, she said, "So this Encanto guy is real."

"Yes," Mellie said.

"Oh, this is going to be fun," LaTisha said sarcastically.

The back part of the publishing company was what shocked Mellie. The building, the elevators, the reception area, were all what she expected, but the back was a messy rabbit warren of stuff. Books, manuscripts, ARCs, and cover samples were strewn along the wall because, she realized the deeper she got into the main part of the building, there was nowhere else for them to go.

The hallway led to tiny office after tiny office, each of which had one desk, overflowing bookshelves, two chairs, and paper everywhere, even in this digital age. All of them had computers too, most decorated with little trinkets.

None of the offices had windows, which would have driven Mellie bonkers.

Then, the hallway emptied into what had once been a lot of open floor space. Now, however, someone had set up cubicles, which looked just like the offices, only with carpet walls and no ceiling. Papers everywhere, no bookcases (of course) but books littering every surface, and that ubiquitous computer decorated with personal trinkets.

LaTisha rounded a corner. Mellie followed, and finally saw offices again, these a little larger, and all with windows (overlooking the buildings across the way). Those offices were a bit better, but not much, and certainly not as glamorous as those portrayed in the movies. For one thing, no desk was polished, and none had an empty surface.

Finally they got to the corner of the building, and there again was something Mellie expected: a gorgeous conference room—windows on two walls with a view of the city, a lovely long conference table with comfortable chairs on all sides, a sideboard covered with coffee, tea, bottles of water, and pastries.

Mellie's stomach growled. Her agent had called her at the airport and asked her to lunch. She had turned him down because she had been too nervous to eat and because she hadn't met this person, although she had talked to him on the phone. He hadn't known about Charming either, except as a friend who "helped" with the book, and Mellie was afraid she'd hear recriminations all over again.

"Have a seat," LaTisha said as she opened the door to the conference room. "I'll let everyone know we're here."

Mellie walked in. The conference room was cooler and smelled of recycled air. She resisted the urge to sit at the head of the table, going, instead, to the windows and looking out.

On the street below, New Yorkers walked with purpose. She had never seen a town where people walked so fast and with such determination. They all seemed to have somewhere to go—in a hurry.

The door opened, and she turned, hoping it was Charming.

Instead, a man she had never seen before came in. He wore a well-tailored suit, and he had silver hair, which would have made him look distinguished if he weren't short and round (with a ketchup stain on his lapel).

"Marcus Hall," he said.

Her agent. She hadn't escaped him after all.

"I'm glad we have a moment," he said. "I've been watching the news coverage. It was a bit of a surprise."

"Yes, it was," she said.

"They won't pull the book," he said, apparently trying to be reassuring. "It's making too much money for them, and now, with this controversy, it'll make even more. But they might want some kind of retraction from you, maybe a statement—"

"You believe the press coverage then," she said.

That stopped him. "I don't know what to believe," he said.

At that moment, a team of other people came into the room, led by LaTisha. A thin man in shirt sleeves, a heavy-set man in a three-piece suit, three women in blouses and skirts, and a harried looking woman wearing khaki pants and a summer sweater with the sleeves rolled up.

She was the only person who introduced herself.

"I'm Mary Linda McIntosh," she said.

She looked like Mellie imagined an editor would look—a serious, bookish woman who worked much too hard. She had a worry frown between her intelligent eyes.

She extended her hand, and Mellie took it, introducing herself even though an introduction wasn't necessary.

"This took us all by surprise," Mary Linda said.

"Me, too," Mellie said.

"I understand someone is joining us?" the thin man said.

"Ch—Dave is here?" Mellie asked, trying not to sound too eager.

"I just heard from reception. They're sending him back," the thin man said. "I'm Anthony Phillips, by the way, the president of this division."

"Mr. Phillips," Mellie said.

The others then introduced themselves. The man in the suit was the corporate lawyer. One of the women was a publisher, another the head of publicity, and the third the head of sales.

Mellie didn't understand the hierarchy or who exactly did what, but she noted that LaTisha sat at the far end of the table as if she felt that she didn't belong. She probably didn't, since she wasn't the head of anything.

"Yesterday *did* surprise us," Phillips said.

"Yes, I'm sorry," Mellie said.

"How much of what she said is true?" he asked.

Mellie's heart was pounding. She was much more nervous than she expected. "Can we wait for my friend?"

"Is he your lawyer?" the lawyer asked.

"No," she said.

"He's Dave Encanto, one of the people Cindy Jordan mentioned," LaTisha said.

Mellie felt a bit of irritation. She had thought she and LaTisha had become friends. But ever since the interview, LaTisha had treated her like damaged goods.

Mellie probably should have expected that. After all, it wasn't the first time people believed the worst of her.

"So this is all true?" Phillips asked.

"No," Mellie said. "Not exactly."

"No or not exactly?" the attorney asked.

"Can we just wait?" she asked.

"Our contract is with you," the attorney said. "So, no, we can't wait."

Mellie swallowed hard, feeling completely on the spot.

At that moment, the door opened, and Charming stepped in.

He looked perfect in his gray suit. It brought out the highlights in his hair, accented his broad shoulders, and made him seem even more handsome than he was.

His gaze met hers for a brief moment, warming her, then he smiled at everyone else in the room.

"Hi," he said, "I'm Dave Encanto. I hope I'm not too late…?"

Then he walked to the table, letting the door close behind him.

Chapter 43

CHARMING HURRIED AS FAST AS HE COULD TO GET TO THE meeting. The train arrived at Penn Station a few minutes early, but he had trouble getting a cab. Then he made the mistake of telling the driver to step on it, a mistake he would never make again.

He had faced knights in battle, he had jousted with real lances, he'd fenced with real swords, but he had never been so scared in his entire life as that cab—with his daughters inside it—bounced its way across Manhattan, hurtling through spaces between cars he thought too small for a vehicle to get through.

The cab nearly creamed one bike messenger, and another kicked the side, screaming a profanity that Charming hoped the girls hadn't heard. Imperia loved the ride, and Grace clung to him, looking as terrified as he felt.

Still, they managed to arrive safely, even if Charming thought his heart rate would never return to normal, and he managed to find his way to the correct floor of the multistory building.

The girls seemed cowed by New York and the large building in general. He kept forgetting how little they had seen of the Greater World. But he didn't have time to explain things to them. He had to get to that meeting.

He felt bad that he had to leave the girls in the reception area, but he knew he couldn't bring them with him.

Still, he probably freaked out the receptionist by stressing that no one, and he meant no one, could take the girls from the building without him being there.

She said she understood and then smiled at him—he did have his charm on full blast—and offered to take him to the back. He said he could find the room on his own, which turned out to be a lot harder than he thought, since the place was filled with cubicles and offices that looked exactly the same.

Finally, he stumbled on the conference room, and only because he saw Mellie's worried face. She was leaning back in one of the plush chairs around a large desk, looking like she expected to get slapped.

He pushed the door open.

"Hi," he said, "I'm Dave Encanto. I hope I'm not too late…?"

He had the charm on as high as he could crank it, his voice warm, his eyes warmer. He only looked at Mellie as he came in the door, and she seemed even more upset than he imagined she would be.

The man at the head of the table—too thin by half—and the man sitting next to him both frowned.

"Mr. Encanto," the man at the head of the table. "And here I was hoping you were a figment of Cindy Jordan's imagination."

"No such luck," Charming said with a smile. "Would you all mind if I sat down?"

He didn't want for an answer as he walked to Mellie's side. He pulled out the chair next to her, touched her knee under the table, and gave her a soft reassuring smile.

She didn't smile back.

"That's, um, Mr. Phillips," she said to Charming as she indicated the thin man, "and Anne Groton, the head of publicity. And that's the company's lawyer—"

"I'm Mary Linda McIntosh," said the woman across from Mellie. "I edited the project."

As if he didn't know who the editor was. They probably assumed he didn't know. They had no idea exactly who he was or what his role was. Mary Linda McIntosh introduced everyone else—a publisher, the head of publicity, and the head of sales, as well as the agent he and Mellie had hired at the suggestion of Sheldon McArthur. The only person who didn't get introduced was the woman at the end of the table who was trying to disappear.

"I saw the interview," Charming said, deciding he would take over this meeting. He knew that his charm would go a long way to defusing the tension he felt in the room. "It was a hatchet job."

"Are you saying that it's not true?" The lawyer was the one who spoke for everyone.

"Parts of it are true," Charming said. "That's what makes it so devastating."

He turned to Mellie.

"Did you bring the paper?" he asked.

She fumbled with her purse. She had a copy of their agreement on her laptop and her one assignment, besides coming to this meeting, was to print it out.

She pulled out a copy of the agreement, folded into a small square. She handed it to Charming, who held it for just a moment.

"Let me tell you what's true, and let me tell you what's not," Charming said. "The short version, anyway."

He paused just long enough to create a little drama, but not long enough for anyone to interrupt him. Everyone stared at him, including Mellie.

"This is Mellie's book," he said. "It's her idea, her life fictionalized in fairy tale format, her cause. She tried to write it on her own, but writing isn't her strong suit—that part is true. She asked me to help. We met at a coffee shop, where we also met Dave Bourke, who overheard us talk about this. Mellie had the idea to turn it into a screenplay, but after talking with Bourke, decided that wasn't feasible."

Charming tapped the paper on the desk. Everyone continued to watch him. Good. They couldn't take their eyes off him, often a sign that the charm was working.

"So we thought that I could teach her to write, but the problem was that she felt the timing on this book was now, and I thought she was right. So I offered to ghost the book, using her ideas, her words, and her story. We were on the phone constantly, always updating, and a lot of the dialogue as well as the opinions are all hers, word for word. We drew up an agreement—"

He stood and handed the paper to Phillips, the president, bypassing the lawyer on purpose.

"—in which she paid me to write the book. She would own the content and the manuscript. I would be in charge of the words, she was in charge of everything else including promotion. Initially we thought she would have to pay for the promotion part herself, but she was willing. She wanted this book out there. We didn't expect the big sale, but we're happy about it."

"You have no claim to the book?" Mary Linda asked Charming.

"None," Charming said. "I wrote it for a fee, like any other ghost writer."

Phillips read the agreement. He said nothing as he handed it to the lawyer.

"It would've been nice to know the book was ghosted," Phillips said to Mellie.

"I didn't—I'm sor—I'm new to this," she said. Her entire body was tense. Charming wanted to put his arm around her and calm her, but he didn't dare.

"We weren't sure about procedure," Charming said. "I'm a bookseller and I asked some other bookseller friends. We all knew that publishers hired ghost writers for people, but we also heard of people by themselves hiring ghost writers on spec. That's what we set up."

"You didn't get paid very much," the lawyer said to Charming.

"I don't need money," Charming said. "I have family money. This was a favor for a friend."

"We needed to know this up front," the lawyer said.

"I'm sorry," Mellie said before Charming could say anything. She sounded horrified.

He wished she'd stop apologizing. But he couldn't tell her that either.

"Did you know this, Marcus?" Phillips asked the agent.

"No," he said.

"Because that reporter made it sound like fraud," Phillips said.

"It's not," the lawyer said before Charming could say anything. "They had an agreement. This is legally binding. The manuscript is hers. She had the right to sign the contract and to warrant that she owned it. She does."

"But what about all the charges Cindy Jordan made?"

Anne Groton, the head of publicity, asked. Her voice was soft but had an edge.

"The charges?" Charming said just as softly. "You mean the *accusations* that woman made?"

"Yes," Groton leaned forward. "She made it sound like you people were out to hurt everyone you know."

Charming sighed deliberately. "That reporter was good. Everything she said had a slice of truth."

He softened his expression and looked at her as if she were the only person in the room. That kind of look, combined with his charm, used to make women swoon.

He didn't make her swoon, but he got her shoulders to stop hunching forward.

"These slices of truth," he said, "are exactly what you'd expect, given the book. Mellie does not have a good relationship with her stepdaughter. Their relationship was the spark for the novel."

"Her name is S. White," said the woman at the far end of the table.

"Essy White-Levanger, LaTisha, I told you," Mellie said. She was getting irritated, which wouldn't help anything.

"And that name is the inspiration for using Snow White," Charming said smoothly. "It works, since Mellie *is* her stepmother, and they *do* have a bumpy relationship, although, of course, Mellie's never been accused of murder."

In the Greater World, anyway, but he didn't add that.

"It's all fodder, and Mellie used it for the book. She even tried to tell her stepdaughter she was doing this, but her stepdaughter wouldn't take the messages, so she was blindsided."

"This is a mess," Phillips said.

"Yes, it is," Charming said. "But people's lives are messy. I've been following the publicity around this book, and up until yesterday, it's Mellie's understanding of that mess that readers love."

Mellie glanced at him. She gave him a small, grateful smile. He smiled back, a real smile, just for her.

"Mr. Encanto is right," Groton said. "It *is* the mess that readers love. The fact that sometimes the people who love us the most aren't people we're related to, but people who join our family later. The book acknowledges how difficult family relationships are, and this fuss just proves it."

Mellie started to say something, but Charming brushed her leg, silencing her. The publishing people were already headed in the right direction. Better to let them come to their own conclusions.

Groton turned to the lawyer. "I need to know if we're in legal trouble."

The lawyer looked at Charming and Mellie, a small frown on his face. Then he turned to Groton.

"If everything they've just told us is true, no, we're not."

"It's true," Mellie said, a tad more desperately than Charming would have liked.

No one looked at her.

Groton nodded. "Good. Because we can use this entire mess to our advantage."

She smiled at Charming. "You, sir, are very charming. Do you know that?"

There was a sparkle in her eye that he didn't like.

"So I've been told," he said dryly.

Mellie tensed beside him.

"We'll send you out to explain this whole thing," she said. "You have charisma and—"

"No," Charming said.

Everyone in the room looked at him. They seemed surprised.

"No?" Phillips said.

"No," Charming said. "This book is Mellie's. It's got a lot of traction, because of her. I'll just screw that up. Besides, I have no agreement with you people. Mine's with her, and it explicitly states that I'm the ghost on this. I stay hidden."

Phillips said, "But—"

"No," Charming said.

"He's right," the lawyer said. "He has no legal obligation to us."

"It'll save the book," Groton said.

"The book doesn't need saving," Charming said. "I checked. I own a bookstore and I have a lot of bookseller friends. We all sold out of *Evil* in the last twenty-four hours. Ingram has copies on back order. So do all the other distributors. This book is selling like crazy because of the publicity. So you guys need to manage it. You have the agreement. That's all you need."

"He's right about the numbers," the head of sales said.

Phillips nodded. Charming had a sense the man already knew how well the book was selling.

"I'd like you for one interview," Phillips said to Charming. "Just one."

"No," Charming said. "I'm not sitting next to Mellie on some talk show, fielding questions about her book. It gives the wrong message."

"What message do you think it would give?" the head of sales asked.

"I want this to be seen as Mellie's book one hundred percent," Charming said. "Because it is. If I sit next to her on some show, then it's *our* book, and that's just wrong."

Phillips sighed. "How about a print interview then? Just about process. I'm sure we can get a reporter from the *New York Times* to come over here and talk to you—briefly—with one of us in the room. It would save the book."

"The book doesn't need saving," Charming said.

"But its reputation does," Phillips said. "We need people to know it's legit."

Charming looked at Mellie. The word "reputation" got him. That was what had concerned her from the beginning.

"I don't want to take anything away from you," he said softly, hoping she would understand. He didn't want to be on a television show for another reason, one he couldn't express here.

His charm would make him the only person the camera saw. It had happened before, on *Book TV*. No matter how good Mellie was at publicity—and she was damn fine at it—she'd pale in comparison. No one would see her.

He didn't want that.

"You won't take anything away from me," she said, and his breath caught. He willed her to take that phrase back. She was missing the problem. He was going to have to fight this thing by himself.

But she continued. "I think everyone is right. One interview in print only would help."

She stressed "in print." So she saw the charm problem as well. And she thought print was the solution.

Charming didn't want to do any interviews, but talking to one print reporter (and charming that reporter) was a risk he could take. There wouldn't be film of this, and even if the reporter became besotted, Charming could use that to his advantage.

He could manipulate the reporter into telling the story Charming wanted to tell, not the story that everyone believed after Cindy Jordan's hatchet job.

He sighed again, and this time, the sigh was heartfelt.

"All right," he said. "When do you want me to do it?"

"As soon as we can get someone down here," Groton said. "The sooner we quash this story, the better."

Mellie nodded. Charming's stomach knotted.

"And LaTisha," Groton said to the woman at the far end of the table, "call the interviews we already have set up. Tell them we'll be there, and we'll be sending over a statement beforehand, just so that they know this controversy is bogus."

"Okay," she said and left the room.

Groton looked at Mellie. "Is there any other reason this screenwriter would badmouth you?"

Groton was smarter than Charming would have liked. But Mellie didn't flinch.

"He wanted to date me," she said. "And I said no."

"The truth is," Charming said, "that when she said no, he made a scene in the coffee shop and got kicked out for good. He was a jerk. I'm sure everyone, from the barista to the regulars, will corroborate that."

"And you two," Groton said, looking at Mellie and Charming. "What exactly is your relationship?"

Charming put his hand over Mellie's.

"That," he said quietly, "is entirely between us."

Chapter 44

CHARMING'S ANSWER TO THE HEAD OF PUBLICITY HAD BEEN absolutely perfect—and completely infuriating. Mellie wanted him to tell them that he cared for her, that they were more than friends. But it wasn't any of their business, and besides, he hadn't told his own daughters yet.

She understood, and wished she hadn't.

But she loved the feel of his hand over hers. And she loved the way he had ridden to her rescue, even though she had never been a woman who needed rescuing before.

Charming kept his hand on hers for the rest of the meeting, just resting lightly on her skin, making her feel warm and safe. Anne Groton looked at their joined hands from time to time, and said nothing.

Then when the meeting was over, Groton told Mellie to come to her office to check the revised schedule, while Phillips asked Charming to stay in the conference room. They would have a reporter join him shortly.

"Mellie should stay too," Charming said.

Phillips shook his head. "On this one, they do separate interviews. The important interview is with you."

Charming sighed.

"I'll meet you out front," Mellie said, and he nodded, looking trapped and uncomfortable.

She went to Groton's office. The schedule was slightly different—more interviews crammed into tomorrow than initially planned. Mellie had to do two print interviews here at the publishing house, and she got to see those journalists after Phillips and Groton finished with them.

Mellie had no idea which journalist was interviewing Charming, and she really didn't want to know.

Groton promised Mellie a quiet night, since the rest of the tour would be crazy.

"I'd offer to take you to a spectacular dinner," Groton said, "but I have a hunch you want to spend time with your charming ghost writer."

The way she said it meant she understood exactly how Mellie felt about Charming.

Mellie didn't exactly know how to answer. Groton smiled. "I'd want to have dinner with him too. He seems like a very nice man."

"He is," Mellie said.

"Let me get you some cash," Groton said. "That way we still pay for your dinner—"

"No," Mellie said. "I can afford it."

"I know," Groton said, "but that's not the point. This trip is all on us."

"Then I'll give you the receipt and you can reimburse me," Mellie said.

Groton smiled. "Deal."

Mellie sighed, feeling more tired than she had in days, maybe weeks. The stress of the tour finally hit her. "Am I done for the day?"

"You are," Groton said, "but remember, we need you at 6 a.m. sharp. You're diving in with both feet. Howard Stern in the morning. And he won't be easy on you."

"He wouldn't have been easy on me even if there had been no scandal," Mellie said.

"Exactly," Groton said. "So be rested."

Mellie nodded. She thanked Groton and said she could find her own way out. Which was easier said than done. Every corridor looked the same.

Finally, she had to ask a woman in one of the cubicles how to get to reception. The woman gave detailed instructions, as if Mellie were about to embark on a trip into the wilderness, and then set her free.

Eventually, Mellie found that steel door she had come through in what felt like days ago. As she touched the door, she smiled. Going from the reception to the real world of publishing felt like going from a Grimms' Fairy Tale to the real world of the Kingdoms. The Kingdoms had some elements of Grimm, but it wasn't truly magical and it wasn't pretty and it certainly wasn't what you expected.

Mellie pushed the door open and stepped into the brightly lit reception area. Charming hadn't arrived yet. The receptionist smiled at Mellie from the desk. Mellie crossed to one of the couches. As she sat down, she realized that two other people were in the room.

They sat on the couch which was on the same wall as the door she had just come through, which was why she hadn't seen them. She recognized them instantly.

Charming's daughters.

They were much more beautiful in person. They had the same glamour that most people from the Kingdoms had, a bit of something extra that made them seem more alive than the average person in the Greater World.

The youngest, Grace, sat with her feet tucked underneath her, leaning against the arm of the couch, a book in her hand. She wasn't reading, even though she pretended to be. She looked at Mellie over the top of the book.

Mellie smiled at her.

Grace looked down at the page, pretending not to see her.

The other daughter, Imperia, was much more formidable. She had the reedy thinness girls got just before they headed into puberty. She would be tall and glamorous. She had pale blond hair and her father's bright blue eyes. She was stunning—or she would be if she smiled.

Mellie had a sense that Imperia didn't smile much at all.

The girl seemed desperately unhappy.

"You're the woman who was in our hotel room last night," Imperia said.

Mellie wasn't going to lie to her. "Yes."

The receptionist gave them all a sympathetic look, then grabbed a pile of papers, and excused herself for a moment. She went through a door behind the desk that Mellie hadn't noticed before. The door was the same color as the wall, apparently designed to be unnoticed.

Mellie frowned. It seemed as though the receptionist was trying to give them privacy.

"You know who my dad is, right?" Imperia said.

"Yes, I do," Mellie said.

"You know what they call him." Imperia's spine was straight. She had perfect princess posture. Grace looked over at her with an expression bordering on fear.

But fear for whom? Mellie? Or Imperia? Or just fear of a scene?

"They call him many things," Mellie said.

"He's Prince *Charming*," Imperia said. "He's the *handsome* prince."

"I know," Mellie said. She would not let herself smile. She didn't want Imperia to think Mellie was patronizing her. Because Mellie wasn't. She wanted to hear what Imperia had to say.

"And you know what a handsome prince's job is, right?" Imperia asked.

To live happily ever after? Mellie almost said, but stopped herself in time. Right now, from Imperia's point of view, her father had no happily ever after. He had just divorced their mother.

"His job," Imperia said before Mellie could come up with a second answer, "is to rescue damsels in distress."

"Oh," Mellie said, and felt her heart sink. Of course, Imperia was right. Saving damsels in distress was as natural to Charming as, well, his charm.

"You're not the first one he's rescued," Imperia said.

"Imp," Grace whispered, as if she didn't want to be part of the conversation.

But Imperia didn't look at her.

"He makes them all feel safe and special and oh, so important, but they're not. They're just damsels, and he's just doing his job." Imperia spoke with great force. She didn't have her father's charm, but she had something stronger. She had certainty.

Mellie's gaze met hers.

"You're just the latest damsel," Imperia said. "There will be another."

And that was the sentence that made Mellie take a deep breath. Suddenly she recognized this emotion. Imperia was only twelve. She was terrified. Her father was divorced, and now he had spent a night with another woman. Even if Imperia didn't know that they had made love, she knew that Mellie had been in the room with him.

Imperia knew that they were more than friends.

And she felt threatened.

Mellie felt her own shoulders relax.

"I know that's what he does," Mellie said. "And I can't tell you how grateful I am that he helped me."

Imperia's eyes narrowed. She had clearly hoped to upset Mellie—and she had nearly succeeded.

"What were you doing in our room?" Imperia asked.

"Trying to figure out how to solve a problem with my book," Mellie said. "We had to have a meeting on it today, and last night was the only time."

"He kissed you," Imperia said.

Mellie nodded. "I kissed him back."

"Do you love him?" Imperia asked.

Mellie looked at the girl. Mellie didn't want to lie to her, but she also didn't want to tell her the truth. In Imperia's life, she had probably seen dozens of women fall for Prince Charming. *This* Prince Charming.

The real Prince Charming.

Her father.

Mellie leaned back, trying to think of the best way to answer.

Chapter 45

CHARMING HAD JUST LEFT HIS INTERVIEW WITH THE *New York Times* reporter when he saw the receptionist scurry by him. His heart started pounding.

Why had she left her post?

Why had she left the girls alone?

He pushed his way past the cubicles, not stopping in the publisher's office like he'd been asked to do. They had already let him know what they wanted: they wanted him to write a book under his own name—

Anything you want, Phillips said, *so long as it's fiction. You're a spectacular writer.*

I told you, Charming said, *it's Mellie's words.*

And your ability to make them clear, Phillips said. *Not to mention your ability to tell a story.*

Charming didn't want to think about that right now, just like he didn't want to think about the reporter he saw. At least he'd been able to sway her. Charm had worked beautifully, helped by the fact that she had no respect at all for ghost writers. She was perfectly willing to believe that it was Mellie, and Mellie only, who made *Evil* work.

Her news story—"An Interview with a Ghost," she said she'd call it—would go a long way to repairing the damage done by Cindy Jordan. *Besides*, the *Times* reporter told Charming, *Cindy Jordan had been fired from two stations for embellishing her research. I wondered, when this story broke, if she had embellished here.*

And she made it seem like she would check. He would let her. Everything would work out. The tension in the publishing house had eased. Now he just had to tell Mellie, and gather up his girls.

If, indeed, they were okay. The threat from Ella had ended, but that didn't mean his girls should be left alone in the reception area.

He opened the double steel doors to see Mellie, sitting on the couch, looking a bit bemused. Across from her, Imperia had gone into full imperial mode.

Charming eased the door closed quietly. No one noticed him except Grace. She started to say something, but he put a finger to his lips. Her eyes smiled at him, clearly liking the fact that they had a momentary secret.

"He makes them all feel safe and special and oh, so important, but they're not," Imperia was saying. She sounded angry. "They're just damsels, and he's just doing his job."

His poor daughter. He had no doubt these words had come directly from Ella's mouth, more than once. He had so much work ahead to repair the damage that Ella had done.

"You're just the latest damsel," Imperia said bitterly. "There will be another."

He looked at Mellie. She took a deep breath. His breath caught too. He didn't know what he would do if she believed this nonsense. She already had troubles because of who he was. She felt herself unworthy, as if he was something special.

He was a divorced dad who owned a bookstore. Nothing more. At least, nothing more in the Greater World. In the Kingdoms, he was even more of a failure.

Everyone knew he would never be King, not with his dad hanging on forever.

Mellie tilted her head slightly as if she were assessing Imperia.

"I know that's what he does," Mellie said. "And I can't tell you how grateful I am that he helped me."

Charming let out that small breath he'd been holding. He hadn't expected that answer from Mellie. Neither, he noted, had Imperia.

Imperia's eyes narrowed. He privately called that her "incoming" look. It meant she was going to let something nasty fly.

"What were you doing in our room?" she asked.

"Trying to figure out how to solve a problem with my book," Mellie said. "We had to have a meeting on it today, and last night was the only time."

God, Mellie was good. In fact, she was spectacular. She wasn't letting Imperia get to her. Mellie seemed to know exactly what to do.

So, of course, Imperia ratchetted up the tension.

"He kissed you," Imperia said.

Mellie smiled. The smile was warm and a bit personal, as if she had remembered the moment. He remembered it. He loved kissing her.

Mellie nodded. "I kissed him back."

Imperia's frown grew. She was getting angry because she couldn't control Mellie.

"Do you love him?" Imperia asked.

Good question, he thought. He finally was beginning to understand what Mellie had said about Snow White. Snow had been slightly older when Mellie had married into the family. And Snow was grieving the loss of her mother.

Snow had challenged her, just like Imperia was doing. This must have felt very familiar to Mellie.

He wanted to hear the answer, but he knew that any answer—yes, no, maybe—would only make Imp angrier. He wanted Mellie in his life. And that meant teaching his girls how to get along with her.

So he spoke up.

Chapter 46

"THAT'S REALLY NONE OF YOUR BUSINESS NOW, IS IT, IMP?" Charming was standing near the steel doors. For the first time in their entire acquaintance, Mellie hadn't noticed when he entered the room.

Imperia glared at him. Charming seemed unfazed. He just looked at her, calmly. His daughter's moods didn't seem to upset him.

And that was a good thing.

"I happen to care about Mellie," Charming said.

Mellie's breath caught. She hadn't expected him to say that, particularly to his daughters. She heard the warmth in his voice.

He did care for her.

And that meant more than she could say.

"Are you going to marry her?" Grace asked, sounding scared.

Mellie winced. She didn't want to threaten these girls in any way. She had been shoved into a family before. She didn't ever want that to happen again.

"We haven't discussed it," Charming said, his gaze meeting Mellie's. His eyes smiled at her—yet another version of that smile!—and she could sense the tenderness. "So that means the answer, at the moment, is that we have no plans to marry."

Perfect answer. It didn't bother her at all, not the way his answer in the meeting had bothered her. This answer kept the door open—wide open, actually—to some kind of future.

And Imperia caught that.

"That doesn't mean anything," Imperia said. "You could make plans."

"Do you want us to?" Charming looked at his oldest daughter with great amusement. He knew she wouldn't want that, but he also didn't seem to mind teasing her.

Of course, Imperia didn't seem to know she was being teased.

"No, I don't want that," Imperia said, giving Mellie a sullen glance.

Mellie said nothing. She didn't dare. She was going to have to be gentle with those girls, help them accept her slowly, not quickly.

Charming grinned at Imperia, then looked at Mellie. "So I see you've met my girls."

The amusement in his voice made her want to smile. But she didn't dare. She needed to do this introduction correctly.

"We haven't met formally, no," Mellie said.

"In the Greater World," he said, "the Charming family does nothing formally."

Grace clutched her book to her chest, blue eyes wide as they looked at Mellie.

"But we're formal in the Kingdoms," Grace said. "Grandfather insists."

So she wanted formality. Mellie noted that.

"But your grandfather's not here," Charming said, "so we don't have to do things his way."

Grace took a deep breath. Clearly she had grown up

with her grandfather as the ultimate authority. A frightening authority. Something more to work on.

Something Mellie didn't dare tackle in this reception room. Instead, she would discuss it with Charming later.

In fact, all of this would be better discussed later, over that dinner the publisher was going to pay for, maybe. Or in Charming's room after the girls had fallen asleep.

Mellie looked at Charming.

"Did the interview go all right?" Mellie asked.

Charming shrugged. "I hope so because I'm not doing another."

Mellie stood. It felt good to be on her feet. Imperia leapt to hers, but Grace stayed down as if she didn't want to be noticed.

"I have the evening off," Mellie said.

"Goodie for you," Imperia said.

"Imp," Charming said, a warning in his voice.

"It's all right," Mellie said. "I worry her."

"You do not," Imperia said.

Mellie smiled at Charming. He smiled back.

"She should worry," he said softly.

"Why?" Grace asked, that fear still in her voice.

"Because there might be a stepmother in our future," Imperia snapped.

Charming nodded, then raised his eyebrows, as if he had just caught himself agreeing with Imperia.

"Imperia reminded me," Mellie said, "that you are Prince Charming. There are a million distressed damsels in need of your services."

Imperia made a noise that sounded like strangled words. If Mellie had to guess, what Imperia had strangled was the urge to tell Mellie to shut up, and not let her father know what she had said.

"Are you a damsel in distress?" Charming asked Mellie, using that tone he'd had the night before.

When they were alone.

"Not anymore," Mellie said.

"Then I should feel no compunction to be with you," he said. "And yet I do."

Her heart rose. She wanted to go to him, but she didn't. Not in front of his daughters.

"You realize this isn't how the fairy tale ends," Mellie said softly.

"I've had the fairy tale," Charming said. "The fairy tale sucks."

"Da-ad!" Imperia said. Grace looked up, obviously shocked.

Charming didn't look at them. He was looking at Mellie.

"I prefer the Greater World," he said, "with its hard-edged reality."

"And its books," Mellie said with a smile.

"Oh, yeah," Charming said. "I used to think the books were the best part."

"What's best now?" Grace asked.

"My girls," Charming said, still not looking at her. "All three of my girls."

Then Charming slowly and deliberately walked across that reception area, stopped in front of Mellie, and took her chin in his hand. He gazed in her eyes.

The intimacy of the movement surprised her. She thought he'd wait until later to touch her. Maybe wait a few weeks before letting the girls know exactly how he felt.

But apparently, he didn't feel like waiting.

"I don't believe in happily-ever-afters," he said to Mellie.

Neither did Mellie. His words made her smile. "Happily-ever-afters are too easy," she said.

"I think relationships take work," he said.

"All the time," she said.

He bent his head toward hers. His lips hovered near hers. He was almost—almost—kissing her. If she moved just a little, their lips would touch.

But she didn't want to make the first move in front of his daughters.

"Dad," Imperia said. "She's the *evil stepmother*."

"She's no more evil than the rest of us," Charming said without looking at his daughter. "In fact, once you get to know her, she's an amazing woman."

Then his lips brushed hers. His hands slipped down to her shoulders, then along her arms, putting them around him. He pulled her close, and kissed her, really kissed her.

Mellie melted into him. To hell with his daughters. Mellie wanted to enjoy this kiss, and she was going to.

She was.

"Gross," Imperia said.

"Shut up," Grace said.

"No," Imperia said.

"Dad likes her," Grace said.

"So?" Imperia said.

"So I do too," Grace said.

Charming smiled. Mellie could feel the smile on his lips as he continued to kiss her.

"You're not going to marry her," Imperia said.

Charming pulled away from Mellie for just a moment. "Not this week."

"Next week?" Imperia asked.

"She'll still be on tour next week," he said, continuing to hold Mellie close.

"The week after?"

"We'll see," he said.

Mellie smiled. She couldn't help herself. She leaned into his arms. He was letting his daughters know that Mellie was going to be part of their lives, and they needed to get used to that.

"I hate 'we'll see,'" Imperia said. "'We'll see,' means 'Yes.'"

"It means we'll see," Charming said, and kissed Mellie again.

"Oh, yuck," Imperia said.

Mellie eased out of the kiss. "They're not ready," she said softly.

"Not yet," he said.

"I won't be forced on anyone again," she said.

"I know," he said. Then he touched his brow to hers. He whispered, "I love you."

She leaned close. "I love you back," she whispered.

It felt liberating to say those words. She had wanted to tell him how she felt for a long time.

"That's a start," he said.

"In a fairy tale, that's the end," she said.

"And this isn't a fairy tale," he said.

She laughed. "Thank God," she said. "Thank God."

About the Author

Before turning to romance writing, award-winning author Kristine Kathryn Rusch edited the *Magazine of Fantasy & Science Fiction* and ran Pulphouse Publishing (which won her a World Fantasy Award). As Kristine Grayson she has published six novels so far and has won the *RT Book Reviews* Reviewer's Choice Award for Best Paranormal Romance, and, under her real name, Kristine Kathryn Rusch, the prestigious Hugo award. She lives in Oregon with her own Prince Charming, writer Dean Wesley Smith (who is not old enough to be one of the original three, but he is handsome enough) as well as the obligatory writers' cats. www.kriswrites.com.

Watch for the next Charming book
Utterly Charming
Coming October 2011
From Sourcebooks Casablanca